MARKED UNDER THE MIDNIGHT SUN

BLACK ROCK GUARDIANS

SUSANNA STROM

THE BLACK ROCK GUARDIANS SERIES

Secrets of Shooting Star Lake

Havoc Under the Hunter's Moon

Marked Under the Midnight Sun

Visit my website at https://susannastrom.com/
https://www.facebook.com/susannastromauthor/
https://www.facebook.com/groups/1572291033136914

Developmental Editor: Christina Trevaskis
www.bookmatchmaker.com

Interior Designer: Jovana Shirley
Unforeseen Editing, www.unforeseenediting.com

Proofreader: Brittany Meyer-Strom
brittanym.edits@gmail.com

Cover Designer: Lori Jackson Designer
www.lorijacksondesign.com

Photography: Golden Czermak
www.furiousfotog.com

Cover Model: Nick Pulos

ISBN ebook: 978-1-960382-09-2
ISBN paperback: 978-1-960382-10-8

Published by Cougar Creek Publishing LLC

Chapter One

Viggo

Sweeney pulled the sedan onto the side of the old logging road, cut the engine, and turned to me. "You brought the jammer?"

Irritation sliced through me. Like there was a chance in hell I'd go on a mission and forget to bring a vital piece of equipment. I cut the coyote a dirty look but didn't dignify his question with a reply.

"Well, did you?" he persisted, ignoring my scowl.

My alpha had ordered me to play nice with the coyotes, at least until our alliance had outlived its usefulness. Their proximity to our wolf enemies and their alpha's willingness to use his soldiers as cannon fodder was the only thing of real value they brought to the relationship. Once we got our hands on the wolves' Black Rock, we could kick the coyotes to the curb and beat a hasty retreat out of Washington state. Until then, we had to string our so-called allies along.

Sighing, I patted the pocket holding the black market signal-blocking device. "Got it."

"Good." He nodded. "Remember, even if you jam their security cameras, the woods are crawling with guards."

The wolves ran security patrols on their land? No shit.

"Keep your eyes peeled for trouble," he added.

At that final, unnecessary piece of advice, my last nerve snapped. Who did this little pissant think he was talking to? I was a grizzly enforcer, for chrissakes. A member of the most powerful shifter pack in Alaska. Maxim Medved's top lieutenant. I was the boogeyman who haunted our enemies' nightmares.

And Sweeney?

An accountant, not a soldier. The number two man in a bush-league pack of coyote shifters led by an alpha with delusions of grandeur. Yet none of those shortcomings stopped Sweeney from acting like he was some kind of tactical genius, and I his clueless underling.

Turning sideways in the passenger seat, I fixed him with a death glare.

Color drained from Sweeney's cheeks. He clamped his lips together.

I stood six-feet-six and was built like a tank, but I brought more than physical intimidation to my role as an enforcer. I'd heard the whispers, had seen folks scuttle the opposite direction when I glowered. The look in my eyes and the expression on my face scared men shitless.

Hey, whatever worked to get the job done and to keep me in Medved's good graces.

"Stay here," I ordered, allowing the pissed-off grizzly to show in my eyes. The coyote bobbed his head and kept his trap mercifully shut.

Yanking my hood up over my head, I stepped out of the car. Clouds covered the moon and stars. Snow drifted down from the dark sky. Gravel and ice crunched beneath my boots. I reached into my pocket and toggled the button on the powerful signal jammer. The high-tech gizmo would disrupt the wolves' security cameras, but my boot prints in the snow still might give me away. Sometimes the simplest stuff derailed the most elaborate plan.

Couldn't be helped.

Ducking my head to avoid a low branch, I stepped between the trees and crossed into the Black Rock Guardians' territory. Their pack headquarters—a hundred year old lodge built on the shore of Shooting Star Lake—lay two miles to the south.

My mission was a straightforward snatch and grab. Medved texted this evening and ordered me to nab a hostage, a bargaining chip to use against the young wolf alpha. Easiest thing would be to take one of the soldiers patrolling their pack land. Give me five minutes in the woods, and some unlucky sap would find himself trussed up in the trunk of Sweeney's car.

But no. Medved wanted a noncombatant, which meant I had to sneak past the patrols and make my way toward the lodge that housed the members of the pack. Once there, I'd break in, lie in wait, and kidnap the first civilian who crossed my path.

Sigh.

Boss never made things easy, did he?

Cocking my head to one side, I listened hard. No small animals scurried through the underbrush. Cold had driven them into their burrows, or maybe they'd sensed my presence and had hunkered down in place. Tree branches swayed and cracked under the weight of the snow. Safe in his roost, an owl hooted a protest at my incursion. I didn't hear any footsteps, but that wouldn't last. I had to get cracking before the wolves crossed my path or figured out that I'd disabled their cameras.

On silent feet, I hurried toward the lodge. The wind blew inland from the lake, carrying my scent away from the wolves who patrolled near its shores, a stroke of pure luck. A hundred yards from the lodge, I cut to the west and carefully worked my way toward the water, intending to approach the structure from the rear.

Splash.

The sound of a pebble plopping into the lake brought me to an abrupt halt. I scanned the shoreline.

A solitary figure wearing a boxy parka stood silhouetted against the water. Bare feminine legs gleamed in the dim moonlight. Shivering, the woman rubbed her hands together.

I drew in a slow breath, capturing her natural fragrance. Beneath my skin, my bear stirred, lifted his head, and sniffed the air. What was that delectable scent? A honeyed sweetness cut with something sharp, something with an acrid bite. It reminded me of the tangy scent of citrus oil that lingered on my fingers after I peeled an orange. I licked my lips, savoring the bittersweet perfume, then startled.

What the hell. The woman was human, not a wolf.

I shook my head, smiling at my good fortune. I'd done my research. The only humans in the Black Rock Guardians pack were the Hagen women, the alpha's mate and her two cousins. What were the odds that I'd stumble across a member of the wolf alpha's family?

Medved would fucking love this. And nothing insured my longevity more than keeping the boss happy.

I snuck between the trees and planted myself on the rocks, cutting off her path to the lodge. She turned around and spied me. Her eyes grew wide with shock.

My bogeyman persona slipped naturally into place. "Keep quiet." I imbued my voice with menace. "Don't fight, and you won't get hurt."

I expected the woman to react like every other target I'd confronted. To shrink back in terror. To tremble and comply with my orders. Instead, she clenched her jaw and drew her dark brows together. Her eyes flashed.

Was she… shit… was she actually going to put up a fight?

She sucked in a breath. Before a scream could escape her lips, I lunged and slapped a hand over her mouth. The little human bit me—*bit me*—sinking her teeth deep into the pad of my thumb. Blood dripped down onto my wrist. With the sharp tip of her ankle boot, she walloped me in the shin. The pain was nothing—I could handle physical pain, and her blow barely registered—but surprise smacked me upside the head.

I wrapped my free hand around her throat and hauled her struggling body against my chest. Her shoulder bore no sign of a claiming bite, so she wasn't the alpha's mate or the cousin who had recently mated one of his top lieutenants. By the process of elimination, it was Liv Hagen who bucked and writhed against me, refusing to give up the fight. Amazement blasted through me. Most enemies whimpered and surrendered when I growled an order, but not this fragile human.

Disobedience wouldn't do her a lick of good. Not in the long run. Not when she stood face-to-face with my unforgiving, hardass alpha. It would be a kindness—a mercy—to allow her to learn that lesson from my hand and not Medved's. Time to shut this insubordination down and let her know who was in charge. I tightened my grip on her vulnerable neck, careful not to do serious harm as I cut off her breath.

I brought my mouth to her ear. "Don't *want* to hurt you. Doesn't mean I won't." I paused, breathing in that enticing orange peel scent.

For fuck's sake. She's a job. Pull your head out of your ass.

Her oxygen-deprived body stilled as she gave up the fight.

"You gonna be good?" I demanded.

She jerked her head in a yes. I eased my grip on her throat and slid my hand away from her mouth. Big mistake. Her chest rose as she filled her lungs with air. The stubborn woman was getting ready to scream.

Covering her mouth again, I shrugged. Enough was enough, dammit.

"Have it your way," I muttered.

With one hand, I grabbed handcuffs from the pocket of my cargo pants and slapped them onto her wrists. I forced one end of my scarf past her lips then wrapped its length around her head, silencing her with a makeshift gag.

She kicked me again, a hard strike to the side of my knee that would have knocked a human off his feet. Against a grizzly shifter, the blow was little more than a love tap.

My luck avoiding the wolf patrols wouldn't hold. I had to get to the car with my prisoner before they spotted me. I tossed the woman over my shoulder, took a step, then remembered Medved's instructions.

"Boss wants me to leave a calling card," I told her, pulling a metal canister out of another pocket. I dropped down on one knee and spray-painted a single word across the rocks.

MEDVED

It was a mocking "fuck you" to a young wolf alpha who had absolutely failed to keep his family safe. A blatant reminder that bears could run rings around wolves anytime and anyplace. An insult aimed at the heart of the Black Rock Guardians.

Pivoting on my heel, I strode away from the lodge. My prisoner arched her back and squirmed. Her coat and short dress rode up, exposing her bare thighs.

What was a human thinking coming outside in this weather with naked legs? I tugged the fabric down, then clamped a hand against her thighs, pinning both her and her skirt in place. The gag kept her from crying out, but she grunted loudly enough to catch the ears of any nearby wolf.

I shook my head. Did the woman have *any* sense of self-preservation? I smacked her pert, round ass once, just hard enough to get her attention. "Quiet," I ordered in a low voice.

She huffed a protest and redoubled her efforts, thrashing wildly and making rumbling sounds deep in her throat.

I dropped her onto her feet. She wobbled. I grabbed her shoulders, steadying her. Above the scarf that covered the bottom half of her face, her brown eyes shot daggers at me. She pulled back her foot.

"You won't like what happens if you kick me again," I warned.

Narrowing her eyes, she considered my threat, saw I meant business, and slowly placed her boot back on the ground.

Well shit. Maybe self-preservation and the little human weren't strangers after all.

"Good girl," I breathed.

She nodded, acknowledging my praise. Her cuffed wrists blasted up, and she punched the underside of my chin with balled fists.

I blinked.

Did she… did she seriously think she could knock me off-balance and escape, or was striking out nothing more than a defiant fuck you, like Medved's message to the wolf alpha?

Didn't matter. What mattered was getting my captive out of the woods undetected. What mattered was teaching her to mind her manners and do as she was told, otherwise the foolhardy human wouldn't survive her first meeting with Medved.

Five minutes in her company and the woman had already proved to be a major pain in my ass. I shouldn't give a damn about what happened once I turned her over to the boss, but I did. The pesky human had snuck right under my defenses.

What was up with that?

I tightened my grip on her shoulders and leaned over till we were nose to nose. "Listen up," I snarled. "Hold still. Keep quiet, or I'll make you behave."

Her cheeks flushed a pretty pink. A mutinous expression crossed her face. She snorted and rolled her eyes.

Not intimidated, was she?

Reluctant admiration wound through me, a sentiment I mercilessly quashed. I knew exactly where my loyalties lay. The absolute last thing I could afford was to see her as anything other than a job.

I banded one hand around her nape and cupped her throat with the other. Her bewitching orange peel scent flooded my nostrils. Beneath my fingertips, her pulse quickened. Mine sped up to match it, echoing her own.

What the hell?

I shook my head, trying in vain to banish my troublesome reaction to the woman. My fingers tightened on her slender neck. I lowered my voice. "I mean it. Give me trouble, and I'll choke you out then carry you out here unconscious."

At the threat, her eyes widened and she froze. I held still, too, my face set in unyielding lines. This was a battle of wills I didn't want to lose. I didn't want to cut off her air. I didn't want to watch the light fade from her pretty brown eyes when she slipped into unconsciousness.

When was the last time I hesitated during a mission?

My self-control is out of whack, dammit.

Seconds ticked by. Her shoulders slumped and her defiance melted away as the fight went out of her. I forced her chin up and locked eyes with her, mesmerized by the hazel flecks that glittered in her irises.

What is wrong with me?

"Don't want to hurt you." I deliberately gave my voice a hard edge. Still, the words held a ring of truth.

She jerked her head in acknowledgment and didn't resist when I slung her over my shoulder once again. She hung limply, as quiet as a mouse. I knew better than to trust this meek act. Victims often cooperated to avoid pain. If she caught sight of a wolf, her bogus submission would evaporate and she'd raise a ruckus, bringing the wolves down on my head.

Disappointing Medved was not an outcome I wanted to entertain.

I slipped into the trees and stealthily worked my way back to the road. Twice I heard the distant sound of paws slapping the ground. Both times I halted and braced myself for a fight, but the wolves moved on without detecting our presence.

As soon as I emerged from the forest, I settled my prisoner on her feet. Sweeney stepped out of the car and rushed to my side.

"What do we have here?" Catching her chin between his stubby fingers, he tilted her face up and pushed the scarf aside, baring her shoulder.

At the sight of the Sweeney's hands on her body, irrational rage heated my blood. I grabbed hold of his wrist and yanked it away from her throat. "Back the fuck off."

Unfazed by my anger, the coyote cackled and glanced my way. "A human. Not mated. Gotta be Liv Hagen. You've done all right for yourself, son. Vilhauer will be pleased."

Son? I bristled at the patronizing moniker. And I didn't give a damn whether the coyote alpha was pleased or not. "She's going with me," I reminded him.

He rocked back on his heels. "Well, now. We might need to rethink that plan. There's nothing Vilhauer would like better than getting his hands on one of the Hagen bitches."

Liv's knee shot up and she nailed the coyote jackass in the balls. He doubled over, cupping his junk with both hands.

"Why you little—" he spat.

Biting back a grin, I stepped between them and held up a warning hand. "*My* prisoner."

"We'll just see about that," he sniffed.

Ignoring him, I opened the passenger door, guided the woman onto the front seat, and secured the seat belt around her. With her arms pinned down and her wrists bound, she couldn't reach the buckle to free herself. She wasn't going anywhere.

"You can get in the back," I called to Sweeney over my shoulder.

He grunted an indignant protest.

"Or not." I shrugged, perfectly willing to leave him on the side of the road on the outskirts of wolf territory. I climbed into the driver's seat, slid it way back, then gave him ten seconds to make up his mind. When he didn't move, I turned the key.

Muttering under his breath, Sweeney opened the door and crawled onto the back seat.

I pulled a U-ey and steered toward Belle Reve, the riverside resort town an hour away where I'd made my base during my assignment in Washington state.

While I drove, I made a plan. After a quick stop at the motel to pick up my duffel and my rental car, the Hagen woman and I would start the long trip home. We'd drive to a small airport north of Seattle where I'd stowed one of the pack's bush planes, a 1950 de Havilland DHC-2 Beaver. From there, we'd fly directly to central Alaska.

Touching down in Canada was impossible. No way could I smuggle a kidnap victim through Canadian customs. I'd modified the Beaver to carry extra fuel in the wing tips and rolled a 55-gallon drum into the cabin. With that and what it carried in the fuselage tanks, we should just be able to make it home without stopping to refuel. If all went according to plan, we'd land at the pack's airstrip in early evening.

I'd turn my prisoner over to the alpha and walk away without a backward glance. Exactly what I'd always done. My out-of-left-field pity, respect, attraction—whatever you wanted to call it—be damned. I had my orders.

I cut a glance at my captive. She sat up straight, vibrating with tension. Her eyes scanned the woods outside the car. If she was hoping for rescue—for a wolf to bound out from between the trees—she was shit out of luck. I'd put the hurt on any fool who tried to stop me from completing my assignment. That included my quote unquote ally who sat sulking in the back seat.

We rode in silence till I turned off the logging road onto the state highway leading to town.

"Mmmh." Liv made a guttural sound, jerked her chin up, and stomped her feet. "Mmmh."

"You having trouble breathing?" I'd jammed a big wad of fabric into her mouth. Despite my threat to choke her out, I had zero interest in actually cutting off her air.

She bobbed her head.

"Okay." I pulled the car onto the shoulder of the highway and turned to her. I couldn't trust any promise she made to keep quiet, so I didn't ask for one. "I'm gonna take out the gag, but if you scream or pitch a fit, I'll shut that shit down." Eyes locked on hers—so she'd see I was serious—I took a bottle of pills from my hoodie's pocket and gave it a good shake. The rattling sound pulled her attention from my face to the knock-out pills. "One of these will put you under for six to eight hours. Keep quiet or go nighty-night. You decide."

With the scarf covering her mouth, I couldn't see her lips turn down, but from her narrowed eyes and furrowed brow, the woman was scowling at me. Let her. I didn't expect her to be happy about being kidnapped. I did expect her to obey me.

The woman was a fighter. I knew with one hundred percent certainty that she was biding her time, waiting for an opportunity to escape. If I knew what was good for me—and I did—I wouldn't give her the chance.

One reluctant nod of her head signaled her compliance.

"All right." I unwound the scarf and tugged the ball of fabric from her mouth.

She sucked in a deep breath, coughed, then smacked her lips. "Yuck."

I grabbed a bottle of water from the console and held it up. "Drink?"

"Yes," she croaked. I screwed off the cap and held the bottle to her mouth. She tilted her head back and opened her mouth. Her lips closed over the bottle top. She took three deep swallows.

My traitorous cock twitched. I adjusted my pants, hoping she didn't notice.

She slumped against the seat. "What now?"

I cleared my throat. No harm in telling her. "Now I take you to Alaska."

She swallowed and cleared her throat. "To Medved?"

"Yeah." I watched closely for her reaction. Panic flared behind her eyes before she banked the emotion.

Smart woman. Medved was one scary son of a bitch, a trait he inherited from his father. In the 1950s, the senior Medved had come within spitting distance of exterminating the Black Rock Guardians. After launching a surprise attack on the wolf pack, he'd driven the survivors out of Alaska and seized their land and goods.

The wolves had retreated to the lower 48 with their greatest treasure in tow, their Black Rock, the boulder sized meteorite that imbued shifters with extra speed, power, and stamina.

Every member of the wolf pack wore a leather bracelet holding a wire-wrapped chip of the black rock against their skin.

A handful of grizzlies wore similar bracelets, taken from dead wolf soldiers during the war. Medved hoarded the chunks of stone like a miser's gold, but as his top enforcer, I was allowed to wear one. He wanted a piece of the meteorite for every one of his soldiers. That was the only reason he'd allied with the wolf pack's coyote enemies.

From the back seat came the sound of Sweeney's voice speaking low into his phone. "You won't believe who landed in our laps, Mr. Vilhauer." A pause, then, "We got Liv Hagen, sir." Glancing into the rearview mirror, I saw Sweeney vigorously nod his head in agreement with whatever his dipshit alpha was saying. "You're absolutely right. This changes everything. You can finally get payback for your boys."

A month ago, somebody had murdered Vilhauer's two sons. Medved ordered me to look into it. I discovered that the men had turned traitor, believing that their father was leading the coyote pack to destruction. They'd reached out to the new wolf alpha, Adam Landry, and offered to overthrow their father and broker a peace between their packs. When Landry showed up to their meeting, he'd found the coyote dissidents with their throats slit.

Vilhauer knew nothing of his sons' double-dealing and blamed the wolves for their deaths. I had no clue who killed the men, but I doubted Landry was responsible for the deaths of his would-be allies. Preemptive murder wasn't his style, but Vilhauer was champing at the bit, eager for revenge. Bet he'd like nothing better than to kill a member of Landry's family and toss her body onto wolf pack land.

Anger flooded my veins once again. Not going to happen on my watch.

Twisting around in the seat, I snatched the phone from Sweeney's hand and crushed it in my fist.

"What the hell?" he sputtered.

"Get out of the car," I ordered.

"It's *my* car," he protested. "You got no right to kick me out of my own vehicle."

"Yeah, well, Liv Hagen is *my* prisoner," I countered. "My alpha ordered me to bring her to Alaska, and that's what I'm gonna do."

"But Vilhauer—"

I didn't bother to hide my contempt. "Vilhauer can take it up with Medved."

If he dared.

Sweeney gaped at me, his mouth hanging open.

I'd mastered the menacing scowl. No need to raise my voice to get my point across. "Get out of the car."

He opened his mouth to argue some more, but the look on my face shut him up. He scooted across the seat, scrambled out, and slammed the door.

"Good riddance," I muttered, pulling onto the highway.

"Amen," the woman breathed.

Sharing a moment, were we?

I cut her a sideways glance. "If Sweeney shifts and runs, he'll be in Belle Reve in no time. Best thing for both of us is to be long gone before he meets with Vilhauer and rallies the coyotes."

She made a face. "You're telling me I'd be better off with the grizzlies than the coyotes?"

Well, now, I couldn't guarantee that, could I?

"My orders are to deliver you safe and sound to Medved. You'll be better off with me." That was true. Ish. For now anyway.

She sniffed and slouched down onto her seat. I swore I could see the wheels turning in her head.

Liv Hagen wasn't going to make this easy on me, was she?

Chapter Two

Liv

"You'll be better off with me," the giant said.

Maybe.

Coyotes or grizzlies, both were bad news. The coyote alpha blamed Adam for the deaths of his sons. Killing me would settle the score. But Medved was the ultimate bad guy, the leader of the same grizzly pack that almost wiped out the Black Rock Guardians decades ago.

I needed a better option than either of the pack's sworn enemies, a door number three if you will.

Where the hell were the wolves?

Huddled against the car seat, I kept one eye on my captor and one eye on the landscape flying past outside the window.

Patience and I weren't friends. We were barely acquaintances. If you don't believe me, ask my twin sister, Annika. When the powers that be doled out virtues, Annika inherited a double dose of sweetness and serenity, while I got a shit ton of irritability and impatience. According to the wolves I played cards with every week, I possessed the world's worst poker face.

Restlessness and aggravation ate a hole in my stomach. I had to fight the urge to chew my bottom lip and squirm, but I didn't want to give away my fear to the mammoth grizzly behind the wheel.

I'd lost all sense of time. It felt like hours instead of minutes since I'd ducked out of the birthday celebration in the lodge's noisy and stuffy party hall. Wolves partied hard. Music played nonstop and the dancing shifters threw off a lot of heat. That second piece of cake I scarfed down—on top of a giant margarita and the pounding percussive beat of the music—unsettled my stomach.

And to top it all off, I felt like a fifth wheel at my own birthday party. My sister snuggled on the lap of her new mate, Zane. Marit and Adam kept making goo-goo eyes at each other. I laughed and danced with my teenaged cousin Xander and with Zane's brother, Remy, but nobody looked at me the way Zane and Adam looked at their mates. Not that I begrudged them their happiness. I wasn't that selfish, but still…

I needed fresh air and a short break from the commotion and my blissed-out, partnered-up relatives. Grabbing my parka, I slipped outside into the snowy night. I wandered down to the lake shore and came face-to-face with one of Medved's minions.

How anybody managed to sneak past the patrols and the security cameras was beyond me. Carrying me through the woods without tripping an alarm should have been impossible, yet my kidnapper pulled it off.

And now, restrained by both handcuffs and a seat belt, I scanned the forest, desperately searching for any sign of help. Annika and Marit must have realized I'd been gone too long. Somebody would follow my footprints down to the lake. They'd see the message the grizzly spray-painted on the rocks.

The Black Rock Guardians would come to the rescue. Any minute now, wolf soldiers would burst through the trees and surround the car. Or maybe I'd look in the rearview mirror and see a convoy of pack vehicles bearing down on us. Adam and

Zane would rally the troops and chase us to the ends of the earth.

All I had to do was delay things till they showed up.

I glanced at my captor. He'd shoved down his hood, revealing a shaved head, heavy brows, a Roman nose, and a short, dark beard. Exactly the kind of rugged features that made my girl parts perk up and take notice. He was built like a heavyweight MMA fighter, with ridiculously wide shoulders and hard-packed muscles. Again, exactly my type.

Too bad the hot guy was a card-carrying dirtbag.

Think.

Maybe… maybe I could chat him up. Act friendly. Then once he let down his guard, I could swing my legs around and kick the steering wheel, forcing the car off the road.

"What's your name, big guy?" I asked.

A moment of silence while he debated whether or not to answer. "Viggo Creed."

"Viggo." I subtly shifted my weight. "That's a nice name. Not one you hear very often."

He grunted and kept his eyes on the road.

I tried again. Angling my knees away from the door, I asked, "How long have you been working for Mr. Medved?"

He turned his head toward me. His brows drew together in an impressive scowl. "No."

"What do you mean 'no'?" I fluttered my lashes, attempting to impersonate my harmless, amiable sister.

He heaved an impatient sigh, and his fingers strangled the steering wheel, the same way he'd threatened to choke me. "*I mean*, you already tipped your hand. You've got all the charm of a wolverine. No way I'll buy your sweet and innocent act."

I gasped, fake-smiled, and painted a stunned expression across my face. Then, before my smile faded, I quickly drew my knees up to my chest and kicked at the wheel.

Viggo caught both of my ankles in one beefy paw and shoved my feet down onto the floor. He braked hard. As I bounced against the back cushion, he reached into the pocket of his hoodie and pulled out the bottle of pills. He popped off the top and plucked a green tablet from the bottle.

Slamming my lips together, I shook my head back and forth.

"Unh-unh," I protested through clenched teeth.

"I warned you," he countered.

With one hand, he squeezed my nostrils shut. With the other, he forced the tablet between my lips and past my teeth. Choking, I tried to spit out the pill. He covered my mouth with his palm.

"Swallow," he ordered, his tone implacable.

I resisted for thirty seconds before the need for oxygen forced me to give up. I choked down the pill, opened my mouth, and hauled in a lungful of air. Viggo held the water bottle to my lips again, and I drank greedily.

"Asshole." I glared at the grizzly.

He lifted a shoulder. "Not the first time I heard that."

"Eat shit and die," I piled on.

"Heard that one, too," he said.

"I bet." I shuddered. "I can't believe you roofied me."

"Roofied?" The handsome jerk had the gall to look both pissed off and offended. "Your—uh—*virtue* is safe with me. You're a job, sweetheart, nothing more. The only thing I want from you is cooperation and obedience. The sooner I turn you over to my alpha, the better."

Well, that stung. Not his assurance that he wasn't some kind of date-rape creep, but his absolute indifference to what would happen to me when he handed me off to Medved. Viggo Creed truly was a coldhearted bastard.

I slumped back in the seat, a ridiculous sense of hurt and disappointment settling in my chest.

Viggo's nose twitched, like he smelled something bad. He cut me a glance, opened his mouth, then snapped it shut without a word.

Fine. I was in no mood to chit-chat with my kidnapper.

I squeezed my eyes shut and took stock of my physical symptoms. Did I feel any different? How long till the pill took effect? My pulse was slowing down, but that could be because I'd stopped fighting. Or maybe the sedative was kicking in. Maybe the margarita amplified the effect.

I had no clue what to expect.

Shit.

I sat very still and listened to my heart beat, painfully aware of the minutes ticking by. Pursing my lips, I blew out a slow, calming breath.

"You okay?" a deep voice rumbled.

Seriously? The man abducted and drugged me—said he didn't give a damn about my well-being—then had the nerve to ask if I was all right. Held prisoner. Doped up. At the mercy of the pack's oldest enemy. My world was spinning out of control, and I was anything but okay. Tears pricked my eyes.

Don't you dare cry.

I had to… I had to… you know… assert myself. I was Liv Hagen, dammit. The granddaughter of Freya Hagen. I trembled and cowered for no man. Time to… time to set the record straight.

I forced my lids open and focused my gaze on my kidnapper's face. "I'm not afraid of you."

He leaned toward me, invading my personal space. I went cross-eyed and my vision swam. Viggo had *two noses.* I bit my lower lip, suppressing a sudden giggle. He pinched my chin and tilted my face up till we were eye to eye. The grizzly looked almost sad, as if he carried the weight of the world on his broad shoulders.

"You should be."

I frowned, confused. "What?"

"You should be afraid of me, Liv."

Fear. Oh. Yeah. Right. That's what we were talking about. I slow-blinked.

"And Medved. You gotta be careful around the boss."

"Humph," I snorted.

His expression turned deadly serious. "I mean it. If you defy or disappoint him, he'll make you pay."

"You… um… you speaking from s'perience?" The last word slurred.

"No." He shook his head. "I got too much to lose to risk disappointing Medved."

I'd think about what that meant later. Right now, I couldn't hold onto my train of thought. Everything slipped away like sand through clenched fingers. My head tipping to one side, I watched him shrug out of his hoodie. He draped it over my bare legs. It covered me from my ankles to my hips, and still held a hint of his body heat. I sighed, savoring the warmth.

"Thanks." Due to my parents' relentless reminders, the polite response came automatically to my lips.

"You're welcome."

My eyelids drooped. Unconsciousness surrounded me, inching closer and closer. Reluctant to render myself helpless and vulnerable, I battled to stay awake.

"Don't fight it," he said. "I won't let anything bad happen to you while you're asleep."

My *kidnapper* promised to keep me safe. The irony bit deep. He'd stolen me from my family. He planned to turn me over to the devil. Still, a small part of me believed him. I didn't think he'd hurt me while I was knocked out.

My head fell back against the seat, and all the strength ebbed from my limbs.

"Crap," I moaned.

My vision narrowed, and I surrendered to the darkness.

"Whoops-a-daisy," a deep voice rumbled.

Daddy used to say that when he swooped in and picked me up after I fell. Of course, I was—what?—four or five years old when that happened. I turned twenty-six yesterday. I was a grown-ass woman, not a kid. And that wasn't Dad's voice. But the sensation of being swung up in a man's strong arms was the same.

Whoops-a-daisy.

I chortled, too tired to open my eyes.

"Shhh," the same voice murmured.

My head lolled to one side, and my cheek rested against a hard chest, just like that time years ago when I fell off the monkey bars at the park. I'd howled from shock and pain, the skin on my knees and elbows scraped raw. Dad came running. He cried "whoops-a-daisy," lifted me up, and cradled me against his chest. Then, like now, came the sensation of being carried while a man strode from one place to the next.

Creak. A car door opened. The man—Viggo—deposited me inside and pulled a seat belt across my chest.

I tried to force open my eyes, but the stubborn things refused to cooperate.

The car door slammed shut. A few seconds later, the driver's-side door swung open. The car bounced as the man settled his bulk behind the wheel. I heard him fumble in the back seat, then he wedged something soft between my head and the passenger side window. A pillow.

The engine purred to life. The car lurched forward and picked up speed.

"Got my duffel," he said. "Switched cars. Now we're heading out of Belle Reve."

"'kay," I mumbled.

"I'll get the heater going."

Soon, hot air poured from the vents, surrounding me in a cocoon of warmth.

Something was wrong. I knew it. I knew I should kick up a fuss, but couldn't exactly remember why. I was so freaking tired. I couldn't find the energy to resist the absolute exhaustion that promised to drag me under.

"Go to sleep," Viggo ordered.

Yeah. Good idea.

"'kay," I repeated and burrowed into the pillow.

I came to curled on my side on a hard bench. The cushion I lay on was too thin to provide much padding. My entire body ached, and it felt like somebody had driven an ice pick into my skull.

Viggo hadn't dropped me onto the seat like a sack of potatoes, as Grandma used to say. No. My head rested on a pillow, and he'd wrapped a blanket around me.

Guess he's a considerate jerkwad asshole kidnapper.

He'd also rearranged the handcuffs. My left hand was free and tucked under the blanket, but the right lay on the pillow, still braceleted by the metal shackle. I tugged, but something held my hand in place.

Slowly opening my eyes, I squinted up at a chain connecting the cuff to a ceiling-mounted bracket. If I wanted to, I could sit, but otherwise I couldn't go far. I twisted my head around and got a better look at my surroundings. I lay on a curved bench seat in the back of a small airplane, in what should have been the third row of seats. The second row had been removed and replaced by a barrel secured in place by heavy straps. A headset covered my ears, muffling but not eliminating the drone of a powerful engine. Beneath me, I felt the small vibrations of a plane in flight.

We were in the air, on our way to Alaska.

Fuuuck.

My pulse kicked, shooting my headache into the stratosphere, like the airplane I rode in. No, I corrected myself. Small planes didn't fly that high, did they? I knew squat about private aircraft, other than what I'd gleaned by watching TV. And we all knew how reliable that information was. Even if I somehow managed to free myself and to overpower the big grizzly, I had no freaking clue how to land a plane or call for help.

My gaze darted to the front of the vehicle. My captor sat in the left seat in the cockpit—the pilot's seat—facing an old-fashioned instrument panel full of dials and switches. Beyond him, a dark sky filled the plane's windshield.

"There's water and a bottle of ibuprofen in a bag by your feet."

I jumped when Viggo's voice came through the headset.

Water. The word triggered a visceral reaction. My mouth felt absolutely parched, my tongue thick and gummy. I wobbled to a seated position and groped one-handed for the small paper bag at the opposite end of the bench seat. Checking the contents, I found water, a bottle of pills, a pair of mittens, and bag of gummy bears. I shoved the last two into the pocket of my parka for later.

Fluid and pain relief came first. The safety seals on both the water bottle's cap and ibuprofen appeared intact. I dumped two round red tablets onto my palm. They looked right. I opened the water bottle and sniffed. The water smelled fine, but what did that prove? I shook my head then winced at the pain.

The truth was, if Viggo wanted to drug me again, he wouldn't be sneaky and tamper with the water or medicine. Brute force was more his style. He'd plug my nose and force the tablet into my mouth.

Before I could second-guess myself, I popped the red pills onto my tongue and took a big swig of the water.

"We got hours of flight time ahead of us." Viggo's voice came through the headset again. "You might as well lie down and get some more sleep."

Grandma used to say I was born with a burr under my saddle, leaving me prickly and argumentative. Doing as I was told ran counter to all my instincts. The prospect of obeying my kidnapper galled me, but his advice was sound. Whatever lay ahead, I'd handle it better with more sleep under my belt.

"Asshole," I repeated on principle. Not sure if he heard me through the headset. In any case, he didn't react to the insult.

My mind churning, I lay down and tried to make myself comfortable on the hard bench. Thanks to the message spray-painted on the rocks, Adam knew for certain that the wolf pack's old enemy had struck. Kidnapping a member of the alpha's family was tantamount to a declaration of war. Adam was smart, brave, and a skilled fighter. So were the rest of his soldiers. But could they take on the largest, most feared pack in Alaska? What if something happened to Annika and Marit's mates during a rescue attempt?

"Don't get yourselves killed coming after me. I'll find a way to save myself," I whispered to myself.

Viggo glanced over his shoulder at me. Had he heard me whisper? I'd better keep my mouth shut and not blab my plans to the enemy. Closing my eyes, I willed my tense body to relax. I fell back on an old trick, mentally counting backward by sevens.

"Three hundred," I whispered. "Two hundred and ninety three. Two hundred and eighty six. Two hundred and seventy nine. Two hundred and seventy two."

By the time I got below one hundred, I was already half asleep.

A hard bump jostled me awake. The plane shuddered and rattled as it bounced over ground far too unstable to be an actual runway. Without warning, it made a sharp turn to the left and tipped over sideways.

I slid and ended up sprawled across a window.

Icy water poured into the compartment. My heart stuttered. We must have crash-landed into a lake or river. Scrambling up onto my hands and knees, I strained to keep my head above the rising flood.

Outside the opposite window, dancing flames lit up the night. Holy hell. When the plane flipped, the wing must've crumpled, rupturing a fuel tank. Whoever said fire and water didn't mix had never seen jet fuel burning on the surface of a river. With the hot engine and fuel spurting everywhere, soon the entire fuselage would be engulfed. I had to get out before I either drowned or burned.

I yanked frantically on the chain that secured me in place. It held fast.

Crap. What do I do?

I barely felt my chilled fingers as I fumbled for the bracket which was now by my feet. If I could unclip the chain, I might be able to escape the plane. My clumsy fingers finally found a small padlock.

My heart sank. Screwed. I was screwed. Another minute and my head would be under water.

"Dammit," I gasped, panic squeezing my chest.

"I got you." Viggo's voice boomed through the headset.

Glancing toward the cockpit, I watched him splash toward me. Relief hit me like a sucker punch. Who would've guessed the sight of my kidnapper would fill me with such joy?

Chapter Three

Viggo

The Beaver was one helluva fine bush plane. A warhorse. A beast. But as strong and reliable as she was, the weather in Alaska was a fickle bitch. Forecasters predicted a wet warm front to push into the central part of the state some time after midnight, bringing with it a temperature inversion and the threat of freezing rain.

No problem. I'd stay ahead of the weather and be home with my feet up and a glass of scotch in my hand long before the freezing rain hit.

Hah.

The front rolled in hours earlier than expected. Freezing rain pelted the plane. Without a de-icer, I had to drop altitude and find warmer air. I descended into a heavily forested river valley, surrounded on all sides by rugged mountains. Above me, the damned freezing rain didn't let up. At the lower altitude, the engine gobbled up the fuel reserves.

I'd lived in Alaska all my life and recognized this heavily forested valley. At this altitude, I was never gonna clear the pass. And the storm was only getting worse. The sun rode low in the sky, and I didn't have time to search for an open, grassy meadow. A river wound its way through the valley. I flew along it, my eyes scanning for a straight spot along the bank, a place I could set the plane down. Out of the gloom, I finally spied it. A spit of sand, barely a hundred yards long, and as narrow as my landing gear.

I circled around to line up my approach. Visibility was down to less than half a mile, and ice was beginning to frost my windshield.

You'd better land it right the first time.

Settling my hips in my seat, I adjusted my grip on the wheel and set the Beaver down. The beefy wheels crunched across the gravel bar.

Just as I was breathing a sigh of relief, one of the main wheels slipped into the river. Off-balance, the plane veered into the water. I pulled back on the yoke and added power, but I wasn't fast enough. The wheel sunk into the water and gravel, slewing the plane sideways. Forward momentum tipped the plane on its side, and the wing caught the ground. I fought the controls, but the accident had taken on a life of its own.

The wing crumpled. Avgas sprayed into a fine mist, the fuselage sagged into the river, and icy water poured in. I was just unbuckling my belt when a large orange light blossomed out the side window. The fuel had caught fire.

I grabbed my go bag and jumped from my seat.

"Dammit," Liv cried from the back of the plane. The helpless desperation in her voice cut me to the quick. Chained to ceiling, surrounded by rising water, she had to be scared out of her head. No time to waste.

"I got you." I sloshed through the water to reach her.

With her brown hair plastered to her head, Liv looked like a drowned rat as she struggled to free herself.

"Lemme." I fumbled for the padlock that attached the chain to the ceiling bracket. Instead of spinning the dial underwater, I twisted it apart, releasing the chain. I slung an arm around Liv's waist, pulled her to her feet, and tossed her over my shoulder. Reaching up, I opened the aft door and clambered out. Not wanting to plow through the flames that surrounded the Beaver, I let the river carry us a dozen yards downstream, then climbed onto the bank.

I deposited the fragile human on the gravel then turned to wade back into the river.

"What are you doing?" she called through chattering teeth.

"Gotta disable the transponder." Last thing I needed was for the FAA to hone into the rescue beacon and track our location. Keep the humans out of pack business, that was the alpha's rule. I'd use the satellite phone in the emergency go bag to call the pack for help.

Fighting the current, I made my way to the Beaver. I ducked inside the wreck, shut down the transponder, grabbed my duffel, then swam back to the riverbank. For ten seconds I watched fire lick at the crumpled fuselage. Despair shot through me. Medved would be beside himself at the loss of the reliable old girl.

Shaking my head, I turned to my prisoner.

Liv's body shook violently. Soaking wet, with bare legs, and cheeks flushed scarlet from the frigid air, the human was in trouble. I knew of a shelter cabin ten miles to the north but couldn't risk the hike through the woods. Liv would succumb to hypothermia before I could get her there. The sun had dipped below the horizon and the temperature was plummeting. The woman needed shelter and heat *now.* I stomped into the forest, my eyes scanning our surroundings for a promising spot to take cover.

There, straight ahead, I spotted an upturned white spruce. Its root ball stretched a good ten feet across, wide enough to provide shelter from the wind.

"Gonna build a fire," I told Liv, depositing her on her feet. The key to the handcuffs was tucked away safely in my pocket. I freed her right hand from the metal cuff then pulled a waterproof, windproof emergency sleeping bag from the go bag and shook it out. It was flimsy and lightweight, but the Mylar lining would reflect ninety percent of her body heat back at her while I built the fire. I helped her step into it and tugged it up to her shoulders. "You wanna sit?" I asked.

"On the cold ground? No." Her pink cheeks had paled, a warning sign of hypothermia. "I'll stand here out of the wind till you get the fire going."

"I'll hurry," I promised. A lifetime spent in the woods—coupled with shifter strength and speed—meant I could make short work of chopping wood and starting a fire. The emergency go bag held everything I needed: an ax, a knife, and a fire-starting rod. It also held a metal coffeepot and two cups, a pair of snowshoes, a second Mylar sleeping bag, two woolen blankets, a pouch of food, and a satellite phone, among other things.

Like they say, I was loaded for bear.

Ha.

I dragged a crumbling log close to our proposed shelter then quickly gathered kindling and a pile of bigger branches. I shaved curls of kindling wood onto the nest of dry tinder I'd collected and lit the fire. The flames caught and I piled on more branches.

With the lid, I scooped snow into the coffeepot and set it near the fire to heat. There was a hot cocoa packet in the food pouch, and I wanted to get something warm into Liv.

While she huddled close to the flames, I kicked snow away from the fire and the upturned tree roots. Next, I cut away some of the dangling roots that blocked easy access to the shelter. I chopped ten-foot lengths of narrow tree trunks and leaned them against the top of the root ball, creating the skeleton for a sort of lean-to. Wide strips of bark filled in the openings between the logs. A bed of dead pine needles and fresh boughs would help insulate us from the cold ground. Finally, I jammed several short branches into the ground near the fire, creating a sort of drying rack.

I glanced at Liv. "Gimme your coat, dress, and boots."

"What?" she sputtered. "Dude, I'm not stripping in front of you."

My lip quirked. Nobody but this feisty, gotta-be-freezing-her-ass-off woman would dare call me dude. Most packmates cringed in my presence and referred to me as Mr. Creed, or sir.

Not Liv.

"You'll never warm up if you spend the night in wet clothes." I pointed at the sticks wedged into the ground. "I'll put your things close to the fire to dry out."

"Forget it." She yanked the emergency sleeping bag up to her ears.

Shy and ladylike were the last words I'd use to describe Liv, so something else was going on with her. My gut told me the stubborn woman was desperate to retain some semblance of control over her life, and she definitely didn't want to be naked in front of me.

I bit the inside of my cheek. I never got a good look at her body underneath the down parka, but her legs were shapely, and I bet her figure matched.

What the fuck am I doing?

Was there anything more pointless, more self-destructive than being attracted to the woman I was turning over to my heartless boss?

Time to shut this shit down.

I stepped toward her and deliberately shaped my features into an intimidating scowl. "You telling me you'd rather freeze to death than take off your wet clothes?"

She didn't answer, probably realizing how foolish she'd sound if she said yes.

"My orders are to bring you safe and sound to Medved. I can't let you get hypothermia."

"And a flunky like you doesn't dare disappoint his alpha, right?" Scorn dripped from her voice.

"That's right." No point in taking offense when she spoke the truth. I lowered my chin and put command into my voice. "So either you strip, or I'll do it for you."

Color returned to her cheeks in an angry flush. "Try it, buddy, and you'll lose a hand."

I could easily overpower the mouthy woman and peel her clothes off. Grizzly shifter versus human? Hell, no contest. Liv wasn't stupid. She had to realize how powerless and vulnerable she was. Still, she jutted out her chin, and her pretty brown eyes shot sparks.

Rubbing the back of my neck, I debated how to handle the insolent human. I'd ripped her away from everybody and everything she knew. Her next few days were bound to be rough, especially if she shot off her mouth in front of Medved. Why not cut her some slack? If she saw me as a reasonable man, she might be more willing to listen when I warned her to mind her manners in front of my alpha.

"How about I turn around and look the other way while you undress?" I proposed.

The fingers clutching the top of the sleeping bag had turned bone white, and she trembled from the cold. "Fine," she said reluctantly. "Do it."

I put my back to her. "Just don't get any crazy ideas about picking up a branch and clobbering me."

She snorted. "We're in the middle of godforsaken nowhere." I heard rustling as she dropped the sleeping bag and shed her wet clothes. My imagination filled in the details as I imagined her naked behind me. "Even if I managed to knock you out, where would I go?"

"Exactly," I agreed.

"You can turn around." I did. She'd tugged the sleeping bag up to her armpits and held out her sodden clothes and boots. "I put the gloves and gummy bears in the parka's pocket," she added.

I fished the mittens and candy from the pocket then stuck the boots upside down on a pair of branches. After spreading her clothes out on other sticks, I glanced with satisfaction around our encampment. The tree would block the wind. The pile of firewood I'd gathered wouldn't last the night. I'd go out in a few hours and collect more.

Dropping into a crouch, I unzipped the waterproof go bag and pulled out the wool blankets. I handed them to Liv. "Wrap yourself up. I'm gonna spread the other wool blanket on the ground as insulation and tack one of the Mylar sleeping bags up on the root ball, behind where we'll sleep. It'll reflect back heat from the fire. We can bundle up under the other wool blanket and Mylar bag and settle for the night all comfy cozy."

Liv's eyebrows shot up. "Did the big scary grizzly shifter actually say *comfy cozy*?"

Yeah. Yeah I did.

Sometimes the damnedest things popped out of my mouth. I pivoted the conversation, nodding at the coffeepot. "I'm heating water for hot cocoa."

Liv slid a blanket inside her Mylar cocoon and did a little shimmy while she wrapped it around her body. The emergency sleeping bag fell to the ground. She kicked it toward me. I tacked it up on the root ball behind where we'd sleep, then spread the second wool blanket over the bed of boughs. Liv dropped to the ground, drew her knees to her chest, and snuggled down under the wool blanket. I draped the second Mylar sleeping bag around her shoulders.

Now to warm her insides. I fixed the cocoa and handed the cup to Liv. She held it close to her mouth, breathing in the chocolate-scented steam. Her lips turned up, the first marginally pleasant expression she'd shown in my presence.

"Marshmallows," she sighed.

I nodded. "I have it on good authority that marshmallows are non-negotiable in hot cocoa."

"Well, remind me to thank your 'good authority.'" She took a deep swallow. Her eyelids fluttered shut and pure pleasure shone on her face. "It feels amazing to drink something warm."

My chest tightened. This break in hostilities between us—her moment of happiness—wouldn't last. I had no clue what Medved intended for the gutsy human, but I knew down to my bones that it wasn't good.

Medved.

Now that the prisoner was warm and safe, I had to report in. "Stay put," I ordered. "I'll be back in a few minutes." Snatching up the go bag, I marched into the woods. I stopped a short distance away, close enough to keep an eye on Liv, but far enough that she couldn't overhear my conversation.

Thirty seconds later, the sat phone acquired a signal. I punched in Medved's personal number.

"Where the hell are you?" he barked.

Great. Boss was already in a pissy mood, a pissy mood that morphed into a full-on rage when I told him about the accident.

"You fucking crashed the Beaver?" he exploded.

The old plane was more than reliable means of transport. Originally owned by the Black Rock Guardians, it was a prize of war. With all their pilots dead, the wolves had abandoned their small fleet of planes when they fled the state at the end of the conflict. I swear, Medved gloated every time he laid eyes on the Beavers. And now, one of them floated down the river, a crumpled and burned-out hulk.

I squeezed my eyes shut, bracing for the inevitable threats of dire punishment. Medved knew all the chinks in my armor and wasn't above exploiting them. A moment of silence, then he asked, "And the prisoner?"

Looked like the threats of punishment could wait.

"She survived the crash and is secured," I said.

"She?"

Damn. Medved had no clue who I'd captured. "Yes, sir… I took Liv Hagen."

Another longer silence, then, "You're bringing me a member of the wolf alpha's family?"

"That's right." The words came reluctantly. Liv had been giving me grief since the moment I confronted her, but the idea of turning her over to my brutal boss troubled my conscience.

My conscience. That was rich. I'd learned to shut that little voice down years ago. Maxim Medved's top enforcer couldn't afford to indulge any inconvenient sense of right and wrong.

"Well, now." I imagined my alpha gleefully rubbing his hands together. "You make sure she stays in one piece till I get my hands on her."

"Yes, sir." I intended to do exactly that.

"Where are you?" he asked.

I told him, adding, "Come first light, we're gonna hike to a shelter cabin ten miles north of here."

"I know the place," Medved said. "Once you get there, sit tight and wait for an extraction team. When the weather permits, I'll send a chopper. Might take a couple of days to get there. Keep a close eye on the Hagen woman till your packmates arrive."

"Will do."

He hung up without another word.

Pain flared in the back of my head.

"Suck it up," I muttered, rubbing the base of my skull.

I made a quick call home to assure them I was okay, shoved the sat phone into the go bag, and tromped back to our campsite. Liv had finished her cocoa and was holding her hands out toward the flames. Firelight danced across her face, highlighting prominent cheekbones and a slender jawline. The heat had colored her cheeks a healthy pink.

I added another log to the crackling fire then removed my boots and set them by the flames. With my back to her, I peeled off my wet hoodie, long-sleeved tee, cargo pants, and boxers, and spread them out to dry.

"Here."

I glanced over my shoulder at Liv, who held out the second wool blanket.

"You keep it," I said. "Shifters run hot. I'm fine."

"Well, I'm not fine," she countered. "You think I want to watch you walk around like that?"

"Huh?" I whirled to face her.

She held up a hand to block the view. "Dude, seriously. Put your junk away."

The words sounded flip, but I caught a hint of anxiety behind them. I stood still and honed my senses. Her heart rate had sped up, and the scent of fear rode the air.

Being naked was no big deal to shifters. We stripped before assuming our animal forms. I never gave it a second thought. But Liv was a human—a human who'd been taken captive by the enemy, a now naked enemy.

I took the blanket she held out and wrapped it around my shoulders. Softening my voice, I said, "I didn't mean to scare you."

Defiance flashed in her eyes. "You don't scare me, remember?"

Brave words, but I knew better. I'm a master at manipulating fear to achieve my goal, at putting a man on the ragged edge, balanced between panic and hope. I scared her, all right, but I had no need to rub her face in it.

Squatting, I pawed through my duffel till I found two pairs of sweat pants and a sweatshirt. The bag wasn't waterproof and the pants were slightly damp, but the heat radiating from my skin would dry them out eventually. I hiked one pair up over my hips, laid the other pair of pants and sweatshirt next to the fire, then dropped onto the ground next to Liv.

"So what happens next?" she asked.

"We get some sleep," I said. "Then tomorrow morning we make our way to a cabin I know of about ten miles north of here."

Liv moaned. "If I'd know I was going to get kidnapped, I would've worn something more substantial than a short, skimpy dress to my birthday party."

"Your birthday party?"

"Yep." She bobbed her head. "You kidnapped me on my birthday, big guy."

Where did that ridiculous impulse to apologize come from?

I clamped my lips together and busied myself opening the food pouch.

"You hungry?" I grunted.

She leaned close and peered into the pouch. "What do we have?"

"Protein bars, peanut butter crackers, jerky, dehydrated apples and cranberries, almonds, dried chickpeas with sriracha—"

Hey eyes lit up. "I love spicy food. I'll take the chickpeas with sriracha."

I shuddered and handed them over.

"What? You don't like spicy stuff?" she asked, tearing open the package.

"Nope," I said emphatically. "Not the taste. Not the smell."

"Unless you plan to kiss me—which I wouldn't recommend trying—we won't have a problem." She popped a handful of chickpeas into her mouth.

My gaze fell on lips that still held a faint stain from the red lipstick she'd worn to the party. When she wasn't verbally abusing me, Liv's mouth was downright pretty, with a plump lower lip and an extra deep notch in the upper one. When she was nervous, she gnawed on her lower lip, chewing it like a dog with a bone. I knew better than to point that out. Comparing a woman to a dog? Never a good idea. And why let on how easy I found it to read her emotional state?

I tore my eyes away my captive and stared into the fire. For several minutes, the crunch of Liv chomping on her spicy treat was the only sound to disturb the night. Then I heard it, something creeping through the underbrush a dozen yards away. Tilting my head to one side, I focused my senses and detected two heartbeats. Caught a whiff of cat, not the familiar scent of lynx, but something new.

I sat up straight, my eyes scanning the darkness.

"What is it?" Liv spoke through a mouthful of chickpeas.

"Shhh." I held up a warning hand.

Twigs cracked as the pair stalked closer. Within seconds, two big cats crouched in the underbrush, firelight reflecting golden-yellow in their eyes. Cougars. What the hell. I'd heard rumors that Canadian cougars had been encroaching into the state, but this was the first time I'd encountered the predatory beasts inside Alaska.

"Are those wolves?" she whispered, hope in her voice.

The big cats rarely attacked humans. But the mere possibility of them coming at Liv—slashing and biting her vulnerable skin—sent my protective urges into overdrive.

"Cougars." I slowly rose to my feet. I shoved the sweatpants down my legs. Naked, I touched the black rock. Power slammed into me. I sucked in a deep breath and shifted.

CHAPTER FOUR

LIV

For a few tantalizing seconds, hope dangled in front of my eyes. Maybe Adam and his wolves had caught up with us. Or—more likely—he'd reached out to wolf shifter allies in Alaska, and they'd tracked us down. They'd rescue me. Within twenty-four hours, I'd be home in Washington, and I'd put this fiasco—and Viggo—behind me.

"Cougars." The single word stomped out that hope.

The Black Rock Guardians had recently allied with a small pack of lynx shifters in New Hampshire, the same pack who'd helped Zane rescue my sister from a vengeful coyote. When he announced the alliance, Adam mentioned that they were the wolves' first feline allies.

That meant natural cougars—wild predatory animals with sharp teeth and claws—watched us from the shadows. Their bright, unblinking eyes glittered in the darkness. I sensed rather than saw them coil their muscles, preparing to pounce.

Sympathy for every mouse cornered by a cat spiked through me. I had absolutely no intention of ending up kitty chow. I crawled sideways and wrapped my hand around one of the branches forming our lean-to. If it came to a fight, I'd go down swinging.

Viggo stood and kicked off his pants. The air surrounding him shimmered, and I smelled ozone, both signs of an impending shift. A grizzly took shape among the sparkling lights.

No more than three feet away from me, the beast reared back on his hind legs, towering over me. Tawny brown fur glinted in the firelight. He huffed a clear warning at the cougars.

A year ago I had no idea supernatural creatures existed. Since then I'd wrapped my head around the reality of wolf and coyote shifters. Coyote shifters didn't spook me. Wolf shifters in animal form were bigger than their natural counterparts, but I'd lost my anxiety around them. After witnessing my brother-in-law trot across a room in wolf form and lay his head on my sister's lap, it was hard to think of the wolves as intimidating beasts.

But this freaking huge bear was another matter entirely. Danger oozed from his pores. He raked the air with sharp claws that had to be four inches long. If I were the big cats, I'd turn tail and run.

The bear dropped down onto four legs. His muscles pulsated, like a powerful engine building up steam. A deep, earsplitting growl erupted from his throat. I shivered, the hair on my forearms bristling. Scooting backward, I got as far away from the grizzly as possible. In a blur of movement, he charged, leaping over the flames and scattering sparks. The cats whirled around and bounded away, Viggo in pursuit.

I held my breath, listening for the sounds of battle. Howls of pain. Ripping flesh. I heard nothing, nothing except the crackling fire and branches creaking under the weight of snow.

Three minutes later, a naked Viggo in human form stomped into our campsite. I scanned his big body, searching for injuries. The skin covering his impossibly wide shoulders, broad chest, and chiseled abs was smooth and undamaged, glowing bronze in the firelight. No torn flesh. No blood.

"Thank God," I sighed, relief flooding my veins.

I jerked, startled. Why would I feel an ounce of concern for my kidnapper's well-being?

Easy. Because I'm better off with him than without him. For now, anyway.

For better or for worse, if I was going to survive in the frozen wilds, I needed Viggo, his brute strength, and his skills. Self-preservation, that was all. Those few, brief moments of personal connection we shared—the whoops-a-daisy and the marshmallows and rescuing me from the rising waters—those had *nothing* to do with my sense of relief.

Viggo silently jerked his sweatpants up his legs and dropped onto the ground next to me. As far as I could tell, he hadn't broken a sweat chasing after the cougars. Looking into his eyes, I ignored the expanse of tanned muscle next to me.

"Cats won't be back," he said.

"You mean you killed them?"

He shook his head. "I ran them off. I don't kill without good reason—"

"Except when Medved orders you to," I interrupted, defaulting to snark. "Because you can't say no to the head honcho, right?"

"Yeah. Because I can't say no to my alpha." He dragged a hand over his shaved head.

For the first time, I noticed his bracelet, three strands of woven leather holding a familiar black stone.

I sat up straight and pointed. "Where did you get a chunk of black rock?"

He touched the stone. "From Medved. His father got his hands on several of these bracelets during the Great War."

"You mean… you mean your people *looted* dead wolf soldiers' bodies?" Accusation made my voice shrill.

He lifted a shoulder. "Of course. Wouldn't make sense to leave a valuable asset on a corpse."

I fell silent, my thoughts spinning. Adam knew Medved's endgame. The grizzly alpha wanted to steal the wolf pack's prized Black Rock, the big meteor that for some unfathomable reason worked magic on shifters, boosting their speed, strength, and endurance.

"Is that why Medved ordered you to kidnap one of us? Does he think he can trade me for the Black Rock?"

"He doesn't confide in me, but if I were to guess, I'd say yes, that's his plan. I hit pay dirt when I stumbled across you. Medved's not one to squander an opportunity."

My heart sank. "Adam is family, but he's also the alpha. The good of the pack *has* to come first. He won't give up the Black Rock, not even to save my life."

A grimace twisted Viggo's face. "You might be surprised by what a man's willing to do to protect somebody he loves."

"Is that what you do for Medved?" I asked, my voice tight. "Do you threaten people's loved ones—their family and friends—to get them to toe the line?"

"Sometimes."

Viggo was an enforcer. I shouldn't be surprised he acted like a heartless bastard. Still, disappointment sank claws into me. "That won't work with Adam," I said. "He'd die to protect any member of his pack, but he won't sacrifice the one thing that gives his people an advantage over every other shifter. He won't give that kind of power to the pack's oldest enemy."

"You better hope you're wrong," Viggo muttered, staring into the fire.

"I'm not." I paused and studied his profile, taking in the lowered brows and the determined set of his chin. I'd rather face what was coming head-on. If I knew what to expect, I could make a plan, knowing I had nothing to lose if it failed.

"If Adam refuses to give up the Black Rock, is Medved the kind of man who'd order my death?"

Viggo swung his head around and met my eyes, his expression grim. "Yes."

A stark, unambiguous response. Okay. Now I knew. "Would he order *you* to kill me?"

A moment's hesitation, then, "I don't want to hurt you, Liv."

"That's not what I asked."

Instead of answering, he hopped up and put another log on the fire. He walked to the edge of the light, planted his hands on his hips, and gazed into the dark woods. My question clearly troubled him.

Maybe the grizzly enforcer had a conscience after all.

Didn't stop him from threatening to choke me out, from shoving a pill down my throat, now did it?

Pushing him to answer—to commit to a plan of action—might be a bad idea.

"Come back to the fire," I said. "We have a long hike in the morning, and we need to get some sleep."

"Yeah." He sighed, trudged to our makeshift bed, and dropped down next to me.

Hanging Mylar behind us to reflect heat from the fire had been a stroke of genius. The pile of branches helped insulate us from the cold ground. Our little nest provided shelter from the worst of the elements, but it was far from warm. Cold bit my nose and the tips of my ears, and I couldn't stop shivering.

"Want another cocoa to warm you up before you fall asleep?" Viggo asked.

"No." The offer tempted me, but the last thing I wanted was to wade through the snow if I woke up in the middle of the night needing to pee. And no way in hell would I ask Viggo to carry me to some discreet place behind a bush.

He patted the spot next to him. "Shifters run hot. It'd make sense to share body heat."

Snuggling with my very attractive captor. That had to be the most outrageous notion ever.

"You want to cuddle?" I asked slowly.

He shrugged. "Don't get your panties in a twist. I've got no nefarious agenda. Heat transfer can keep your core temperature from dropping and can prevent frostbite on your extremities."

Well, if he was going to apply logic to the situation…

I weighed my options. Frostbite would be damned inconvenient, not to mention painful. Losing a toe on principle would be downright stupid. I needed rest and I was too cold to fall asleep easily.

"So what do you suggest?" I eyed his big body.

He held out one muscular arm. "Slide over here. Press up against my chest, skin to skin. We'll wrap both blankets around ourselves and trap the heat."

Naked cuddling with my hunky kidnapper.

"I can't freaking believe I'm doing this," I muttered.

I handed him one of the wool blankets and kept the Mylar one firmly around my shoulders as I scooted close to him, my nude body hidden under the reflective fabric. I slipped under his arm and leaned against his side. Viggo spread both blankets over us, covering me from my toes to my chin.

"Ohhh." A bliss-filled moan escaped me before I could hold it back. Touching Viggo was like hugging a hot-water bottle. Welcome warmth penetrated my skin. I wriggled closer, tucking my cold cheek under his chin and splaying my fingers across his chest.

I sniffed, breathing in his scent. The man smelled… nice… like cypress mixed with a hint of black pepper and musk. I rubbed my nose against his throat. The spicy aroma relaxed me, which made zero sense.

Was this how Stockholm syndrome started?

"Don't get any ideas," I warned him—and myself—shuddering with pure pleasure.

He wrapped an arm around my shoulders, securing the blankets in place and holding me close. "You got nothing to worry about on that account, I promise."

I was plastered butt-naked against a dangerous man, an enemy who'd kidnapped, threatened, and drugged me. He might be leading me to my death. But I believed him when he promised to keep his hands to himself.

"We'll leave at first light," he said. "I laid out clothes for you to wear."

I glanced over at the fire and spied a Viggo-sized gray sweatshirt and sweatpants spread out to dry. Looked up into his face, I said, "I'm tall, but you're practically a giant. Your clothes will swim on me. How am I supposed to walk if I can't keep my pants up?"

"You aren't." His palm rubbed a soothing circle on my back. "I'm gonna carry you."

"No, you're not." I ran almost every morning and lifted weights three times a week. I had the endurance and strength to keep up.

"Yeah, I am." His tone was mild, but his voice held command. "Your ankle boots are no good in the snow. The sweatpants might help keep you warm for a while, but they won't keep you dry if you're hip-deep in snow. We've got one pair of snowshoes, and moving shifter speed, I can cover the distance in no time."

I couldn't credibly argue against a single one of his points, dammit. "So what's the plan? Are you going to throw me over your shoulder like a caveman and charge through the woods?"

"Something like that." His lips quirked, betraying a sense of humor. "Or you could ride piggyback."

I groaned a reluctant acquiescence.

"Go to sleep," he rumbled. "You'll need your strength for what's coming."

CHAPTER FIVE

VIGGO

Liv conked out faster than I expected.

Not me. With the pretty human tucked naked against my body, I couldn't relax enough to fall asleep. She made soft, snuffling noises as she burrowed into my heat. Her breath tickled my skin. I was far too aware of her breasts pressing against my ribs. She threw a leg over mine. The soft, supple skin of her inner thigh slid up my leg, from my knee to my groin, a tantalizing friction that stalled the breath in my lungs. Just as I finally started to drift off, her tongue darted out and she licked my collarbone.

She licked me.

Sleep ran for the hills, and I was suddenly wide-awake.

Beneath my skin, my shadow brother opened his eyes. I bit back a groan and hoped to hell that my racing heart and ragged breathing wouldn't wake her. After a long minute, my rioting senses subsided. I lowered my head and sniffed her hair, drawing in that enticing bitter-orange scent.

If I possessed an ounce of sense, I'd keep my distance from this beguiling woman. But I couldn't let her freeze. I was simply doing my job by clutching her naked body against mine.

Yeah right.

"Mmmm." She smiled against my skin, as if caught up in a happy dream. The smile made no sense. She was living a nightmare. I'd have expected fear to follow her into sleep, tainting her dreams and making her thrash wildly in my arms. Instead, she sighed and wriggled close to me, as if all was right in her world.

Maybe her subconscious mind was throwing her a bone, granting her a peaceful respite before reality crashed down on her head once again. If that was the case, best to let her linger in whatever happy place her mind created.

It couldn't last, for either of us.

Tomorrow. Tomorrow I'd shore up my defenses and work on keeping my distance. Tonight, I'd keep her warm and safe.

"Shhh," I whispered, stroking my hand through her silky dark hair.

Three times during the night, I untangled my limbs from Liv's, got up, and added logs to the fire. Each time I crawled back onto our makeshift bed and pulled Liv's pliant body close to mine. Fatigue finally got the best of me, and I drifted off. At first light, I jerked awake and found my arms empty.

Where was she? She knew better than to take off on some foolhardy dash through the woods, didn't she?

I cocked my head at the sound of a branch snapping underfoot, followed by a whispered, "Dammit."

Through half-closed eyes, I watched her approach the fire. She dropped her blanket on top of my duffel and bent over to pick up the now-dry sweatpants, exposing a perfect, upside-down heart-shaped ass.

My ticker kicked, but I kept quiet. Letting her know I got an eyeful would only anger or embarrass her. I might as well keep my mouth shut and enjoy the view.

She yanked the pants up and tied the extra fabric at her waist into a knot. Shivering in the chill morning air, she slipped the sweatshirt over her head and rolled up sleeves that hung inches below her fingertips. Her parka and boots came next. Following my example from last night, she scooped clean snow into the coffeepot and set it on the coals to heat. Without a backward glance, she marched away from the campfire and into the woods.

I'd give her five minutes to follow the call of nature before I got concerned and gave chase. In the meanwhile, I threw on my own clothes and boots. I was stirring instant espresso into a cup of hot water when she returned.

"Coffee?" I held out the cup.

"Come to mama." She snatched it up and breathed in the potent aroma.

I lifted an eyebrow. "Come to mama?"

"My sister says I'm an antisocial, grumpy ole bear before my first cup of coffee," she explained.

"A grumpy ole *bear*?" I emphasized the word. "That bad, huh?"

Her cheeks flushed, either from the frigid air or from the inadvertent insult. My money was on the former. Liv Hagen never held back with the insults. She shut her eyes and took a deep swallow of the piping hot brew.

"You close with your sister?" I asked before I could stop myself. So much for my vow to keep my distance.

Her eyes flew open and she glared at me, suddenly furious. "Am I close with my sister? Jesus, what kind of a question is that? Annika is the best person I know, and I love her more than anybody."

Where did this abrupt, out-of-left-field anger come from?

She waved her arm and coffee sloshed over the side of the cup. "The only good thing about this fucked-up situation is that you grabbed me and not Annika. My sister is safe. As long as I know that, I can handle anything you throw at me."

"I understand," I said slowly.

"No, you don't," she scoffed. "A man like you couldn't possibly understand."

I could dispute that claim till the cows came home, but there was no point. We each had a role to play in this—what did she call it?—fucked-up situation. In my experience, wishing things were otherwise never made a damned bit of difference.

We should get on with it.

"We need to head out," I said. "Finish your coffee. Grab something to eat while I put out the fire and pack up."

I cleaned up the campsite and packed the go bag and duffel while Liv chowed down on a bag of almonds. Fastening the snowshoes onto my boots, I gestured for Liv to join me. I wrapped one of the wool blankets around her shoulders and knotted it under her chin. We donned goggles to protect our eyes from snow glare.

I put my back to her and crouched down. "Hop on." She grumbled but complied. "Hold tight." She hooked her arms around my neck and her feet around my waist.

I slung the bags over my shoulders and took off. Running at a smooth and steady clip, I reached the cabin in less than half an hour. The heavy door opened with a loud creak. Liv slid to the floor and landed on legs that wobbled a bit. She clutched my arm for support and regained her balance then slowly turned around and surveyed the place.

Built from spruce logs, the one-room structure provided a spartan shelter against the elements. A wood stove, a square table flanked by a pair of benches, shelves holding emergency supplies, and simple bunk beds were the only furnishings. On the wall next to the door hung a first aid kit and fire extinguisher. A deck of cards and a few paperbacks sat on the table. Long nails studded the walls. Thank fuck the last person to visit the cabin left a good-sized stack of split logs and kindling in the firewood rack.

I took Liv's parka and my hoodie and hung them on nails to dry, then checked the stove's flue and started a fire.

"Who uses the cabin?" she asked.

"Hunters. Villagers traveling across the state. Occasionally, snowmobile or dogsled racers. This cabin is way off the beaten track. We're not likely to run into anybody, so you can forget about asking a stranger for help."

Ignoring my warning, Liv wandered across the room and ran her fingers along one of the wooden sleeping platforms. "No mattresses?"

"Nope. Bedding would mildew. They expect folks to bring pads and sleeping bags."

"I guess that makes sense." She glanced at the shelf above the table, the one that held a sauce pan, three bowls, and a half dozen spoons. "You think somebody would have left some canned food. You know, in case people get stuck here without supplies."

"Cans of food might expand and explode when the temperature drops," I explained. "The smell could attract mice and squirrels, maybe even bears. Natural bears, I mean, who might break in to get to the food."

"So, no bedding and no canned food. No bathroom, either?"

"There's an outhouse out back."

She wrinkled her nose. "Annika would say 'look at the bright side.' At least we're warm and dry, and the dangerous wild animals are on the other side of the cabin door."

"Not all of them." I flashed my teeth.

She shot me a reproachful look. "Here we are having a nice, friendly conversation and you go and ruin it by threatening me. What kind of a dick move is that?"

"That was a reminder, not a threat," I said. "Threats are explicit—at least mine are."

"Like I'd ever forget." She dropped her voice mimicking mine. "'Give me trouble and I'll choke you out.' 'Keep quiet or I'll drug you'."

Yep. I'd said that. My chest tightened and regret poisoned my blood. How the hell had I become a man who threatens women with bodily harm?

"How about we declare a truce?" I suggested. "Until the extraction team gets here, you and I play nice. You won't give me grief, and I won't resort to scare tactics."

Liv tilted her head to one side, frowning as she considered my words. After a long moment, her brow smoothed and she stuck out her hand.

"I accept your proposition," she said. "Let's shake on it."

My big mitt swallowed her small hand, her fragile human fingers cool against mine. Inside me, my grizzly brother yawned and lifted his head, roused from sleep by my captive's touch. He tilted back his head, tasting the air, then lumbered to his feet. Unlike natural bears, grizzly shifters don't hibernate in the winter, but our animal selves often lapse into a drowsy torpor.

Until something wakens them.

Let go of her hand.

I had to force myself to release her fingers, a fact that made not one lick of sense.

"That was no proposition." The words fell out of my mouth before I could rein them in. "My propositions—like my threats—are explicit."

Many women would blush or back down when confronted with innuendo. Hell, most women in her position would freak out if their captor said anything remotely sexual. And who could blame them? Liv stood her ground. That stubborn chin jerked up, and a small smile curved her lips. The tightness in my chest eased at this evidence that she didn't fear my intentions.

"Well, now you've made me curious. How exactly *does* Viggo Creed proposition someone?"

I lifted a shoulder. "No games. No pussyfooting around the subject. I tell her exactly what I want to do. Ask what she wants. Wait for her to decide if she's on board."

Liv pursed her lips. "And that lay-it-on-the-line approach works? Do many women hop on board the Viggo train?"

"I've had no complaints."

Liv snapped her jaw shut, biting off whatever she was tempted to say. Her gaze traveled around the room, settling on a gray, eighteen-gallon, plastic storage container sitting on one of the bunks. She pointed. "What's in there?"

Smart move, changing the subject.

"Not a clue," I said. "Let's see."

I pried the lid off the heavy plastic tote. Inside, I found a large, bear-proof storage canister, the expensive type hikers buy at fancy outdoor equipment stores.

HELP YOURSELF

Block letters on the side of the container spelled out the message. I unscrewed the cap and held the canister out to Liv.

"Ho-ly shit," she exclaimed, pawing through the contents. "Lasagna with meat sauce. Teriyaki chicken with rice. Pad Thai. Blueberry granola and lots more." She looked me, a stunned expression on her face. "These freeze-dried meals are hella expensive. Who would leave them here with a note to help yourself?"

I rubbed the back of my neck. "Dunno. Maybe a snowmobiler or hunter trying to pay it forward."

"Remind me to send a big box of pastries to the food bank when I get home." Liv snapped her eyes to mine, her happy expression evaporating. "*If* I get home, that is."

The three Hagen women owned Freya's Bake Shop in Belle Reve, named after their late grandmother. I'd never darkened its door—not with wolf shifters standing guard whenever it was open—but folks in town raved about their baked goods.

"If Landry cooperates, you'll be home in no time," I said.

If the wolf alpha turned over the Black Rock, I'd use whatever pull I had with Medved to persuade him to send Liv back to her people in one piece.

I had more than enough blood on my hands.

"I told you," she said. "Adam will never give up the Black Rock."

"We'll see."

"Yes, you will." She sighed and looked down at the floor for a long moment, then lifted her head, a strained and unconvincing smile on her lips. "This might be one of my last days of relative freedom. Let's not waste it. How about we eat that blueberry granola, then settle in and get comfortable while we wait for the extraction team."

"Fine by me," I said.

After chowing down on blueberry granola, we went out to gather dead fern fronds and fir boughs to use as makeshift mattresses. We whiled away an hour sitting at the table, playing gin rummy. Liv tried and failed to talk me into doing yoga with her. She twisted herself up like a pretzel while I watched her over the top of the paperback I pretended to read. The woman was *very* bendy.

A mental image of her ankles locked around my neck while I—

Nope.

I leapt to my feet, startling Liv.

"Firewood," I grunted, rushing outdoors. Ax in hand, I attacked a round section of log. I aimed for a crack and split the wood in two, then split it again. Log after log, I exorcised my—uh—demons. I'd left my hoodie inside, but still sweat poured from my body. I stripped out of my shirt, swung the ax, and kept at it till I produced a sizeable pile of firewood. When I was done, I scooped up handfuls of snow and rubbed it over my chest and arms, sluicing away sweat. All the while, Liv stood at the window, eye-balling me without a hint of self-consciousness.

I carried an armful of split logs inside and loaded them into the firewood rack.

Liv cocked her head to one side, studying me with a thoughtful expression on her face. "If you ever want to give up your enforcer gig, I know how you could earn a ton of money."

"How's that?" I stood and faced her.

"Chopping wood."

"You mean working for the pack's lumber company?" I'd do that in a heartbeat if Medved would allow it.

"No." She waved a dismissive hand. "Haven't you watched any of those lumberjack videos on social media?"

"Huh?" I had no clue what she was talking about.

"Seriously? Do you live under a rock?" She warmed to the subject. "You could post videos of yourself—all bare-chested and muscly—swinging an ax. I bet you'd have millions of followers in no time. Monetize those skills and assets, big guy."

I frowned. Folks made money posting lumberjack videos? Was she messing with me?

At my silent befuddlement, she threw her hands in the air. "Never mind. I don't suppose you'll be quitting your enforcer job anytime soon."

"Don't suppose I will," I agreed, unable to keep the bitterness out of my voice.

"What do you want for dinner?" She changed the subject so quickly my head spun.

"You choose."

"How about teriyaki chicken and astronaut ice cream?"

"Fine by me."

"I figured you'd be thirsty after chopping wood. I melted snow and mixed up a package of powdered drink mix." She nodded toward the table, where a glass of an unnaturally orange-hued liquid sat. "It's not real OJ, but it's better than a poke in the eye with a sharp stick, like Grandma used to say."

This unexpected kindness surprised me. Feeling awkward, I took a seat at the table and drained the glass. Liv was right; it didn't taste like orange juice, but it was cool and sweet and quenched my thirst.

"Thank you." I nodded to Liv.

"No problem."

She took a seat opposite me and folded her hands together on the tabletop.

I leaned forward onto my elbows. "How soon do you want to eat?"

Liv shrugged. "Whenever you like."

The physical exertion from chopping wood wore me out waaay more than I would have expected. I felt light-headed. Guess I'd more than burned off the calories from the beef jerky I'd scarfed down for lunch. Maybe the night's sleep I lost at our campsite was catching up with me, too.

"Might want to hit the sack early tonight," I mumbled.

"Maybe you should lie down and take a short nap before dinner," she suggested.

"Yeah." I slapped my face, trying to fight off fatigue.

"You okay?" Liv's smug smile raised the hairs on the back of my neck.

Pressing both hands flat against the table, I stood. My left knee buckled, and I swayed.

"What did you do?" I rasped.

Liv pulled a familiar bottle of pills from her pocket and shook them in my face. "Gotcha."

CHAPTER SIX

LIV

So… *I lied* and *I drugged Viggo.*

Whatever.

Lying to him didn't bother my conscience one bit. And sending him nighty-night with his own knockout pills? Nobody could blame me for giving him a taste of his own medicine. Literally.

"All's fair in love and war," after all.

I was a prisoner of war, and the first duty of every prisoner of war was to escape. At least, that's what I remember from an old World War II movie my cousin Xander and I watched a few weeks ago.

Viggo didn't want to hurt me. He said as much and I believed him, but he was a company man, and he'd follow orders. *I can't say no to my alpha.* His exact words.

The absolute last thing I wanted to do was to come face-to-face with the grizzly alpha. Hurting me—killing me—would probably make Medved's day. Every time I allowed myself to think about him, I shuddered, shoving back the panic that nibbled away at my composure. If I let fear sink its teeth into me, I might end up crawling into a corner and blubbering.

Liv Hagen doesn't blubber.

I was a realist. Escape was impossible. Even if I could sneak past Viggo, I lacked both the expertise and the equipment necessary to hike out of this snowy wilderness and to make my way to safety. I'd freeze to death curled up under a bush. Nobody would ever find my body. Cougars or other hungry animals would see to that. Annika and Marit would never know exactly what happened to me. The mystery would haunt them for the rest of their lives, a wound that never healed.

My second best option? To get a hold of the Black Rock Guardians and let them know what was going on. At that thought, homesickness hit hard. I wasn't a sentimental person. Snark—not declarations of love—came naturally to me. There was nothing like the likelihood of impending death to make a girl reassess her behavior. If I could hear a friendly voice, tell my sister I loved her…

Viggo had a satellite phone. I found it when I snooped in the go bag while he was visiting the outhouse. I turned it on, but from inside the cabin, I couldn't get a signal. I needed to take the sat phone outside and climb to a higher elevation. Once again, Viggo posed a massive impediment to my plans.

My only hope was to take him off the playing field, even temporarily.

When he told me his body ran hot, he wasn't lying. He left his hoodie hanging on a nail inside the cabin when he went outside to chop wood. I kept one eye on him through a window while I checked the pockets. My fingers closed around the bottle of pills he'd used to dope me. Triumph brought a grin to my face. The big bad grizzly enforcer had finally made a mistake. One of these pills had knocked me on my ass. For a man Viggo's size, I ground up two and stirred them into a glass of orange-flavored drink.

And now, he lay sprawled on the floor, down for the count. When he came to, he'd be furious. He'd blame me for betraying our truce. My future held confrontations with *two* deadly grizzlies.

"Great. Just great," I muttered.

Yet another worry I'd wrap up tight and thrust into the darkest corner of my mind. Avoidance was fast becoming my default coping strategy.

Gritting my teeth, I shoved my feet into my boots, threw on my parka, and snatched up the satellite phone. I stepped carefully over Viggo's spread-eagle limbs, half expecting him to snake out an arm and grab my ankle, like the monster under the bed in a child's nightmare.

He didn't move a muscle, didn't so much as twitch. At the door, I paused and glanced over my shoulder at the motionless man.

He was still breathing, right? Two knockout pills couldn't kill a shifter, could they?

As if they had a mind of their own, my feet took a step toward the downed grizzly. His eyes rolled beneath his eyelids, proof-of-life enough for my conscience. I backed up, eased the door open, stepped onto the porch, and shut the door with a quiet *snick.*

I bolted toward the back of the cabin, leaving a clear trail of boot prints in the snow. No matter. Viggo could track me by scent alone. I couldn't escape him. The best I could hope for was to make my call before he regained consciousness and caught up with me.

Behind the outhouse, the land sloped upward. I raced up the hill, kicking through the powdery snow and gulping mouthfuls of frigid air. Halfway up the hill I stopped. My eyes and nose dripped in the bitter cold, and my clumsy fingers struggled to toggle the phone's power button.

"Please, please, please." I waved the phone up over my head as if an additional two feet would make a difference. After an interminable half minute, I acquired a signal.

My hands shook as I punched in Adam's personal number. "C'mon. C'mon. Pick up."

"Landry." The sound of Adam's voice dropped me to my knees. Snow soaked through my borrowed sweatpants.

"Adam," I croaked.

"Marit, it's Liv. Get Annika," he shouted. He dropped his voice. "Where are you?"

"Alaska. Someplace south of grizzly pack land. I don't know exactly where. The plane went down during an ice storm. Medved's sending an extraction team to get us."

"Are you hurt?" he asked.

"No. The plane is toast, but I'm okay."

Adam sucked in a breath. "Listen to me. We're coming for you. Hang tight. Pretend to cooperate. Don't say or do anything to anger Medved."

Don't go shooting off my big mouth. That's what he meant.

I ignored his warning and got down to business. "Adam, Medved is going to offer to trade me for the Black Rock."

"Liv—"

"You're the alpha," I interrupted, scanning the trees for any sign of my kidnapper. "We both know the good of the pack comes first. Don't give up the Black Rock, and don't get yourself or anybody else killed coming into the heart of grizzly territory."

A few seconds of silence, then, "I'm not gonna leave you in the hands of the enemy."

"I want to come home." My voice broke, dammit. "If you can figure out how to rescue me without getting our people killed, great. But if you can't, don't blame yourself, Adam. And know that I'll *never* blame you for doing what you have to do to keep the pack safe."

"We're coming for you," he repeated. "Your job is to stay alive till we get there. Do whatever you have to do. Any chance you could try to get on the good side of the man who took you?"

"Work my wiles on Viggo Creed?" I scoffed. "I don't think so."

"Viggo Creed?" Adam groaned. "He's Medved's number one enforcer for a reason. The man is a stone-cold killer. You be careful around him. Don't mouth off. And for chrissake, don't do anything to push his buttons."

Oh? Like spiking his drink and stealing his sat phone?

L-I-V. That spells screwed.

"Give me the phone," my sweet-natured twin sister ordered the alpha of the Black Rock Guardians pack. Her voice trembled when she came on the line. "Are you… are you okay? Did he hurt you?"

Tears flooded my eyes. I furiously dashed them away.

In the background, I heard Zane murmur soothing words. I imagined him wrapping an arm around her shoulders and pulling her close, the way he always did when she needed comfort. He'd kiss her forehead and nuzzle her nose, the world's biggest grouch turned into the world's biggest pussycat by my gentle sister's love.

Good. Whatever happened to me, Annika had a strong, capable partner by her side, a man who absolutely adored her. Even if I never made it home, she'd be all right, eventually.

Annika was older than me by twenty-five minutes, but I'd always slipped naturally into the role of protective big sister. Squaring my shoulders, I firmed my voice. "I'm fine. Warm and well-fed. The man who took me—" I paused and swallowed the lump in my throat. "He says he doesn't want to hurt me, and I believe him."

"I just want you to come home, to be safe." Tears clogged her voice.

In the distance, an angry roar—human, but tinged with a grizzly's fury—shattered the afternoon silence.

"You're the best sister anyone could ever ask for," I said, desperate to get the words out while I still had the time. "I love you, Annika. And Marit, and Adam, and Xander, and Zane, and Grandpa Matthew, and Remy. You tell them all that I love them, okay?"

"I will," she sobbed. "I love you, too, sister."

I didn't want her to hear whatever happened when Viggo found me. "Gotta go. Goodbye." I ended the call, dropped my arms to my side, ready to face my captor.

A blur of movement as a huge form stampeded up the hill then skidded to a stop next to me. Eyes blazing, Viggo snatched the sat phone from me. I half expected him to crush it in his hand, the way he'd demolished the coyote shifter's cell phone. Apparently, he thought better of it, opting not to cut off his only means of communicating with his pack.

I met his eyes and lifted my chin, refusing to cringe. "Bring it, big guy."

Without a word, Viggo bent forward and tossed me over his shoulder.

Chapter Seven

Viggo

I've stared down countless enemies. Made grown men whimper and beg. Hell, made them piss themselves. No one—*no one*—had ever confronted me with as much reckless defiance as this small human. If she pulled this shit with Medved, she was a goner.

"Bring it, big guy."

Did the woman have a fucking clue what would happen to her if I *brought it*?

Shaking my head, I threw her over my shoulder then marched down the hill to the cabin. She bucked, arching her back. I caught a whiff of her enticing bitter-orange scent, mingled with anger and fear.

Focus.

Once inside, I dropped her onto her feet. She glowered at me while I unzipped her parka, peeled it off, and hung it on a nail to dry. I dropped onto one knee and reached for her boot. She pulled back her foot like she was aiming to kick me. My eyes shot up to meet hers.

"Don't. You. Dare," I warned.

Liv tilted her head to one side, considering my words. Sass warred with common sense in her expression. Finally, with a long-suffering sigh, she lowered her foot.

"Good girl." I knew the praise would get under her skin. That was the point. I had to see if sound judgment would prevail when I deliberately chose words that would irk her.

She snorted but held still when I tugged the boots off her feet.

Good.

I hopped up, stepped outside, and flung the boots onto the cabin roof.

"What the—" she exploded, rushing toward the door.

I held out an arm to stop her. "If I can't trust you, I gotta make sure you stay put."

If I had to, I could retrieve her boots and dry them out by the wood stove. She didn't need to know that.

"But… but..." she blustered. "How am I supposed to walk outside with bare feet?"

"You aren't." I chuckled. "That's the whole idea."

Liv backed away from me and threw both arms in the air. "Unbelievable."

"Why? You had to know there'd be consequences when you drugged me and took the sat phone." I kicked the snow off my boots then turned to face her. "So, did you get a call through to your people?"

A moment's hesitation. "No. I couldn't get a signal."

I tapped the side of my nose. "You should know better than to lie to a shifter. I can smell deception, baby girl."

"Baby girl?" Her lip curled in disgust.

Shit. I'd better watch my words so I didn't give myself away. "Don't try to change the subject. You promised not to give me grief. We shook hands on it. From where I stand, that makes you a liar."

"You can't be serious," she cried. "If you were in my shoes—captured by the enemy—what would you do?"

She had me there. To get home to my family, I'd lie, steal, and do violence. Liv tried to hide her feelings, but she was terrified by the prospect of coming face-to-face with the boss. Her fear soured the air whenever we talked about him. Honestly, I couldn't blame her for taking her shot.

"Was it worth it?" I asked. "Did you get what you needed from the conversation?"

That stubborn chin lifted again, and her hands squeezed into fists. My nostrils twitched as I scented both anger and despair.

"Yeah, it was worth it. I told my sister I loved her, and I told Adam absolutely positively *not* to give the Black Rock to Medved."

I sighed and scrubbed a hand over the back of my neck. "If Landry refuses to hand the rock over, this won't end well for you."

She frowned. Her lips trembled. She squared her shoulders and all emotion fell from her face. "Not everyone gets a happily ever after."

"Ain't that the truth," I muttered, locking eyes with my captive. In that instant, I recognized—not exactly a kindred spirit—but another soul who'd made peace with a harsh reality. Some of us do the best we can with the hand fate dealt us. Liv had seized the chance to say goodbye to the people she loved, and she told her alpha to put the needs of the pack first.

Got to respect that.

"I'm sorry," I blurted out.

Her eyebrows snapped together and she gave me the once-over, her gaze searching my face for the truth. "Why?"

Wasn't it obvious? "I'm sorry I dragged you into this mess."

She studied me for a long minute. "If you're really sorry, do the right thing. Let me go. Use the satellite phone and call the authorities for help. A chopper could get here before the extraction team shows up."

Halfway through her speech, I started to shake my head. Regret curdled in my stomach. "Can't do that."

Her pretty brown eyes flashed with anger, and color slashed across her cheeks. "Apologies without action are meaningless. You know it's wrong, but you're still going to hand me over to Medved. In my book, that makes you a hypocritical wuss."

I listened, misery hunching my shoulders. Liv's words stung because they held truth. Years of doing the alpha's dirty work had tarnished my soul. I *was* damned. No simple apology could erase my guilt or make things right. I'd managed to draw a curtain across this knowledge, to act like it didn't matter, to pretend I was serving a greater good. But hell, I knew better.

I bit back the idiotic urge to apologize again and turned my mind to practical matters. "We should eat—"

"Because I need to be well-fed and well-rested to face whatever happens when Medved gets his hands on me. Right?" Scorn dripped from her voice.

"Right," I agreed, all business.

She clamped her jaw shut. Silence descended on the cabin, broken only by the crackle of the logs in the wood stove. I boiled water and reconstituted two packages of freeze-dried teriyaki chicken. Instead of sitting across from me at the table, she took her dinner and retreated to her bunk. Once finished, she walked over to the wood stove and held her hands out toward the heat.

Orange light flickered across her face and brought out the coppery highlights in her dark hair. Her lean, lithe body was swamped by my baggy sweats, but underneath the heavy gray fabric, small shivers racked her frame. She looked more like a lost soul than the tough-talking spitfire who'd pulled a fast one on me. I clenched my fists to stop myself from reaching out to her. Shifters were tactile beings, but my touch was the very last thing that would give her comfort.

Why did I care about comforting her?

Gotta shut this shit down.

"You cold?" I asked.

She ignored me.

The sun had slipped below the horizon. A dusky twilight gloom that matched our moods settled over the cabin. I added another log to the fire and lit the battery-powered LED lantern that sat on the table. A circle of light fell across the wooden surface and onto the floor.

"You wanna play a couple rounds of gin rummy?" I asked.

She shook her head.

A few minutes later, I tried again. "Need me to carry you to the outhouse?" With her boots on the roof, she wouldn't be walking there by herself.

She shot me a scathing look but kept her lips pressed together.

"That's how you're gonna play it," I observed. "You're gonna pout."

Her lips drew back in a snarl that would do any shifter proud. Disdain poured off the woman, imbuing the air with a bitter bite. "I'm going to bed," she said. "I need my strength for what's coming, isn't that what you said?"

"Yep," I agreed, feeling like the asshole she'd called me earlier.

With a *humph*, Liv wrapped a woolen blanket around her body and lay down on her makeshift mattress. She wriggled, probably trying to find a comfortable position, then settled into the bed of fern fronds and fir branches.

I sat at the table, reading a paperback and keeping one eye on my prisoner as she took her time drifting off. She heaved a heartfelt sigh, then another. Gradually, her shoulders relaxed and her breathing grew deep and regular. I laid the book face down on the table.

"You're going to break the book's back." Clear as day, Hallie's voice popped unexpectedly into my mind.

"Yes, ma'am," I uttered under my breath, turning the book over so I wouldn't crack the spine.

I made a point of not thinking about home when I was on a mission. Best way to come back safe and sound was to focus on the job and nothing else. The beautiful woman sleeping a dozen feet away disrupted all my carefully constructed rules of behavior. I couldn't afford to second-guess my choices or to allow conscience a foot in the door.

Rolling my neck, I tried to loosen my tight muscles. I always carried tension in my upper back and shoulders. Whenever I completed a mission, I got a deep tissue massage. This time, after I turned Liv over to Medved, I suspect I wouldn't feel much like rewarding myself.

If only our Good Samaritan had left a bottle of scotch along with all the freeze-dried food. Stashing a bottle of booze would've made a certain sense. According to legend, St. Bernard dogs had small barrels of brandy strapped around their necks when they went out on alpine rescue missions. Scotch—or even brandy—sure would hit the spot right now.

Liv whimpered in her sleep, an unexpected sign of vulnerability from the feisty woman. A minute later, another low sound of distress.

Beneath my skin, my grizzly brother woke up.

"No," Liv mumbled. "No."

The bear cocked his head to one side then lurched to his feet, growling. He shoved against my skin, demanding to be set free.

I slowly stood and took a step toward Liv's bunk.

She sucked in a shaky breath and held it.

I froze in place, waiting on tenterhooks for her to exhale. "C'mon," I urged her to breathe.

She expelled the air in an explosive *whoosh*. My relief was short-lived. Sound asleep, sobbing, she dragged in a shallow breath and curled into a fetal position.

My agitated shadow brother snapped his jaws, ready to fight, ready to take on an unseen enemy.

What was up with him?

"Easy, brother," I murmured.

Go to her, he huffed.

"I got this," I assured him, sidling close to her bunk.

Liv moaned and jerked. Tears trickled down her cheeks and dripped onto the fir branches.

My stomach clenched at the sight of this strong woman reduced to uncharacteristic whimpers by a nightmare.

"Shhh," I whispered, running my palm over dark hair that slid through my fingers like satin.

Her breath hitched and she shuddered.

Help her, my bear huffed. His desperation leached into my blood. I wanted to drag her into my arms. To promise her that everything would be all right. To assure her that I'd stand between her and harm. But I wouldn't make promises I couldn't keep. I'd long since traded integrity for safety. My sense of right and wrong lay in tatters, but the one principle I held tight to was honesty. I didn't lie, not to myself and not to others.

Liv jerked. Both of her arms shot out, batting at the air. "No," she cried. "No. No. No."

Dammit.

Gripping her shoulder, I gave a gentle shake. "Wake up, Liv. Wake up."

She twisted away and nailed me with a right cross to my chin.

"Whoa." I reared back, rubbing my jaw.

Her eyes flew open. "What happened?"

"You were having a bad dream."

"Oh." In one smooth motion, she sat up. Frowning, she touched her tear-streaked cheeks then pulled her hands away and studied her wet fingers. Her face twisted. "I'm not some fragile damsel in distress. I hate crying."

"Under the circumstances, you've got every reason to feel scared and uneasy," I said.

She rolled her eyes. "Well, that's helpful."

"Would you rather I spin some pretty story about how it's all going to be okay?"

"No. I don't want false hope," she said emphatically. "I want you to pull your head out of your ass and do what you know is the right thing."

This again. "I can't."

She threw both hands in the air. "You said you don't want to hurt me." Reproach filled her voice. "What do you think will happen to me when you hand me over to Medved?"

"You're a bargaining chip," I said slowly. "My alpha needs you alive if he's going to trade you for the Black Rock."

"And when Adam refuses, what then?"

I had no good answer to that one. Medved's temper was mercurial at best. He might fly into a rage and order her death. Or he might put her on ice till he figured out another way to make use of her.

Dammit. I hated this job.

I had some sway with the old man. I'd use whatever clout I possessed to keep her from harm. "If I can help you, I will," I vowed.

"You *can* help me, but you *won't*." She raked both hands through her hair, clearly exasperated by a promise she considered worthless. She flopped down onto the bunk, wrapped the blanket around herself, and turned her back to me.

I'm sorry. I bit back the useless words.

Regret flooded my veins, leaving me twitchy and on edge. "I'm gonna walk the perimeter," I announced, not expecting a reply.

To my surprise, Liv lifted her head and glanced over her shoulder. "Did you hear something? Is it the cougars again, or the extraction team?"

"No. I just want to stretch my legs."

"Okay… Be careful."

Be careful? Grizzly shifters were the king of the jungle, so to speak. Nothing in the Alaska wilderness put the fear of God into me. Still, her concern felt good. She didn't want me to get hurt. Or she didn't want to be left alone to fend for herself in the wild.

I grabbed my hoodie and stepped outside. Twenty minutes spent stomping through the snow cleared my head. Maybe I'd overreacted. Maybe leaving Liv without shoes wasn't a good idea after all. I climbed up onto the roof and retrieved her snow-crusted boots. Back inside the cabin, I set them to dry then glanced at Liv's bunk. From the soft, snuffling noises she made, she'd managed to fall asleep.

I sat at the table again and picked up the book, but couldn't focus on the story. My mind spun with thoughts of the woman sleeping ten feet away. Liv had gotten under my skin in a big way.

"What am I gonna do with you?" I asked under my breath.

CHAPTER EIGHT

LIV

A bough poked my ribs, and I jerked awake. Groggy and disoriented, I lifted my head and looked around. I squinted as the one-room cabin swam into focus. Fingers of morning sunlight slanted through the east-facing windows. Dust motes floated in the air. A fire burned low in the cast-iron stove. On the floor, a few feet away from the stove, sat my boots.

Viggo must have fetched them from the roof when he went out last night. He figured out that I couldn't function in snowy Alaska with bare feet. He wasn't one hundred per cent unreasonable. Good.

My gaze skated over to my captor, who slept on a bunk five feet away. He lay flat on his back, with one muscular arm thrown over his head. I studied his profile. He wasn't conventionally handsome, like my sister's mate. Zane left a trail of slack-jawed women in his wake wherever he walked down a street. Viggo's face was more rugged, his chiseled profile carved in harsh, masculine lines. Physically, he was exactly my type, all hard edges and power.

He hadn't shaved his head in a couple of days, and dark-brown bristles now covered both his skull and chin. I was a sucker for scruff. Few things turned me on as much as the sandpaper kiss of stubble brushing over my skin. And don't get me started on muscles. When I fell asleep in his arms the night before last, I had to clench my fists to stop myself from petting his solid chest and shoulders. The enemy who took me prisoner had no business being so damned attractive.

Viggo was a stone-cold killer, and I had to be careful not to get on his bad side. Adam's words and he should know. Still, the grizzly enforcer's brutal reputation didn't paint a complete picture of the man.

I wasn't a count-your-blessings girl like my sister. And never in a million years would I follow her example and keep a gratitude journal. But I was a realist, and I looked at the big picture when forming my judgments.

He could have been *much* worse. I was nothing more than an instrument to Medved, a means to an end. As long as Viggo delivered me to him in one piece, I doubted if the alpha would give him grief about how he treated me.

Viggo made sure I was warm, dry, and fed. He kept his hands to himself. No matter how hard I pushed his buttons—and I definitely pushed his buttons when I drugged him and stole the sat phone—he never responded with violence.

I winced.

I'm giving a man brownie points for not hitting me? That's the rock-bottom, bare minimum of decent behavior.

I sighed.

Focus on the big picture, remember?

The man who did Medved's dirty work was no stranger to violence, but cruelty wasn't his default. He said he didn't want to hurt me. He promised to help me if he could, yet he still intended to turn me over to his boss. What was up with that? For the life of me, I couldn't figure him out. Was he acting out of loyalty? Greed? Fear?

I muffled a snort. Viggo didn't strike me as the kind of man who was afraid of anything.

I rolled over and my bladder protested. I probably should've taken Viggo up on his offer to carry me to the outhouse last night, but at the time the need wasn't extreme and I was too pissed—ha ha—to consider it. I sat up, slid quietly off the bunk, and padded across the room. Leaning against the cabin door, I slipped my feet into my boots.

"Going somewhere?" Viggo asked.

I jumped and pressed a hand to my chest. "Scare me to death, will you?"

He stood and pulled his right arm across his chest, stretching his shoulder muscles. He repeated the exercise with his left arm.

"I'm stiff," he groaned, rolling his neck.

"Sleeping on a pile of boughs on a wooden platform will do that to you," I observed.

"Yeah," he agreed. "I miss my bed."

"Me, too."

A wave of homesickness swept over me. I longed for my cozy room in the wolf pack's lodge and my comfortable bed covered with soft sheets and one of Grandma Freya's hand-stitched quilts. For my birthday present, Zane had built a red oak rocking chair for my room. Annika told me about it at our birthday party, but I hadn't seen it yet.

Now, maybe I never would.

God, I missed Annika and Zane and all the people I loved. The thought of never seeing them again made me weak in the knees. I couldn't afford to be weak. Not now. Not when I had to figure out a way to survive Medved and get back home. Balling my fists, I wrapped my fear up tight and pushed it away.

Put one foot in front of the other and keep moving forward. Grandma used to say that. That motto probably kept her going after she lost the love of her life and had to raise their twin sons by herself.

"I got this, Grandma," I whispered.

I snagged my parka and slid my arms into the sleeves.

"What are you doing?" Viggo yawned and shoved his feet into his boots.

"Relax. I'm not up to anything. I just need to pee."

"I'll come with you."

My eyebrows shot up. "To the outhouse? I don't think so."

He shot me a reproachful look. "I want to check the perimeter and the weather."

"Suit yourself."

I stepped outside into a bracingly cold morning. Frigid air stung my nose and ears. Shivering, I yanked up my hood. I trudged to the back of the cabin, squinting against the bright sunlight that sparkled on the snow. Nobody wants to linger in an outhouse, so I quickly took care of business.

I emerged to find Viggo standing under the cloudless blue sky, head tilted back, nostrils flared. Shifters possessed an unrivaled sense of smell. If a natural wolf, bear, or cougar came within a mile of the cabin, I bet Viggo would scent it.

"What do you smell?" I craned my neck and scanned the woods. "Are there any predators nearby?"

"Only one." He flashed a smile.

I rolled my eyes. "Are there any predators besides a cocky old grizzly bear?"

"Old?" he protested. "Just how old do you think I am?"

I shrugged and added a decade to my best guess. "I don't know. Forty? Forty-five?"

He dropped his chin. "Try thirty-two."

I pursed my lips, bogus skepticism painted across my face. "If you say so."

Splat.

Icy shards peppered my face as a snowball crashed against my chest.

I blinked and sputtered, narrowing my eyes. A grinning Viggo balanced another giant snowball in his right hand.

I couldn't match a shifter's speed or strength, but I'd be damned if gave up without a fight.

"Oh, it's on." I dove into a shoulder roll, scooped up a handful of snow, and hurled it at Viggo's face.

A bellow of laughter erupted from his throat.

Splat.

He nailed me with another snowball.

What do they say? The best defense is a good offense.

I danced sideways, scraped up a double-handful of snow, and rushed him. Lowering my head, I tackled him to the ground and landed on my knees, straddling his waist. I leaned forward and rubbed the snow onto his face. My fingers threaded through his short beard, and my thumbs came to rest on his firm lower lip.

No way could I have knocked a six-and-a-half-foot behemoth off his feet unless he allowed it. I tilted my head and studied him. "I wouldn't have taken you for a man who likes to start snowball fights with girls."

He chuckled and wrapped his big hands around my hips. "Goes to show you don't know me very well."

We locked eyes. Even through the heavy cotton fabric, I was very aware of the strength and warmth of the fingers clamped around my upper thighs. The harsh lines of his face had relaxed, and he appeared younger than his thirty-two years. Not boyish. Viggo Creed couldn't pull off boyish if he tried. But he looked less like a man staggering under the weight of a heavy burden.

If I were smart, I'd follow Adam's advice. I'd try to get on Viggo's good side. *Work my wiles.* Make him fall for me so he'd be reluctant to hand me over to Medved. If I were willing to play him, I could oh-so-innocently shift positions and press up against his crotch. Send out signals that I was attracted to him, that I was DTF, like the kids said.

I've never been a player. Not even to save my life could I use sex to manipulate a man. As a strategy, seduction was out, but I could try to encourage a more intimate connection. The more he saw me as a person he liked, the less likely he was to follow through with whatever heinous orders his alpha gave him.

"You're right. You know way more about me than I do about you," I said slowly. "You know I work at a bakery and that I'm super close with my sister and cousin. What about you? What do you do when you're not on a job for Medved? Do you have family and friends back at the grizzly village?"

His body stiffened. I felt him withdraw from the conversation, as if I'd crossed some invisible line by asking about his personal life. His fingers slid from my hips to my waist. He lifted me off his body, leapt to his feet, and offered a hand to pull me to mine.

"To answer your earlier question, I don't smell any other predators in the area." He angled his head toward the trees. "I do scent a couple of snowshoe hares over there in the bushes."

I glanced toward the woods. "Unless they're armed and dangerous, I'm not going to worry about bunny rabbits," I said, brushing snow off my knees.

He shook his head. "I was thinking about fresh meat. A snowshoe hare weighs three or four pounds. A couple of them make a fine meal. I could go hunting. You could help me field dress the hares. We'll fry 'em up and have a nice lunch."

"Ho-ly shit," I burst out, shuddering.

I won't pretend to have some high-minded objections to eating meat. Give me a rib eye or a juicy pork chop, and I was a happy girl. But there was a world of difference between ordering a steak at a restaurant and skinning and gutting a still-warm animal.

Was I squeamish? Hell, yes. A hypocrite? Guilty as charged. My sister was a vegetarian, a choice dictated by her principles. I was able to enjoy meat because I resolutely refused to think about the animal's journey from the field to my plate.

Maybe denial and avoidance weren't such new coping strategies after all.

Viggo's heavy brows pulled together, and he frowned. "What's the problem?"

"You want me to field dress a hare."

"Yeah," he drawled, genuine confusion on his face. Of course he was perplexed. Grizzlies are predators and eating game came naturally to them.

"I can't do it. I'd puke," I confessed.

He shrugged. "No problem. I'll clean 'em."

"Can't we just eat the freeze-dried food and let the snowshoe hares go on about their business?"

His forehead creased. "Why?"

I opened my mouth then paused before answering. Danger and the possibility of death hung over my head. Fear tried to smother me, and it took all of my willpower to keep it at bay. I'd fight to survive. But I didn't have the heart to do harm to innocent creatures, not when I felt such a keen sympathy for their plight.

"What's going on?" His gaze penetrated my defenses. The man was an experienced interrogator, and he could smell deceit. I could either refuse to answer or speak the truth.

"I know what it's like to feel trapped, to be scared someone might kill you. I… um… shit. The truth is, I don't want to hurt the hares." The confession rendered me tongue-tied and self-conscious. I was supposed to be a hardass, not a sentimental wimp.

Viggo stepped close and I caught a whiff of his cypress-and-black-pepper scent. With gentle fingers, he brushed a strand of hair off my cheek. His hand slipped down and captured my chin, tilting my face up so I had no choice but to meet his gaze. Understanding, not judgment, filled his golden-brown eyes.

A tenuous connection bridged the gap between us, filament thin, fragile, but with substance. I fought the crazy urge to take shelter in his arms, to press my cheek against his chest, to burrow in his strength. Instead, I forced my limbs to stay still and resolutely held his gaze.

"You might kick, bite, and scratch, Liv Hagen. You might call me an asshole and heap abuse on my head, but underneath it all, you're a softy," he pronounced.

"I am not soft," I said.

"Don't get me wrong. I know you're a strong woman, but beneath that prickly exterior, you have a heart."

"How about you?" I laid both hands on his chest. His heart drummed against my fingertips, his pulse picking up speed.

"Tell me, Viggo Creed. Under that tough guy exterior, do you have a heart?"

An anguished expression flickered across his face. Regret and resolve tightened his masculine features.

"Well, do you?" I persisted.

Whop. Whop. Whop.

As one, Viggo and I turned our eyes to the clear blue sky. A helicopter hovered over the cabin, sunlight glinting off its metallic fuselage. Viggo sucked in a breath. His hands slid down to my arms, and he gave a reassuring squeeze.

"The extraction team is here."

Chapter Nine

Viggo

I led the way toward the clearing where the helicopter set down. Liv trailed behind me. The Garvey brothers—Jasper and Hank—climbed out of the chopper and sauntered toward us, shit-eating grins on their beefy faces.

Well, fuck. Of all the men at his disposal, why did Medved send these two jokers?

Jasper whooped and clapped me on the arm. “Good to see you, buddy. We got socked in by freezing fog and couldn’t lift off till this morning. Hope you had some fun while you waited for us to show up.” He waggled his eyebrows, gave a suggestive wink, and nudged me with his shoulder.

I bristled, offended by both the familiarity and the innuendo. “I’m not your buddy, asshole. I’m the man in charge of this mission.”

Ignoring my protest, he leaned sideways to get a better look at Liv, who stood behind me. “Remember us, sweetheart?” He cocked his thumb at Hank. “Because we sure do remember you.”

Liv stepped up to my side and lifted her chin. Defiance and contempt seeped from her pores. “How could I forget? You’re the bozos who tried to kill my sister, my cousin, and me. I'll always remember how you tucked your tails between your legs and ran away when Zane showed up."

Last summer, before I was assigned to Belle Reve, the coyote alpha's second-in-command asked for grizzly help with his vendetta against the Hagen women. The operation devolved into a major clusterfuck. The coyote threatened to rip out Liv's throat. Her sister, Annika, shot him. When the wolf lieutenant showed up, Jasper and Hank turned tail and skedaddled. After the botched mission, Medved ordered them back to Alaska. I eventually took their place in Belle Reve.

Jasper and Hank must've wormed their way back into Medved's good graces.

The humor slid from Jasper's face. "Watch your mouth, woman, or we'll give you something better to do with those purty lips."

"Try it and see what happens." She peeled back her "purty lips" and snapped her teeth.

My bear roared his approval, even while homicidal impulses swept over me.

Touch her and die. I barely managed to bite back the words.

"Enough." I raised a hand to silence them then turned to Liv. "Wait for me inside the cabin." She narrowed her eyes, clearly unhappy at being ordered around. I couldn't afford to lose face in front of the Garvey dipshits, not if I wanted to keep them in line. I put on my finest I-mean-business expression and shot her a stern look. "Go. Now."

She huffed out a protest then turned on her heels and flounced toward the cabin.

"She's a handful," Hank observed. He picked something out from between his nicotine-stained teeth then wiped his finger on his plaid flannel jacket.

"If you need help keeping her in line, all you have to do is ask," Jasper added, elbowing his brother.

Inside me, my unhappy bear growled low.

I jabbed a finger at Jasper. "You men are gonna keep your hands off my prisoner. Don't touch her. Don't talk to her. Hell, don't even look at her."

"Why you gotta be that way?" Jasper scoffed. "Medved wants a warm body to trade for the Black Rock. If we bring her in a little worse for the wear, boss won't mind."

My shadow brother roared and scrabbled against my skin. My temper threatened to boil over. As if it had a life of its own, my hand shot out. I grabbed Jasper by his throat and squeezed. His face turned a mottled red, and his eyes bugged out.

"Whaddaya doing?" Hank cried, tugging on my arm.

I shook him off and leaned forward till my nose almost touched Jasper's. "Lay a hand on her and I'll rip out your windpipe, you feel me?"

Over Jasper's shoulder, I spied Liv watching us from the cabin's window. She couldn't know exactly why I was losing my shit on the Garveys, but I bet she could guess.

Jasper couldn't talk, but his head jerked up and down. I waited a beat—so the bastard would know I absolutely was not playing around—then let go. He stumbled backward, clutching his neck and gaping at me google-eyed.

Hank sputtered and patted his brother on his back. "What the fuck, man," he protested.

"Respect. The. Chain. Of. Command." The furious grizzly blazed in my eyes as I punctuated each word.

"Yeah. Yeah. You got it," Jasper croaked, rubbing his throat.

One brisk nod, acknowledging his capitulation, then I pivoted and marched toward the cabin. "Wait outside," I called over my shoulder.

I stepped into the cabin, shut the door, and sucked in a slow, calming breath, willing my anger to recede.

Liv stood in the middle of the room, her arms folded over her chest. "Was that about me?"

"Nothing for you to worry about," I assured her. "I can keep those jackasses in line."

Her mouth twisted. "I'm used to being the one to keep the jackasses in line."

"I bet you are." Not once since I'd taken her had my captive groveled in fear. Hell, she'd taken me on at every turn. In her ordinary life, I had no doubt she could put men like the Garveys in their place. Her ordinary life had taken an extraordinary turn. She had to face up to her new reality. "But times have changed and you need to be smart and keep your head down. Let me handle the Garveys."

She growled—she actually growled—and my bear tossed his head in admiration.

"I'm not even a little bit hungry," she said, "but maybe we should eat something."

I've been harping on her about keeping her strength up. Sounded like she took my advice to heart.

"I'll put water on to boil," I said. "Pick out something for breakfast."

"And what about the Garveys?" she asked.

I snorted. "They can cool their heels."

A small smile ghosted across her lips. "Well, all right. Let's take our time."

While Liv picked out our breakfast, I fixed two cups of powdered espresso. We sat at the table and sipped our coffee. Once we got caffeine in our systems, I rehydrated a protein-rich breakfast skillet made with freeze-dried eggs, sausage, potatoes, and red peppers. Afterward, Liv packed the emergency go bag, and I closed down the air vents on the wood stove to limit the air intake and slowly extinguish the fire.

"You ready?" I asked. If she needed more time to prepare herself mentally to meet Medved, I'd give it to her.

She squared her shoulders. "We can't put it off forever. Let's go."

Two hours later, the chopper set down on the outskirts of the village. Under ordinary circumstances, I'd have taken the controls from Hank for the flight home, but I didn't want to leave Liv in the rear of the chopper with the Garveys. Couldn't trust the dipshits not to say something that would set her off. Better I stick by her side and let Hank fly. The flight passed in relative silence. Liv didn't say a word. Jasper kept his trap shut, too. We all sat and stewed in our thoughts.

Jasper had left his car at the small airstrip a mile outside of the village. During the short drive to grizzly headquarters, Liv's eyes eagerly scanned the surroundings. She had to be curious about the buildings and forestland that used to belong to the Black Rock Guardians. A hundred years ago, the wolves had built the town and lumber mill with money they'd earned mining gold. Pack headquarters, the houses, the school, the community center, the store, Howling Jack's bar, all the buildings were constructed by the Black Rock Guardians. Her grandfather had been a member of the pack, this place the centerpiece of the bloody history between the wolves and the grizzlies.

Jasper drove slowly down the main street. Few people were out in the middle of the day, but the handful of folks we passed craned their necks to look in the back of the car. Word must've gotten out that I was bringing in a prisoner. We parked in front of headquarters, a squat two-story office building that butted up against the larger community center where we gathered for communal meals, pack meetings, and parties.

I took Liv's elbow and escorted her into the lobby, Jasper and Hank on my heels. I looked like nothing more than a loyal grizzly enforcer delivering an enemy hostage to his alpha. In reality, I kept Live close because I didn't trust anybody else near her.

Medved's secretary, Evelyn, looked up from her computer and nodded toward my prisoner. "I see you had a successful trip."

"I did." I nodded. "The boss in?"

She shook her head. "He flew to Fairbanks this morning, called away on urgent business. I expect him to return tomorrow. In the meantime, he said you should keep a close eye on the prisoner."

Jasper turned to me. "You've had a rough couple of days what with crashing the plane and all. If you want to head home and get some rest, Hank and I can lock the prisoner in the Hole and stand guard."

Lock Liv in a dark, dank basement cell? Abandon her to the Garvey brothers' tender mercies? Not gonna happen.

"I'll take her to my place."

"Is that smart?" Jasper scratched his beard. "What if she makes a break for it?"

I filled my smile with menace. "You suggesting a small human woman is gonna get the best of me?"

She *had* got the best of me, but they didn't need to know that.

"No. No. No." He raised both palms in an *I surrender* gesture. "Just trying to be helpful, to step up and do my bit." He glanced at Evelyn. "You'll tell Mr. Medved that Hank and I did our bit, won't you?"

The secretary looked to the heavens, apparently having no more patience for the Garveys' bootlicking than I did.

"Call me when Medved gets back," I said to Evelyn.

"Will do."

Taking Liv's arm again, I led the way to the car. I grabbed my duffel and the go bag from the trunk. "My house is half a mile away. You mind walking?"

"After sitting for a couple of hours, I'd like to stretch my legs," she said.

We walked north for two blocks, past the school and the clinic, then we turned right onto a residential street lined with tidy bungalows. My house was the last one on the left, the only one whose front walk was lined with wild Nootka rosebushes that perfumed the yard in early summer. Hallie loved the pink roses and filled the house with bouquets when they bloomed.

At the thought of Hallie, I picked up the pace, suddenly desperate to be home.

I trotted up the front walk—Liv close behind—then dug in my pocket for my keys. My hands shook as I put the key into the lock. Inside the house, Bosco barked a raucous welcome. The mutt always recognized my heavy tread across the porch.

I swung the door open and stepped into the front hall. A small figure with her mama's light-red hair flew out of the kitchen and rushed me, a rapturous Bosco on her heels.

"Daddy," Hallie shrieked, waving both hands in the air.

I swung her up into my arms and whirled round and round, both us laughing like hyenas. Finally, I sank to the floor, holding my giddy, giggly daughter on my lap. Hallie patted my shoulders and peppered my cheeks with kisses. Bosco licked my face.

"I missed you, Daddy."

My heart turned over. "I missed you, too."

Home. I was home.

I glanced toward the doorway where a white-faced Liv stood gripping the edge of the doorframe.

CHAPTER TEN

LIV

D*addy.*

Viggo was a father.

My stomach flip-flopped and I grabbed the doorframe for support.

I'm a freaking fool.

Why hadn't it occurred to me that Viggo might have a mate, a child? Why did I presume a drop-dead-gorgeous thirty-two year old shifter was single? I'd checked the man's magnificent body out, for chrissakes. Fantasized about—well, shit—never mind what I'd fantasized about.

From the back of the house, a timer buzzed, followed by the unmistakable sound of an oven door slamming shut. The smell of freshly baked chocolate chip cookies wafted through the air.

Dear God, we'd walked into a cozy scene of domestic bliss.

Maybe I could ask Viggo to put me in the Hole, whatever that was. Anything would be better than crashing this family reunion.

I shot Viggo a dirty look. Why the hell hadn't he mentioned that he was mated?

He squeezed his daughter's shoulders and pointed to me. "Hallie, this is Liv. She's going to be staying the night with us."

Hallie hopped to her feet and walked up to me, a welcoming smile on her face and her hand extended for a proper shake. "Hi. It's nice to meet you."

Somebody had taught the kid manners. Probably her mother, the woman I didn't know existed until thirty seconds ago, because Viggo sure as heck wasn't brimming over with the social graces.

I shook her hand and rallied my wits. "Nice to meet you, too, kiddo."

Footsteps. I braced myself to meet the missus, to watch Viggo slip his arm around another woman and receive a juicy welcome-home kiss.

A young man emerged from a back room and jogged toward us, wiping flour-covered hands on his jeans. He clapped Viggo on the shoulder then turned to me with a friendly grin. He looked like Viggo, with the same dark hair and eyes, the same strong nose and heavy brow. Only his expression was markedly different, unguarded and carefree. His eyes sparkled with uninhibited goodwill.

"We've got chocolate chip cookies fresh outta the oven if you're hungry," he offered.

"Uncle Owen makes the best chocolate chip cookies in the world," Hallie said proudly. "You want one?"

My head spun. "Sure."

She took my hand and tugged me up the hall, chattering a mile a minute. The dog—a sleek brown-and-white pooch of indeterminate breed—pranced joyfully at her side, his tail curled up and a wrinkle creasing his brow. I caught a quick glimpse of the living room. A plush red sofa and an overstuffed chair flanked a massive stone fireplace. In front of the hearth lay a thick flokati rug, a perfect place to sprawl and soak up the heat. A few paces up the hall, through the open door of the bathroom, I spied black and white tiles and an old-fashioned claw-foot tub.

We walked into a charming kitchen that would have made Grandma's heart sing. Sunny yellow paint covered the walls and contrasted with the white cabinets. Vintage Blue Willow plates were hung below the ceiling line. An antique cookie jar—a bear with fading red paint on his ears and bow tie—sat on the tile countertop. Chocolate chip cookies cooled on a wire rack.

"Here." Hallie handed me a fat cookie.

I took a bite and gave an exaggerated moan of pleasure. "You're right. I'm a cookie expert and your Uncle Owen makes fantastic ones."

"Is cookie expert a real job?" She looked awestruck, as if a glorious new world of possibility had opened up before her eyes.

"It's kind of a real job. My sister Annika and my cousin Marit and I own a bakery. We're all cookie experts."

"What's the name of your bakery?"

"Freya's Bake Shop. We named it after our Grandma Freya. She taught us all how to bake."

Hallie considered that, her eyes wide.

"I was named after my mother. Hallie Rosalie Creed. Rosalie, just like my mama."

"That's nice," I said.

Where are you, Rosalie?

"Do you want to see my bedroom?"

I glanced at Viggo, who'd followed us into the kitchen. I was his prisoner and he might not want me exploring the house with his kid. He nodded permission.

"I'd love to see your bedroom," I said.

"Come on." She tugged on my hand again and led me down the hall to the open door of her room. The coral walls held a mismatched collection of pictures. A poster of a K-pop boy band hung next to a framed print of a fairy gazing at the moon. On the opposite wall, another poster proclaimed "Kindness Is Free, Spread the Word." The odd juxtaposition of images suited a child who was no longer little—I guessed her age somewhere around eight or nine—but not yet a teenager. A tween, that was the word I was looking for.

Hallie threw herself onto her queen-sized bed covered with a mint-green-and-white floral comforter. She patted the spot next to her.

I dutifully sat down. "When I was your age, I had a dinky twin-sized bed. I would've loved a big one like this."

"Daddy and Uncle Owen still read stories to me at bedtime. They're so big they'd fall out if we cuddled up in a little bed, so they got me a big one. We're reading the third Percy Jackson book now."

"Lucky you," I said.

"Yep," she agreed. "There's room for Bosco to sleep by me, too."

"Bosco is your dog's name?"

"Uh-huh." She bounced on the bed. "He's half pug and half sheltie, and he's a really good boy. Do you have a dog?"

"My cousin has a dog named Loki, and my sister just got a new kitten named Eliza," I answered.

"Nice."

"Does your mama read bedtime stories to you, too?" I kept my voice casual, aware of Viggo standing in the hall watching us through the open doorway.

Hallie hopped off the bed and grabbed a framed photo from her dresser. She handed the picture to me. I studied the face of a pretty young woman with the same strawberry blond hair and blue eyes as Hallie.

"That's my mama. She died when I was three months old."

I cut a glance toward Viggo, who looked at his daughter with eyes that held both love and sorrow. In a million years, I never would've guessed that he was a widower, that in his early twenties he'd been left alone to raise a child.

No, I corrected myself. Not alone. At the very least, Viggo had a brother at his side. In the Black Rock Guardians, everyone would have rallied to support a child who lost their mother. I hoped it was the same in Medved's grizzly pack.

"I'm sorry you lost your mama, kiddo."

"I don't remember her. I wish I did, but I don't."

Unexpected tears stung my eyes, and I cleared my throat. "I bet your daddy and Uncle Owen tell you stories about her."

Hallie smiled wistfully. "They do. I know she liked pineapple on pizza. She liked to put together jigsaw puzzles, the big ones with a thousand pieces. And she loved flowers. She planted the wild rosebushes in the front yard. When they bloom, Daddy says she can smell the sweet scent all the way in heaven."

Well, crap. There was no way I wasn't going to cry after hearing that. I widened my eyes but couldn't prevent a tear from escaping and sliding down my face.

Hallie touched my cheek, a serious expression on her face. "It's okay to cry when you're sad. Daddy says so."

My understanding of the world flipped on its head. The big bad grizzly enforcer—the stone-cold killer—the brute who kidnapped and drugged me—was a father who validated his daughter's feelings.

I didn't know what to make of that knowledge. At a loss for words, I nodded at the little girl.

"If you're going to spend the night, do you want to sleep in here with me?" she asked. "The bed's big enough and we don't have a guest room."

"Liv will be sleeping in my bed." Viggo's big body filled the doorframe.

At the prospect of sleeping in Viggo's bed, my heart catapulted against my ribs. "I'll be what?" I demanded, my voice shriller than I liked.

His lips curved. He shot me a reproachful look, but his eyes twinkled. "You take the bed. I'll sleep on the couch."

"You're too big for the couch, silly." Hallie protested with a laugh. "You'll roll off onto the floor and bump your noggin."

"Liv is company. We can't have company sleep on a couch."

"I still wish she could stay with me," Hallie grumbled.

"You'll have plenty of time to talk to Liv," he said patiently.

"How long will she be staying with us?"

Viggo rubbed the back of his neck. "I don't know for sure. She's Mr. Medved's guest, and he hasn't told me exactly how long she'll be with us."

Hallie turned serious eyes to me. "I don't like Mr. Medved," she said in a conspiratorial whisper. "He's mean."

No child in the Black Rock Guardians pack would *ever* call Adam mean. The cubs loved and trusted him. How often had I seen Adam soothing a cranky infant or comforting a toddler with a boo-boo? Sometimes he sat in on the children's story hour, and the little ones clambered all over him.

"Hallie." Viggo's voice was sharp. "What did I tell you about talking disrespectfully about the alpha?"

She rolled her eyes. "I know. I know."

He gentled his voice. "How about you show Liv the rest of the house while I move some of my clothes and toiletries out of my bedroom?"

"Okay." Happiness restored, Hallie hopped off the bed and held out her hand toward me.

We retraced out steps to the front of the house.

"Here's the living room." Hallie's hand swept out to indicate the cozy space.

I wandered over to the stone fireplace and dropped to my knees on the plush flokati rug. Holding my hands out to the flames, I peered into the firebox.

"Wolves," I exclaimed, surprised. A pair of black andirons shaped like wolf heads held the burning logs. Firelight reflected in the cast-iron beasts' green glass eyes.

"Wolves used to live here in the olden days," Hallie explained. "They left some of their stuff behind when they moved away."

Moved away? A deceptively benign phrase. The Black Rock Guardians had been murdered and driven from their homes when Maxim Medved's father launched an unprovoked war against the wolves in the 1950s.

Which wolf family had lived in this house? Did they survive to flee the state? Or had the grizzlies killed them?

Owen had followed us into the room. I caught his eye and he gave a quick shake of his head. Hallie didn't know the bloody history. Whatever happened here wasn't her fault.

I swallowed. "The andirons are pretty."

"I like them," she said. "Wolves are cool."

I glanced around the room, eager to think of anything other than the war. An upright piano was tucked into one corner.

I pointed. "Do you play?"

"A little bit. Daddy plays the piano, and Uncle Owen plays the guitar. They tried to teach me, but I'm all fumbly fingered. Sometimes we have music nights where they play piano and guitar and I sing along."

"What kind of songs do you guys like to sing?" I asked.

"Cat Stevens is Daddy's favorite. We sing 'Morning Has Broken' and 'Moonshadow' together."

Another seismic shift in my understanding of the world.

I had to pause and wrap my head around the image of Creed family music nights where they played Cat Stevens songs. *Cat Stevens.* Grandma Freya would approve. Her musical tastes had been firmly fixed in the '60s and '70s. Grandma and her best friend, Dorrie Mittelmann, had driven across the country in 1969 to attend Woodstock. For years, we believed that her twin sons, Dad and Uncle Nick, were Woodstock babies. Now we knew the truth. Grandpa had been a wolf shifter, and his pack had been driven out of Alaska by Viggo's people.

"Besides singing, what else do you like to do?" I asked, genuinely curious about what a child in a small, isolated community did to pass the time. "Do you go to school?"

"I love school." She gave a happy jump. "I like science the best. Daddy gave me a telescope for my birthday. We look at the stars and planets together. Did you know Mars has two moons?"

"Cool beans." I liked stargazing myself. "Do you know how many moons Venus has?"

"Is that a trick question?" she asked. "Because Venus doesn't have any moons."

"You're right," I said. "Let's try another one. This is harder. How many moons does Jupiter have?"

She preened. "Ninety five."

"Right again. How did you get to be so smart?"

She shrugged. "I like to know stuff."

I could relate to that sentiment. After college, I studied and read whatever interested me, whether it was useful knowledge or not. I knew next to nothing about important stuff like politics or greenhouse gases, but ask me about the history of kickboxing or glassblowing, and I could talk your ear off.

Owen wandered away and Hallie and I continued our tour. I followed her through the kitchen to the pantry. Canned goods and five-gallon plastic bins holding flour and sugar and other staples filled the shelves. A large freezer occupied one corner.

"Uncle Owen and I picked lots of wild blueberries last summer. We froze a bunch, so we can make blueberry muffins and pancakes all year long."

"That's smart," I said. "What else do you have in the freezer?"

"Meat. Moose and elk and venison. Salmon. Chicken. More fruit because fruit's my favorite food. Uncle Owen likes to make double batches of stuff like lasagna and chili, then he freezes the leftovers for quick dinners."

She showed me the hall bathroom and the closet where I could find extra towels. "You have to jiggle the handle on the toilet so it doesn't run," she warned me. "I'm supposed to remind Daddy to fix it."

"Your Uncle Owen isn't handy?" I asked.

"Nope. Daddy's better at fixing broken stuff, but Uncle Owen is way better at baking and video games."

A hall closet held a washer and dryer. I'd been wearing Viggo's sweats for a couple of days. At the sight of the washing machine, I felt grubby and itchy, ready for a shower and fresh clothes.

We walked past the closed door to Owen's bedroom. "You don't want to look in there," Hallie warned in a whisper. "It's messy. Daddy says as long as Uncle Owen doesn't let food rot and stink up his room, it's okay. He's a grown-up and gets to decide if he cleans his personal space. *I* have to keep my room neat." She sighed at the injustice of the situation.

A door at the end of the hallway swung open, and Viggo stepped into the hall, holding a pile of clothes. "It's all yours," he said, tilting his head toward the open door.

"Come on," Hallie grabbed my hand and pulled me into her father's bedroom.

A king-sized bed stood against the far wall flanked by a pair of elaborately carved nightstands. A dark-red comforter lay atop the bed—apparently Viggo really liked red—and a carved wooden trunk sat at its foot. A tall dresser occupied another wall. An overstuffed leather chair and ottoman took up a corner of the room. An open door led to a bathroom. A second door presumably led to the closet.

Hallie dropped to her knees next to the trunk. Her finger outlined an animal shape on the front of the wooden chest. "Daddy said the man who used to live in the house was a wood-carver. He left some fancy furniture behind. Look." She pointed to moose sporting a giant rack of antlers carved onto the lid of the trunk. "There's deer, and elk, and bears, and wolves, and lynx, and eagles, and all kinds of Alaskan birds and animals. The nightstands are fancy, too."

I sank to the floor next to the little girl and gently touched a carved wolf.

"Beautiful," I murmured. Letters chiseled into a corner of the lid drew my eye. I leaned over to get a better look.

Jacob Hunter, the letters spelled out.

My heart did another flip-flop. Hunter. That was Zane and Remy's last name. Remy was a techie with no interest in handiwork, but Zane was a skilled woodworker, and building furniture his passion. Had he inherited that talent from an ancestor named Jacob?

If I survive this mess, I'll ask him.

I traced my fingers over the name, feeling connected to this place and its former wolf inhabitants, feeling not quite so alone here in the hands of my pack's enemies.

Hallie touched my shoulder. "Are you okay?"

The sweet little girl reached out with kindness. Despite the history of enmity between our peoples, she wasn't my enemy. I glanced over her head at her father, who watched me with solemn eyes.

Maybe Viggo wasn't my enemy, either. Or at least, maybe he didn't want to be.

I ruffled her strawberry blond hair. "I'm fine, kiddo. And I'm really happy that I got to meet you."

She threw her arms around my neck. "I'm happy you're staying with us. It's nice to have another girl in the house."

"I keep Rosalie's clothes in the trunk," Viggo said. "She was taller than you, but about your size otherwise. You can take a shower and change into fresh clothes. Help yourself to anything in the trunk."

I looked at Hallie. "Do you mind if I wear your mama's clothes?"

"Don't be silly." She patted my cheeks. "Sharing is good."

Shit, I was already more than halfway in love with this kid. I liked children, but I'd never been one of those women who'd go gaga over babies. The few times I babysat, I was more than happy to turn the rugrats back over to their parents. But Hallie… I shook my head. I was bonding with the girl.

From my knees, I glanced up at Viggo. Once he crossed the threshold into his home, he looked and acted like a different man. He leaned against the door now, his shoulders relaxed, the tension wiped from his face. The implacable, take-no-shit mask he wore cracked to reveal a family man. So… which was the real Viggo Creed? The brutal enforcer or the daddy who adored his child?

Both, a small voice whispered in my head.

I narrowed my eyes, my thoughts racing.

"I don't like Mr. Medved… He's mean." Hallie's words had provoked a strong reaction in Viggo and a warning for her to watch her mouth.

I searched my memory for everything Viggo had told me about Medved.

If you defy or disappoint him, he'll make you pay.

Followed by, *I've got too much to lose to risk disappointing Medved.*

And when I begged him to do the right thing and help me escape, a simple, agonized, *I can't.*

My gaze flicked from Viggo to Hallie and back again, suspicion morphing into certainty.

Medved was using Hallie and Owen to blackmail Viggo into doing his dirty work.

Chapter Eleven

Viggo

"Cats," Hallie said decisively. "Make mine look like cats, please."

Cats were easy. Add ears to a circle, drop chocolate chips in for the eyes and nose, and call it good.

Metal flipper in one hand, batter bowl in the other, I stood in front of the stove, taking requests. I turned my eyes to the pretty woman sitting next to my daughter at the kitchen table. "How about you, Liv? You want cat-shaped pancakes, too?"

Her lips quirked up and pure devilment sparkled in her eyes. She was considering asking me for something stupid complicated—like the map of Italy or a snowflake—I saw it on her face. Instead, she relented.

"How about heart-shaped?"

"You got it."

Butter sizzled and steam curled into the air as I poured batter onto the cast-iron griddle. Three minutes later, I deposited two cat pancakes on Hallie's plate and two hearts on Liv's.

"Meow." Hallie poured syrup on her pancakes and dug in.

I returned to the stove and poured five plain old round pancakes for Owen.

"How come you didn't you ask me what shape I want, bro?" Owen leaned so far back in his chair that it balanced on two legs.

I shot him a dirty look.

Owen clutched his heart. "I'm crushed."

Hallie giggled through a mouthful of pancake.

From the counter, my cell phone pinged with an incoming text.

Suddenly serious, Owen hopped to his feet and took the spatula from my hand. "I'll take over the pancakes. You deal with that." He nodded toward the cell.

I snatched up my phone and retreated to the hallway to read the message in private.

Mr. Medved flies back this morning. Meet him at his office at 11. Bring the prisoner.

Leaning against a wall, I inhaled a slow breath. Bosco had followed me into the hall. I laid a hand on his head. From the kitchen, Owen cracked a joke, followed by a hoot of laughter from Hallie.

My stomach clenched. I'd do absolutely anything to keep my family safe.

Bring the prisoner.

Bile crawled up my throat. I had no choice. I had to comply.

Liv's voice drifted up the hall—every syllable she spoke a dagger to my heart.

I gave myself a few minutes to regain my equilibrium. Sensing something was wrong, Bosco nuzzled my fingers, whining low.

"Good boy," I said under my breath.

Get on with it.

I snapped my spine straight and marched to the kitchen. Owen looked up and met my eyes. His brows drew together as he took in my expression. He nodded in understanding then plastered a big hammy smile across his face. With both hands, he lifted his breakfast plate and swiped his tongue across the surface, lapping up melted butter and syrup.

"Yum." He smacked his lips.

"Ew, icky." Hallie shrieked. "Licking your plate is bad manners, Uncle Owen."

Owen's distraction worked.

"Are you sure?" he asked. "Bosco licks his plate and you never accuse him of having bad manners."

"Bosco is a dog." Hallie fixed him with a stern look. "He has to use his tongue."

"I don't know." Liv spoke up. "Sometimes I like to use my tongue, too. Sometimes I lick my plate clean. Especially when I eat ice cream." Her pink tongue darted out and circled her lips.

A mental picture of Liv straddling my hips and licking ice cream from my bare chest popped into my mind.

Where the hell did that come from?

"See? Liv's on my side," Owen said.

"Harrumph," Hallie sniffed, not at all convinced.

"Hey, peanut," Owen said. "I know that your dad usually walks you to school the first morning after he gets home from a trip. But I was thinking, maybe I'll walk with you today instead."

"How come?" Hallie took comfort in routine and liked surprises about as well as she liked bad manners.

Owen and I had done our level best to shelter her from the fear and stress that percolated through the pack. In a world where safety and peace of mind were hard to come by, we'd made our home a haven, a place where Hallie felt loved and secure. Still, I wondered if at some level, she sensed the peril we lived in. Maybe that was why she followed the rules and valued predictability.

Like father like daughter.

"I need me some extra Hallie time, and I'm heading downtown anyway," Owen said.

Your father needs to prepare Liv for her meeting with his homicidal alpha. No way Owen could speak that truth, so his lame excuses would have to do.

"Okay," Hallie agreed. Like her mother, she was essentially good-natured and easygoing.

"Finish your juice then go brush your teeth," I told her.

She polished off her OJ, hopped up, and set her dirty dishes in the sink. Her arms snaked around my waist, and she gave me a quick hug. I stroked my hand over soft, shiny hair.

"I'm glad you're home, Daddy."

My battered old heart melted into a puddle of goo. "Me, too."

With a little wave to Liv, she scampered toward the bathroom.

"I'll grab her backpack," Owen offered. He headed toward the front door, leaving me alone with Liv.

"She's a good kid," Liv murmured.

My throat grew thick. "That she is."

Liv carried her plate to the sink and poured herself a second cup of coffee. She took a slow sip, studying me over the rim. "Your secret is out, big guy. I've seen you with your daughter and brother. The world might think you're a hard-hearted badass. But the truth is, you're a big ole softy."

"Am not," I harrumphed.

My life was a precarious balancing act, all the disparate pieces held together with spit and bailing wire. I had to be strong—to be a hard-hearted badass—in order to keep my family safe.

"Don't get me wrong," Liv added. "I like this side of you, the big bad alpha male who's a pussycat around his kid."

A pussycat? I groaned

"I understand, you know," she continued.

I frowned. "What do you understand?"

She set the mug on the counter and laid her hand on my arm. At the physical contact, my bear shook himself awake. He jumped to his feet and pawed against my skin.

She's ours, brother, he huffed. *Ours.*

"What did you say?" I asked out loud, shocked to the core by my bear's assertion. He had *never* declared any woman ours. Not even Rosalie. Not even when I'd begged him to.

Liv squeezed my arm and leaned toward me, bringing with her a delicious heat and the scent of citrus. I fought the urge to bury my face in her throat, to breathe in that bitter-orange perfume, to taste her natural musk. My breathing grew ragged. Touching the tip of my tongue to one of my canine teeth, I imagined the fang puncturing fragile human flesh in a claiming bite that would forever mark her as mine.

Whoa.

I barely knew the woman. She was a member of an enemy pack, for chrissakes.

Ours, the bear hissed, undaunted.

"I said, I understand." Liv slid her hand up and down my arm. "I see what you have to lose if you disobey or disappoint Medved. I get it, Viggo. I don't like it, but I get it."

Chapter Twelve

Liv

Viggo's admonitions rang in my ears as I followed him into grizzly pack headquarters.

Keep your mouth shut and your eyes down. Don't give the alpha lip.

I'd ignored the whispers and sideways glances from the people we passed on the sidewalk. I expected folks to glower, to give me the stink eye when Viggo paraded me—an enemy, a member of the wolf alpha's family—past them. Most of them appeared more curious than hostile. One woman stared at me with undisguised pity. More than anything, that look of sympathy made me trip over my boots.

Crap. What did she know that I didn't?

Viggo caught my elbow and steadied me, his hand warm and reassuring on my arm. My mind skipped back to high school, to a US history class, where the teacher told us that treason included giving aid and comfort to the enemy.

By that reckoning, Viggo was a traitor.

I yanked my arm out of his grasp so no one would see him helping me.

"Go straight through to his office," the secretary called as Viggo strode into the lobby.

People fell back against the corridor wall, beating a hasty retreat when they saw us coming. The grizzly soldier clearly struck fear into the hearts of his packmates. What had Medved ordered him to do that inspired that kind of dread?

My imagination ran riot and ice crept up my spine.

You don't know him, I wanted to shout. *You don't know why he does what he does, or what it costs him.*

Or maybe they did. Maybe they all cowered and hopped to when Medved snapped his fingers. What a sorry, fucked-up way to live.

The injustice of the shitty situation rankled deep.

Turning my head, I studied Viggo's implacable profile. Nothing in his posture or expression revealed his feelings. He was glacier cold, his emotions walled off. The perfect hatchet man. The perfect enforcer. Yet after only four days in his presence, I knew better than to accept his hardass performance at face value.

Our gazes met briefly when he held open the door to Medved's office. I jerked my chin up, assuring him that I was okay, that I could handle whatever happened. Respect flickered in his honey-brown eyes, a warmth he quashed when he turned to his boss.

"Take a load off," the grizzly alpha said, gesturing toward a pair of chairs facing his massive mahogany desk.

I kept my head down, peeking sideways through my lashes as I shuffled across a surprisingly opulent room.

Maxim Medved or his father must have redecorated the office once they took over from the Black Rock Guardians. I couldn't imagine the wolves surrounding themselves with such garish furnishings. Comfort and function ruled in Adam's office at wolf HQ. Adam didn't think twice about the dings on the corner of his desk or the worn spots on his leather chair. One of Grandma Freya's landscape paintings hanging on a cream-colored wall was the only embellishment. Well, that and pictures he'd tacked to the walls drawn by pack children.

Medved had what Grandma would call highfalutin taste. Gaudy black-and-gold damask wallpaper covered all four walls.

Heavy black velvet curtains with gold trim were pulled across the windows, blocking out the view. Adam kept the windows in his office uncovered, showcasing the stunning view of Shooting Star Lake.

I dropped down onto a hard wooden chair and folded my hands together on my lap, playing the part of a timid, intimidated prisoner.

"She give you any trouble during the trip home?" Medved asked.

"No, sir." Viggo stretched out his long legs and settled back in his chair. "Meek as a mouse."

He must've mastered the art of suppressing his emotions and true thoughts, because Medved didn't catch the lie. Now *that* would be a handy skill.

I glanced up from my lap.

"Ho-ly shit!" I exclaimed, all of Viggo's warnings about keeping my mouth shut and not swearing in front of the alpha forgotten.

Behind Medved's desk, three taxidermied wolf heads were mounted on the wall. Their lifeless glass eyes stared straight ahead. The dark-gray wolf in the center had his lips peeled back in a permanent snarl, his sharp fangs powerless to do harm. They were massive beasts—shifters—not natural wolves. Mounted deer heads were creepy enough, but taxidermied wolf shifters were positively obscene.

My shoulders crawled up to my ears.

"You like?" Amusement colored Medved's voice. "Wolf soldiers, killed by grizzlies during the war. I don't know their names, but I call 'em Larry, Moe, and Curly."

I gaped and met the gaze of the dreaded Maxim Medved. Intelligent gray eyes in a broad, craggy face swept over me. He wore a plaid flannel shirt with wide suspenders. He looked more like a lumberjack than an evil kingpin.

"For a human you're a pretty enough little thing," he observed, his dismissive tone like nails on a chalkboard. "What is it you do for a living? Decorate cupcakes?"

I forced myself not to rise to his bait. "That's right."

I took care of the business side of Freya's Bake Shop, keeping the books and ordering supplies, but baking was in my blood. My eyes squeezed shut. For a few seconds, I imagined my sister's contented face when she piped decorations onto a cupcake. She created little works of art that brought joy to customers. Bringing others happiness was of value, dammit, and didn't deserve Medved's contempt.

His insult to my family's business pissed me off big-time.

He clucked his tongue. "A Black Rock Guardian knocked up your grandma, right? That makes you one-quarter shifter."

Knocked her up? Who talked like that? Medved knew how to push my buttons. A tsunami of anger swept over me. Grandma and Aleksandr had been crazy in love. When he died, he took a part of her soul with him.

I slipped my hands under my thighs and hooked my feet around the chair legs, resisting the impulse to fly across the desk and punch the bastard out. He was a massive grizzly, with wide shoulders and a barrel chest, but with the element of surprise on my side, I might be able to get one good hit in before he stopped me.

Viggo's long leg slid sideways on the fancy oriental carpet. He tapped my foot with his, warning me to keep calm.

"Tainted with wolf blood but unable to take animal form." Medved heaved a fake sympathetic sigh. "You got the worst of both worlds, girl. But at least—" He tilted his head to one side and eyed me speculatively. "At least with your part shifter DNA, if one of us knocked *you* up, your child could take animal form."

Only children with more than fifty percent shifter DNA could transform into animals. After losing most of their members during the Great War against the grizzlies, the Black Rock Guardians had banned mating with humans. Adam abolished that law, but not before it almost derailed his budding relationship with Marit. Once we discovered that our grandfather had been a wolf shifter, the prohibition was moot. Unlike most humans, I could give birth to a shifter.

The grizzly alpha was goading me, trying to get a rise out of me. Viggo gently kicked my foot again, his warning clear.

Don't give the fucker the win.

I pressed my lips together, but my fingernails bit hard enough into my palms to draw blood.

"Have you heard from Landry about trading her for the Black Rock?" Viggo changed the subject.

"I have." Medved's lips turned up in a contemptuous smile. "It's just like I thought. The young wolf alpha is soft or maybe pussywhipped by his human mate. Doesn't matter. What matters is that he's willing to give me the Black Rock in exchange for *her*." From his expression, he clearly thought Adam was getting the raw end of the deal.

"Hell, no," I cried, unable to hold back the words.

More than anything, I wanted to go home, but not if it meant the grizzlies getting their hands on the meteorite. Giving that kind of power to Medved was as foolish as handing a nuclear weapon over to terrorists. He'd deploy it without mercy, crushing vulnerable enemies and disrupting the balance of power in the entire shifter world.

The Adam I knew would never agree to that. My death would haunt him, but he'd put the needs of the pack first. What the hell was he thinking by agreeing to negotiate? He promised not to leave me in the hands of his enemies, but he couldn't imagine I'd want this.

Medved snorted at my outburst. "You got bigger balls than your alpha, girl."

"She's got a mouth on her all right, but she's harmless." Viggo's unconcerned tone made light my protest. "I'll have no trouble keeping her in line till the meeting."

"See that you do," Medved warned.

"Yes, sir. When and where is the meetup?"

"Day after tomorrow. Two wolves representing Landry will take a commercial flight into Fairbanks. You'll pick 'em up and fly 'em back to grizzly HQ for the negotiations. Landry said they'll bring a chunk of black rock as a sign of good faith."

"Wolves, returning to their former home, the site of their greatest defeat. That has to sting." Viggo chuckled. "Kudos, sir."

If I didn't know better, I'd swear he was proud of his alpha's machinations.

Medved slapped his leg. "Sucks to be them, don't it?"

Viggo dipped his head in agreement. "Always."

The good humor fell from Medved's face. "The Garveys tell me you took the prisoner to your place instead of putting her in the Hole."

"Yes, sir." Viggo leaned back in his chair, a man confident in his actions. He cut a sideways glance at me and smirked. "Like you said, she's a pretty enough little thing. I took her home with me and put her in my bed. Didn't think you'd mind."

A pretty enough *little thing*? Fighting words. On behalf of women everywhere, I was offended. And he *put me in his bed*? I should be… I should be… appalled. Instead, an incriminating heat warmed my face as I imagined sharing a bed with the big bad grizzly enforcer. The thought of gliding my hands over those firm muscles, of pressing my mouth against his skin, scratching my nails through the dark hair that dusted his chest…

"Nah, I don't mind." Medved's coarse smile grated on my last nerve. "You earned a little fun, son. Take your prisoner home and show her what a grizzly enforcer is made of."

"Exactly what I have in mind."

An unreal conversation. The fact that I sat through it without throwing punches was a testament to my faith in Viggo, a man who'd kidnapped and drugged me. A man I'd known for all of four days.

When you know, you know.

Marit's reply when I'd asked her how she fell for Adam so quickly. Of course, despite my lurid fantasies, I hadn't fallen for Viggo. Not exactly. But I trusted him. I was either shockingly naive or an astute judge of character.

Viggo stood and held out his hand, wordlessly ordering me to take it. Medved watched us with avid eyes.

Meek as a mouse, I reminded myself. Harmless. I had a role to play, a woman who wouldn't give her captor one lick of trouble.

I wobbled to my feet and slipped my hand into Viggo's, his fingers warm against my skin. He pulled me toward the door. I followed him into the corridor.

"Hey," Medved called after us.

Viggo paused and looked back over his shoulder. "Sir?"

"Don't break her," Medved cackled. "Remember, we need her in one piece for the trade."

Viggo laughed. His big hand swooped down and smacked me on the ass. Startled, I whirled around, clutching my tingling butt cheeks with both hands. My jaw dropped and my eyes grew wide. All the people in the crowded corridor froze in place, staring at us.

"No worries." Viggo chucked me under the chin. "I got other things in mind for this one."

Bending forward, he tossed me over his shoulder and clamped a hand across my thighs, pinning me in place. From the back of the crowd, a man whooped.

"Out of my way," Viggo barked.

The sea of people parted as he swaggered toward the exit.

Chapter Thirteen

Viggo

"What just happened?" Liv demanded. She wriggled and I dropped her onto her feet on the sidewalk in front of the store.

"Theater."

She raised her brows and threw her hands into the air, unsatisfied with my one word reply.

"Bears gossip," I continued. "I gave them a show. By now half the town has heard that I took you to my bed. That means it's hands off for everybody else. The Garvey brothers will keep their distance. Nobody else will touch you now that I've claimed you as mine."

Liv's eyes flashed. "As your what, precisely? Your personal prisoner? Your reward from the alpha for a job well done? Your human sex toy?"

I lifted a shoulder. "What does it matter what anybody calls it? If you're under my protection, you'll be safe till Medved meets with the wolves."

She growled her displeasure.

My bear tossed his head and grunted, pleased by her spirit and animal-like vocalization.

Shifter blood, he huffed with satisfaction.

Maybe her shifter blood *was* asserting itself. She'd licked me after all, in her sleep, that first night in the woods. A very shifter thing to do.

A woman scuttled past us, her wide, curious eyes fixed on Liv.

Liv lowered her voice. "You said bears gossip. Have you considered what Hallie will think when she hears that her daddy is keeping a woman prisoner in his bed?"

I dragged a hand over my freshly shaved skull. "Shit. I hope folks will have the good sense not to say anything like that in front of a child."

"And what if Hallie tells her school friends that you're sleeping on the couch so that company can have your bed?" she asked. "This little show we're putting on could go sideways fast."

"You're right," I conceded. "Tonight and tomorrow, we'll sleep together in my bed. That way Hallie can't say otherwise to her friends."

She groaned.

A pang of disappointment shot through me at her obvious reluctance to share my bed. Was the attraction I felt entirely one-sided?

"Nothing about this is ideal," I said stiffly. "But we'll get through it and get you safely back home to your people."

Liv puckered up her face and looked like she wanted to protest—wanted to declare once again that Landry would never give up the Black Rock—but she couldn't argue against reality. The wolf alpha had agreed to negotiate a trade.

Liv scrubbed her hands over her face. "I can't believe Adam is willing to give Medved the meteorite."

Frankly, I was surprised, too. From everything I'd learned about the man, Landry was a fine alpha. Smart. Brave. Devoted to his pack. But at the end of the day, he put family first. Medved would call that a fatal weakness, but I couldn't pass judgment when I was guilty of the same thing.

The door to the community store swung open, and Owen stuck his head out. "How did the meeting with Medved go?"

I guess the gossip mill hadn't reached my brother.

"Come on." I took Liv's arm and led her into the store.

Her curious gaze traveled over the shelves filled with foodstuffs, toiletries, hardware, and other essentials of daily life. In one corner of the shop, Owen had installed a small library, where packmates could borrow books. In an opposite corner, he'd created a community closet, where folks traded outgrown or unneeded clothing. Medved had reluctantly agreed to Owen's request to set aside space for the library and clothing exchange. Neither were strictly necessary and Medved was all about the bare necessities. Owen had a way of charming people into doing what he wanted, and sometimes those charms worked on the boss.

"You work here?" Liv asked Owen.

"I run the place." His smile revealed nothing but satisfaction at a job well done.

I knew better.

Liv walked up an aisle, trailing a finger along a shelf. She paused, picked up a bottle of ketchup, and glanced at the price tag. "Are you kidding?" she exclaimed.

"Groceries cost more in Alaska than they do in the lower 48," Owen said.

"I've heard that, but doesn't the pack absorb some of the costs so people can afford to put ketchup on their fries?"

Some shifter packs might function that way, but not Medved's. How do you think he afforded the heated indoor pool he added to his house or the new Range Rover he purchased every year?

"I wish," Owen said. "It's hard to watch packmates have to choose between eggs or milk. And don't get me started on the cost of fresh fruit and vegetables."

Owen played no part in setting the prices. That was all Medved and his cronies. He ran the village like an old-time company town, where the sole employer owned everything and jacked up prices at the only store. The pack's timber holdings, logging company, and gold mining should have provided enough income for all packmates to live well. Still somehow folks struggled to get by.

Medved was a lousy alpha, but loyalty was drummed into every grizzly from birth. Medveds had ruled the pack for centuries. The pack needed a strong, experienced man to hold everything together, we were taught. A leader with the guts and gumption to prevent other packs from doing to us what we did to the wolves. Without an iron-fisted leader, we'd be sitting ducks. Or so the Medveds insisted.

I'd heard the discontented rumblings about the pack needing new leadership, but nobody dared make a move. Not when the alpha's enforcers sniffed out and brutally crushed every whisper of sedition.

No wonder people held their breath and averted their eyes when they saw me coming. Shame and regret had built a permanent home in my heart. I was a lost soul, but down to his bones, my brother was good. I wanted Liv to know that.

"Running the store is Owen's job, but it isn't his calling," I said.

"Oh?" Liv glanced at Owen, waiting for him to pick up the story. When he didn't—when he looked at me with a surprised expression on his face—she turned to me. "What *is* Owen's calling?"

"He's a healer," I said proudly.

A confused frown creased Liv's forehead. "Then why is he working at a store instead of treating patients at a clinic?"

"Simple," Owen said in a light voice that betrayed none of his disappointment. "Because Medved decided that only women can be pack healers."

"What kind of sexist bullshit is that?" Liv exclaimed. "Adam's mother and father are both healers. Gender has nothing to do with it."

"Yeah, well, Medved decreed that only women can be healers and teachers," I said. "The men are needed to work the timber operation, gold mining, and to serve as soldiers."

"You don't have women soldiers?" Liv frowned.

"Medved says women aren't physically or emotionally equipped to be combatants." Owen rolled his eyes, showing how little he agreed with his alpha's assessment.

Liv made an outraged face. "Try telling that to Kyra. I double-dog dare you."

"Kyra is one of Landry's lieutenants," I explained to Owen. "She's highly respected within the wolf pack."

"Wait." Liv turned to Owen, curiosity burning bright in her brown eyes. "If men are expected to be loggers or soldiers, how come you're working in the store?"

A sore subject. Owen shifted his weight from one foot to the other and looked down at the floor.

Shame should be my burden, not my brother's. "He's got a special dispensation from Medved," I explained.

"Part of your compensation for doing the alpha's dirty work?" Liv guessed.

"That's right."

Owen's head jerked up. "How does she know about your deal with Medved?"

"She's smart. She figured it out."

Relief crossed my brother's face. He touched Liv's arm. "Then you know how much Viggo sacrifices to keep Hallie and me safe."

"I know some of it," Liv said.

"Did he tell you that Medved threatened to take Hallie away from him and give her to a childless couple so she could be"—Owen made air quotes—"raised with a mother's womanly influence?"

Liv pressed a horrified hand to her chest.

"Medved's cronies aren't fit to keep a dog," I muttered.

"From what I've seen, the two of you are doing a fine job raising that little girl," Liv said.

Her praise meant the world to me. At least I was doing one thing right. "Thank you."

"There's more," Owen continued. "If Viggo refuses to follow orders, Medved threatened to send him to some remote outpost to stand guard. And the kicker? I'd have to take his place as an enforcer."

Only partially true, but Owen didn't know that.

"Owen could never be an enforcer." I met Liv's eyes, hoping she understood. "His heart is too pure. I'd never put that kind of burden on my brother."

"So you take it on yourself," Owen said, guilt writ large across his face.

"Don't make me out to be a hero," I protested. "If you knew a fraction of the shit I've done for Medved, you'd know I'm the farthest thing from heroic."

"Why don't you run?" Liv asked. "You're a pilot. You could steal a plane and take Hallie and Owen far away."

"Medved had tracking chips implanted somewhere in Hallie's body and in mine," Owen said. "If we disappear, Medved says his number one priority will be hunting us down and making examples of us."

"I can't risk running." My voice was bleak. "We're fucking trapped."

No words could do justice to the sorry situation. We stood together in silent commiseration. After a long moment, Liv stepped close and touched my face.

"I am truly sorry," she said.

I slid my arms around her waist and pulled her close. She came willingly and pressed her cheek against my chest. We rocked back and forth, taking comfort in simple human contact.

How long had it been since I held a woman with tenderness? Not since Rosalie, the good and kind woman whom my bear—my other self—refused to recognize as his mate. Since she died it had been nothing but hookups for me, sex little more than scratching an itch. I'd never known the magic of sex with a fated mate. Folks talked about the blissful communion that followed marking a partner with a mating bite. I'd long since given up any hope of that.

It's her, the bear whispered. *She's our mate.*

Impossible, I shot back. It was far too late for me to find that kind of happiness. I didn't deserve it, and the circumstances couldn't be worse.

Beneath my skin, my shadow brother snorted derisively. His absolute confidence seeped into my blood and undermined my resolve. I dragged my lips across her sweet-scented hair and gently kissed her temple.

Owen cleared his throat. "What… um… what happened with Medved?"

I told him about the meeting with the wolves and that Liv would be staying with us for another two nights. "You're gonna hear stories about what folks saw after the meeting."

Liv detached herself from my arms and tossed Owen a grin. "The word is out. Ask anybody. I'm your brother's sex toy."

Some of the tension in my chest eased. At least she was able to laugh at the god-awful situation instead of wringing her hands and seething with rage.

Owen recoiled. "Viggo?"

"That's right," she continued. "He gets to keep me until the meeting with Adam's representatives. Sleeping with me is his reward for a job well-done."

"What the fuck?" Owen poked me hard in the chest. "You can't do that, bro."

I couldn't take offense at little brother's anger. "Relax. It's all pretend, a show we're putting on in front of the pack. If Liv's mine, nobody else will dare touch her."

"Especially the Garvey brothers." She made a face.

Owen's mouth hung open, shock and understanding doing battle on his face.

"It's okay, Owen." Liv bumped her shoulder against his. "Viggo and I are on the same page. We're pulling a fast one on Medved and everyone else in the village. Everyone except you."

"What about Hallie?" he asked slowly.

"We can't expect an eight-year-old to keep that kind of secret," I said. "What she needs to know is that Liv and I are sharing a bed, so she won't tell any of her school friends otherwise."

"That could get messy," he warned. "Especially if she thinks it means that you and Liv like each other and that Liv might be her new mother."

Dammit, he was right. We'd have to handle this carefully.

Liv glanced toward the counter, and her eyes lit up. "Are those Flamin' Hot Doritos by the cash register?"

"Yes," Owen said.

She looked at me, her eyes sparkling. "Buy me a package, will you? Call it payment for services rendered."

I turned my eyes upward in a show of exasperation. "Services rendered? Seriously?"

Unrepentant, she dashed toward the counter and tore into a package of the spicy chips.

"Pick up a bag of gummy bears for Hallie, please," I called after her.

Owen grabbed my arm to stop me from walking away. "Hold up. Liv says you're pulling a fast one on Medved and everybody else in the village. But if it's all a ruse—if there's nothing between you—your scent would give you away." He tilted back his head. His nostrils flared and he inhaled a slow breath. The bear glittered in his eyes. "But it's not a ruse. Ever since that hug, I smell desire pouring off both of you."

Chapter Fourteen

Liv

It was one thing to borrow jeans and a sweatshirt. I couldn't make myself wear one of Rosalie's nightshirts, not when I was about to climb into bed with her… with her *what*?

I stopped digging through the clothes stowed in the trunk and sat back on my heels. Now that I thought about it, I realized that I'd just assumed that Viggo and Rosalie had been mated when she died, but I didn't know for sure. There was no tactful way to ask him.

When was the last time I gave two hoots about tact?

I wanted to know if Viggo and Rosalie had mated. It mattered. A shifter mated only once, when they found their soul's other half. Grandma and Aleksandr had mated, even though their happiness was short-lived. Marit and Adam, Annika and Zane, too. My sister and cousin wore the scars from claiming bites on their shoulders. Sometimes, when their fingers drifted to the marks, they exchanged knowing smiles, as if they shared a special secret, a secret I couldn't understand.

Had Viggo found then lost his one shot at true love?

I stood and walked over to Viggo's dresser. In the second drawer I found a neatly folded stack of T-shirts. Taking a black one from the top of the pile, I retreated to the bathroom to change. I brushed my teeth, washed my face, and slipped into a tee so large it hung off my shoulders and grazed my knees.

A knock on the bedroom door.

"You decent?" Viggo called.

"I'm covered up, if that's what you're asking."

The door swung open and Viggo walked in wearing nothing but a faded pair of gray sweatpants. The waistband rode low on his hips, revealing an absolutely delectable V-line. His skin was damp and flushed from the shower he must've taken in the hall bathroom. Dark brown, barely there scruff—one of my very favorite things—covered his skull. At the sight, I shivered and the pads of my fingers tingled with the desire to touch.

His gaze swept over me from head to foot, lingering on the black tee.

"I borrowed your shirt. I hope you don't mind."

He cleared his throat. "Nah, I don't mind." He padded barefoot across the room and threw back the covers. "I sleep here." He pointed at the right side of the bed, the one closest to the door.

"Fine by me."

"You want me to leave the bathroom light on and the door cracked open?" he asked.

"I don't need a nightlight, big guy. Nothing in the dark scares me."

The lamp on the nightstand clicked off, plunging the room into blackness.

"You sure?" Viggo's disembodied voice floated across the wide bed.

I patted the mattress, finding my bearings in the dark, and bumped along the side till I reached the head of the bed.

"I'm a creature of the night," I said in my best Transylvanian accent.

The mattress dipped as Viggo climbed onto the bed. I joined him, sliding between crisp sheets. Heat radiated from his side of the bed. Both Annika and Marit had told me that sharing a bed with a shifter was like sleeping next to a furnace. My feet were always cold. I inched them closer to him.

"A creature of the night," he repeated, mimicking my bad Dracula accent. "I knew you were part shifter. You telling me you're part vampire, too?"

I opened my mouth for a teasing reply, then froze. Sitting bolt upright, I twisted to face him in the dark. "Wait… Are you telling me that vampires are real?"

A year ago, I would've fallen down laughing if somebody tried to tell me that shifters existed or that they'd seen a person transform into a beast. "Lay off the gummies" or "Get your nose out of paranormal romances" would have been my response.

Now I knew better. I counted wolves and lynx as family and friends. If shape-shifters walked among us, maybe vampires were real, too.

"Landry didn't tell you guys about vampires?" he asked in a scandalized voice.

I groaned. My world was about to flip on its head once again. I wasn't sure I could wrap my noggin around a reality that included blood-sucking vampires.

"I'm surprised he didn't tell you," he continued. "Every spring, all the supernaturals send representatives to a big convention in Vegas. You got shifters, vampires, fairies, sasquatches, leprechauns, garden gnomes—"

"Asshole," I sputtered. The dickhead was totally yanking my chain.

Laughter shook his shoulders, jostling the bed. "You surprised? Thought we established early on that I'm an asshole."

I smacked him. I balled my fist and punched his rock-hard abs. The blow landed a little lower than I anticipated—I was flying blind after all—but I felt the gratifying sensation of fist meeting flesh.

Lightning fast, Viggo flattened me against the mattress. He stretched out on top of my body, supporting his weight on his elbows, holding my hands prisoner in his massive fists.

Warm breath skated across my face. I drew in the heady scent of cypress, black pepper, and musk. My tongue touched my lips, savoring the taste. Why did the man smell so damned good?

"Were you aiming at my junk?" he asked.

I tried and failed to flex my fingers. Wriggling proved more successful. He held his body inches above mine, leaving me just enough room to squirm. I slowly inhaled a deep breath. My lungs swelled. Through the thin cotton of his borrowed tee, my nipples grazed his bare chest.

"No." My voice shook. "I have absolutely no designs on your junk."

A sharp intake of breath. A low, satisfied chuckle. "Liar."

Oh God, I moaned. I *was* lying, wasn't I? And he could smell it.

"I don't know what I'm doing," I murmured.

His muscular body lifted a few inches, creating distance between us. "What do you mean?"

"When you first kidnapped me, I hated you. I thought you were a heartless thug, cheerfully doing your master's bidding."

"Most people hate me." No self-pity colored his voice, just a matter-of-fact acceptance of reality.

I tried to tug my hands free. With a disheartened sigh, he let them go. His weight shifted and he started to lift his body off mine.

"Listen to me." I reached up and clasped his face between my palms. "Humans talk about grizzly mamas, mothers who will do absolutely *anything* to protect and care for their children. After getting to know you, I can safely say that grizzly mamas have nothing on grizzly daddies. I see you, Viggo Creed. I see how much you love Hallie and Owen. I understand why you do what you do for Medved."

"I appreciate that, but my motive can't excuse my actions. I don't blame you for keeping your distance."

"Dude, with your infallible sniffer, you have to know I'm attracted to you."

A moment of silence.

"Tell me what you want, Liv," he said. "We might have only a handful of days left together. Once Landry delivers the Black Rock, you'll be going home to the wolves. That's for the best. You'll be safe, far, far away from this dangerous shitshow I call my life."

In the darkness, his eyes suddenly glittered, a sign of the ascendant beast. Apparently his bear had strong feelings about Medved's plan to trade me for the meteorite.

"What do I want?" I sighed. "Honestly, I'd like nothing better than to climb you like a jungle gym. Hang upside down by my knees. Swing from your monkey bars—" I stopped abruptly. I'd pushed that simile well past the point of redemption, hadn't I?

A low growl rumbled from his chest.

Time to be serious.

Sentimental words came easily to my sister. To my ear, they sounded mawkish and cheesy when I attempted them. Still, I tried. "I like you. I respect your devotion to your family. I do feel a connection, an attraction. We could hook up for a few days then go our separate ways. I've done it before, no reason I couldn't do it again. But—"

I hesitated.

"But—" he prompted.

Heat rose in my cheeks, and I forced the next words out. "I suspect I'd have a hard time walking away. That's never happened to me before. I'm not usually a clingy, dependent woman. And you're right. Your life *is* a dangerous shitshow. I can't see any future for us beyond the next few days. I don't want to invite pain in, so I think we should keep our hands off—"

"Daddy!" A loud shriek pierced the darkness, interrupting me. Viggo bolted out of bed and raced across the room. He threw the bedroom door open with so much force that it bounced against the wall. I stumbled after him into the hall then joined Owen outside the open door to Hallie's room.

"She has nightmares," Owen said in a low voice.

Viggo sat on the edge of Hallie's bed, rocking his daughter in his arms. An agitated Bosco paced back and forth in the middle of the room.

"The bad man was in the house," Hallie sobbed. "He chased me. I hid behind the clothes in my closet, but I heard him come into my room, and I knew he was going to get me."

"That sounds scary, sweet girl." Viggo stroked her hair. She bobbed her head and hiccuped. "You know, we've never had a bad man come into the house and chase you, have we?" His voice was gentle.

"No, but in my dream he did."

"Let's see if we can fix your dream. How about we imagine that the bad man knocks on the front door, and you tell him to go away and never come back?"

"What if he won't go away?"

Viggo rubbed his chin, a thoughtful expression on his face. "Maybe you and Bosco can chase him across the yard. Then you can whistle and all the neighbors' dogs will come running to help you. Then you'll push the bad man into a prickly rosebush."

"And then I'll turn the hose on him." Hallie warmed to the notion.

"That's a good idea," Viggo said. "I bet he'll run away, and all the dogs will chase him, with Bosco at the head of the pack. After that, the bad man will never want to come back here and deal with Hallie Creed and Bosco the Wonder Dog."

"Bosco the Wonder Dog." She giggled and patted her leg. Bosco trotted over. She stroked his head. "Will you stay with me till I fall asleep again, Daddy?"

"Of course." He pulled back the covers, and she crawled into bed.

"Can I have a hug, Uncle Owen?"

"Sure thing, peanut." Owen crossed the room in three long steps, bent over, and embraced his niece.

"You too, Liv."

Surprised, I walked to the bed. Hallie flung her arms around my neck. "I like you," she said.

My heart turned over. "I like you, too, kiddo."

Viggo pulled a desk chair close to the bed and carefully sat his big body down on the small wooden chair.

"Sing to me?" Hallie asked.

"What do you want to hear?"

"Hmmm…" She considered her father's question. "How about 'Moonshadow'?"

"You got it."

Viggo cleared his throat. In a rich baritone, he started to sing.

Owen and I retreated to the hall. He gently shut the door to Hallie's room.

I met his eyes. "Viggo is a good father."

"He's the best." Owen leaned toward me and spoke in a low voice. "I was nine when our parents passed. Viggo was seventeen. Dad died in a logging accident and Mom from a broken heart. When Medved suggested that I should be fostered out to another family, Viggo fought back. He insisted he could take care of me. And he did. He practically raised me."

I squeezed his arm. "You were lucky to have him."

"I was." Owen frowned. "I think that's how Medved got his foot in the door, where the manipulation began. Once our parents died, Viggo started doing jobs for the alpha, probably the price he had to pay to keep me with him."

"What a rat bastard," I said.

"Yeah." His eyes grew sharp. "No matter what he thinks, Viggo has a good heart. He deserves happiness and to be loved."

Here was the opening I'd been looking for to get my question answered. "He had that, didn't he? At least for a little while. With his mate."

"Rosalie and Viggo weren't mated," Owen said. "They'd been friends since they were kids. They liked each other, had fun together, and started going out. The relationship probably would have run its course, but she found out she was pregnant. They decided to make it work, but their bears refused to go along with any mating. That happens sometimes. If she hadn't died, my brother would have stayed with her forever, despite their stubborn bears. He told me that sometimes friendship and respect were enough."

Viggo had never mated. Relief shot through me, followed by shame. Why would I begrudge him that soul connection every shifter longed for?

"How did she die?" I asked.

"She went out for a hike. It was early spring and there were still icy spots on the trails. She slipped and fell off a cliff."

I imagined the young mother tumbling to her death, her last thoughts doubtless about the baby she was leaving behind. "How horrible."

"It was horrible," he agreed. "Viggo took it hard, but he set out to give his little girl the best life he could. I've helped as much as I can."

If Annika were here, Owen's story would have my softhearted sister sobbing uncontrollably. I lacked her sensitive nature, but tears gathered in my eyes at the unfairness of it all.

Even if everything worked out for me—if Adam negotiated my release—the people I left behind in Alaska would haunt me. Hallie and Owen and Viggo deserved better than this precarious existence under a despot's thumb. If only they lived in a healthy, functional pack like the Black Rock Guardians. Hallie would thrive. Owen could follow his passion for healing. And Viggo could let down his guard and live a life he could be proud of.

It was so damned unfair.

"You two have done an amazing job with Hallie." I wasn't usually a hugger, but it was a night for them. I held out my arms.

He swept me into a big bear hug, lifting me off my feet before he deposited me once again onto the floor.

"I'm going to go raid the kitchen. You hungry?"

"Nah." I shook my head. "I'm going to head back to bed. See you in the morning, Owen."

"We've got ice cream, mint chocolate chip and cookies-and-cream." He waggled his brows suggestively.

I laughed, resisting his blandishments. "Next time."

"Yeah, next time. Good night." Owen ambled down the hall toward the kitchen.

I stood outside Hallie's bedroom door for another moment and shamelessly eavesdropped. Cocking my head to one side, I listened to Viggo sing his little girl to sleep. He'd moved on from Cat Stevens to James Taylor, serenading her with 'You Can Close Your Eyes,' another one of Grandma's favorites. Dad used to sing it to Annika and me when we were little. Viggo had a beautiful voice. The rich timbre touched something deep inside me. Something tangled up as tight as a Gordian knot relaxed and unfurled, like flower petals opening to the sun. I pressed a hand against my chest.

"What have you done to me?" I whispered.

I tiptoed down the hall and slipped into Viggo's room. I left the door open a crack. A band of light sliced through the darkness and spilled across the bed. I liked this room, the cream-colored walls, the plush red comforter, the fabulously carved wooden chest and nightstands. A tall pile of books sat on Viggo's bedside table. I'd snooped at the titles. Biographies. Mysteries. Thrillers. At the very top sat a copy of *The Discourses of Epictetus*, an ancient Greek philosopher.

When I needed a few more humanities credits during my senior year of college, I took an ancient philosophy elective. The Stoics appealed to my practical, unsentimental soul. Epictetus was a favorite. I couldn't remember the exact quotes that resonated with me, but I was inspired by his injunction to always consider the big picture, think things through, then to commit to a course of action. Good, common-sense advice. I embraced it as a guiding principle. I suspected Viggo had, too.

I climbed into the far side of the bed and lay on my back, squinting at the ceiling.

With a creak, the door swung all the way open. Viggo stood in the doorway, his powerful body silhouetted against the hall light. Once again, the bear shone in his eyes as he looked at me.

I sat up on my elbows. "Did she settle down?"

"Yeah." Exhaustion and concern carved furrows into his brow. "Tonight wasn't so bad. Sometimes it takes her a lot longer to fall back asleep after a nightmare."

An impulse seized me. I rolled onto all fours, crawled toward the foot of the bed, and patted the mattress. "Sit down here with your back toward me."

"Why?"

"Humor me. Just do it."

"Yes, ma'am."

He shut the door, casting the room into darkness. On silent feet, he approached the bed. The weight shifted when he sat.

Rising up onto my knees, I reached out for him. My hands settled on his impossibly broad shoulders then slid toward the base of his neck.

"I hold tension in my trapezius muscle," I said. "And there's nothing I like better than a massage."

He groaned as my thumbs began to press circles against his flesh. I had no training, but I'd received enough massages to know what felt good.

"Relax," I breathed. I rubbed his shoulders and upper back, all the places that got tied up in knots on my body when I was under stress.

If ever a man lived with stress, it was Viggo Creed.

He rolled his head from side to side as I worked out the kinks. When I figured out that he liked firm pressure, I scooted closer and leaned into the task. My palms glided across thick, rounded muscles covered by smooth, firm skin. Beneath my hands, his stiff muscles gradually relaxed. I pressed against him, reached over his shoulders, and worked my fingers across his pecs.

"Fuuuck," he moaned. Sitting up straight, he laid his hands on top of mine. "Thank you. That felt good, but it's time to stop."

"I'm not too tired to keep going," I said.

He laughed softly. "Have pity on a man, will you? Having your breasts press up against my back is taking a toll on my equilibrium."

I jerked backward. "Sorry. It wasn't intentional."

"I know, but if we're going to keep our hands off each other, maybe a massage is a bad idea."

"You're right." I tried to keep the disappointment out of my voice.

I'd fantasized about falling asleep in his arms—like I had that first night in the woods—but it looked like chaste cuddling was out of the question. I crawled to my side of the bed and stretched out, my hands folded across my stomach. Viggo lay down next to me, equally stiff. I held perfectly still, careful not to roll against him.

Sleep was a long time coming.

Chapter Fifteen

Viggo

I woke up lying on my side, my body spooned around Liv's. She'd tucked her head under my chin. Her ass pressed against my groin. The T-shirt she'd borrowed had ridden up. My palm rested on her bare belly, my fingers spanning the distance from hipbone to hipbone.

She fit like we were made for each other.

So much for keeping our distance.

I gave myself thirty seconds to savor the feeling of a woman sleeping in my arms. Under my skin, my shadow brother lolled in drowsy contentment. Liv sighed happily then wriggled backward, burrowing into me.

I suppressed a groan. Lifting my hand from her stomach, I slid my body backward away from hers. She whimpered a protest that almost cut through my fine resolve. I paused then forced myself to abandon my bed and the tempting woman who shared it.

I quietly made my way to the hall bathroom. Didn't want to risk waking Liv when I flushed and ran the faucet. I emerged to find Owen leaning against the wall, two cups of coffee in his hands. He held one out to me.

"I like Liv," he said.

Little brother was getting right to the point, wasn't he?

"Me, too." I nodded my thanks for the java.

We sipped the piping hot brew in companionable silence.

"Do you know what you're doing, Viggo?" he finally asked.

"No." Honesty compelled the answer. "But my bear says she's ours."

"Your bear staked a claim?" Owen's eyes registered shock, followed quickly by concern. "How can that possibly work?"

"It can't. There's no way Liv fits into our world." Bitter resignation filled my voice. "The best I can hope for is that Landry delivers on his promise to turn over the Black Rock, and Medved keeps his word and sends her home safely."

"Dammit all to hell," Owen burst out. "Fuck Medved and the mess he's made of our lives."

"Careful," I cautioned. "Nobody can ever hear you talk like that."

"I know. I know." He clenched his jaw. "It's so damned unfair. The very best case scenario will break your bear's heart."

"It is what it is, brother."

From its charger on the kitchen counter, my cell phone pinged. I rushed to pick it up, scanned the incoming message, and punched in a quick response.

"It's Medved," I told Owen.

"Speak of the devil," he muttered.

"Boss wants me to come to HQ to make plans for the meeting with Landry's reps. He says you're to keep an eye on Liv."

Owen made a face. "I surprised he's not gonna put her in the Hole while you're busy."

"Guess that shows how confident he is that he won," I said. "He said she can spend the day with you at the store."

"No problem. If I need her help with anything, I'll bribe her with spicy chips."

The door to Hallie's room cracked open, and she emerged, yawning and rubbing her eyes. "Is Liv still here?"

"Yep. It looks like she'll be staying with us for a couple more days," I said.

"Good. I like having her around."

"We're having scrambled eggs and toast this morning," Owen said. "Get dressed, peanut, then come to the kitchen and I'll dish you up."

Hallie shuffled toward the bathroom, Bosco on her heels. "Privacy, please." She shut the door in the disappointed dog's face.

"Can you walk Hallie to school?" I asked.

"Not a problem."

"I'll go wake Liv and get dressed. Medved wants me at headquarters ASAP."

Owen frowned. "No time for breakfast with Hallie?"

"No. I'll grab a slice of toast on the way out."

Back in my room, I found the bed empty and the bathroom door closed. I quickly threw on clothes and boots. Liv exited the bathroom in a cloud of steam. She'd wrapped a towel around her damp hair, and her slender fingers were busy cinching the belt on my black terry cloth robe. She stopped in her tracks when she caught me gaping at her.

"I borrowed your robe," she faltered. "Is that okay?"

The spit in my mouth dried up. "Yeah," I choked out, struck dumb by the sight. Did she have any idea what it meant to a shifter to have a woman wear his clothing? To know that his scent would transfer to her skin and linger there, a warning for his packmates to keep their distance?

Beneath my skin, my bear reared up on his hind legs, threw back his head, and roared in triumph.

Don't get your hopes up, brother, I warned.

Humph. He dismissed my concerns.

I cleared my throat. "I'm heading out to pack headquarters. You're gonna be spending the day with Owen at the store, Medved's orders."

"Well if Medved says so." Sarcasm dripped from her voice as she towel-dried her hair.

"Would you like to go to Howling Jack's with me tonight?" I surprised myself by issuing the invitation.

"What's that?"

"The only bar in the village. It was originally built by the wolves."

She held up her palms. "Let me get this straight. You're leaving me with Owen today then you're taking me out to a bar tonight. Isn't Medved afraid I'll try to slip away and make a break for it?"

"Where would you go? We're at the ass end of nowhere—surrounded by a frozen wilderness—and everybody in the village is a grizzly."

She shut her eyes, coming to terms with reality. "Not to mention if I tried to get away when Owen was babysitting me, Medved would blame him and make him pay."

Without a doubt, my alpha would hold Owen accountable if Liv tried something when she was under his care. "He would."

"I promise, I won't do anything to get you or Owen in trouble with Medved." She gave a little laugh. "Not that there's much I could do anyway since I'm stuck at bear central in—what did you call it?—the ass end of nowhere."

"I appreciate that," I said. "Owen will be walking Hallie to school in a little while. Can you get dressed so you'll be ready to tag along?"

"Sure."

I turned to leave.

"Does Howling Jack's serve margaritas?"

I was no fan of tequila, so I didn't know for sure. I glanced over my shoulder. "I think so."

"I want a margarita tonight. A big one."

"It's a date." As soon as the words slipped out of my mouth I wished I could call them back. We weren't dating. We had no future, despite what my bear believed.

Instead of challenging my choice of words, Liv flashed an understanding smile. "It's a date."

After the wolf alpha caved so easily to his demands, Medved had written him off as a lightweight. He was confident the wolves wouldn't try to pull a fast one. I had my doubts, but I kept them to myself. Once he made up his mind, my influence over the boss only went so far.

I blew my wad—so to speak—over the location of the meeting.

It was a hard sell to talk the boss out of holding the meeting in his office, the same room where he'd met with Liv. To my mind, nobody could reasonably expect the wolves to negotiate under glass eyes of their murdered brethren. The idea of Landry's reps facing a wall of taxidermied wolf heads tickled Medved's funny bone, but with the possession of the Black Rock dangling before his eyes, he reluctantly gave it up.

I was in charge of security for the wolves' visit. Medved's instructions were simple and to the point: make sure tomorrow's negotiations went off without a hitch. I spent the day putting security measures in place. My final act before heading home was selecting the half dozen soldiers who would surround our alpha at the meeting. I left the Garvey brothers off that list, a slight the ambitious pair took to heart.

Tough shit.

The delicious smell of meatloaf smacked me in the face when I opened my front door. The aroma drew me to the kitchen, where I found Hallie standing next to Liv at the counter. A pile of carrots lay on a cutting board in front of them. One of her mama's old-fashioned aprons was tied around Hallie's waist.

Spying me, she excitedly waved a vegetable peeler. "Liv is teaching me how to make glazed carrots. We're having mashed potatoes, too, and meatloaf."

"Moose meatloaf." Liv wasn't able to keep the note of skepticism out of her voice. "I slathered it with a sweet-and-sour glaze. I hope it's good." She sounded doubtful.

"Liv has never eaten moose," Hallie said. "I told her it's yummy, but she's not so sure."

"Hey," Liv protested. "I'm willing to give it a shot. After all, Hallie Creed recommends it."

Hallie leaned sideways and pressed her cheek against Liv's arm, a simple, spontaneous gesture of affection. Liv bent over and dropped a kiss on the top of my daughter's head.

"Let's peel another carrot, kiddo."

My bear watched with rapt attention, and my throat grew thick.

Dammit. Liv *fit*. Hallie and Owen liked her. My bear claimed her. He'd never be happy with a sweet, gentle soul. Hell, I loved her sass and spirit, too.

I balled my fists. I'd long since stopped pining for things I couldn't have. Peace of mind was possible only if you accepted reality. Reading Epictetus reinforced that truth.

"Do I have time for a shower before dinner?" I asked.

"It'll be another half hour," Liv answered.

Twenty minutes later—sporting a freshly shaved head—I helped Hallie set the table. The four of us chowed down on one of the best meals I'd had in months. Owen was an above average cook, but Liv was a master. I'm not sure the moose meatloaf converted her into a fan of venison, but she gamely ate her slice.

Once we finished eating, I supervised Hallie's homework while Owen and Liv tidied up the kitchen. Hallie took a long bath. A little before nine, we left Hallie and Owen snuggled up cheek-by-jowl, reading a few chapters of Percy Jackson.

Liv and I walked the half mile into town with only the dim glow of a crescent moon to light our way. After her first stumble, she held onto my arm.

"I thought Alaska was the land of the midnight sun," she grumbled.

"Not in November. You'll need to come back in the summer if you want to see the midnight sun."

"Next time you kidnap me, make sure you do it in June," Liv said, making light of an awkward moment.

Howling Jack's was hopping. Loud voices and raucous laughter poured from the bar. The smell of beer and nachos and cheeseburgers wafted in the air.

Liv paused outside the door, inhaled a deep breath, and squared her shoulders.

"You look like you're getting ready to beard a lion in his den," I observed.

"I am. For most of your people, I'm the enemy."

I couldn't argue. For decades, the enmity between wolves and grizzlies had run deep. I leaned close, breathing in her bittersweet-orange scent. "Nobody will give you a hard time. Not when you're with me."

She lifted her chin. "All right, big guy. Let's do this."

The bar fell silent when Liv and I stepped inside, and all eyes turned toward us. Holding Liv's elbow, I steered us toward an empty table in the back. I pulled out her chair, demonstrating that I expected everyone to treat my prisoner with the same courtesy I did.

The barkeep kept a bottle of my favorite scotch—a Knockando eighteen year old—for my exclusive consumption. No sooner had we sat down than he brought me a glass of my usual.

"Mr. Creed," he murmured respectfully.

"May I?" Liv held out her hand for the glass. I passed it over.

She took a small swallow, hummed happily, then delicately licked the rim of the glass. "I'm not usually a fan of scotch, but that's super smooth." I watched entranced as she took a second sip. She moaned. "Delicious."

"Glad you like it." I shifted positions, adjusting my suddenly tight jeans.

"You're leading me astray, Viggo Creed. I might just abandon tequila for scotch."

The prospect of leading Liv Hagen astray had my vision fuzzing. My turmoil must've shown on my face. She laughed softly and settled back in her chair, clutching the scotch to her chest.

"This one's mine. Order another one for yourself."

I raised a hand, caught the waitress's eye, and pointed at the scotch. She nodded and scurried to fetch it.

"I'm glad to see you're corruptible," I said, proud of myself for keeping a straight face.

One dark eyebrow arched. "Under the right circumstances, you might find that I'm very… flexible."

I moaned, my imagination running wild at mental images of a very flexible Liv.

"You're killing me, woman."

The waitress set another glass of the amber whisky on the table.

Liv's expression sobered. "I wish…" she started.

"I know. Me, too."

We lapsed into silence, staring into each other's eyes, a million words hanging unspoken between us.

Something whizzed past Liv's head—almost grazing her cheek—and embedded itself in the wall five feet from the dartboard.

"Ho-ly shit." Liv jumped to her feet and staggered backward.

Silence descended. Every person in the bar froze in place, watching us.

"Oops. My bad," Hank Garvey drawled. With an infuriating smirk on his ruddy face, the asshole swaggered past our table and plucked the sharp dart from the wood paneling.

"You okay?" I asked Liv.

She touched her cheek, her eyes round with shock, then looked down at her fingers. No blood. "Yeah. I'm okay. It didn't cut me."

I stood and faced Hank. "And that's the only reason you're gonna walk away from here in one piece."

"C'mon, man." Jasper Garvey sauntered over and stood by his brother's side. "You can't get bent out of shape over an accident."

"An accident?" They expected me to buy that line of bull?

Hank snickered. "Yeah, an accident. You think I'd try to hurt your little slut on purpose?"

Slut? A red mist rose before my eyes then burned away, leaving me ice cold and full of purpose.

The smug sneer faded from Hank's face. I grabbed the brothers by their napes and slammed their heads together. Hank slumped to the floor, out cold. Jasper stumbled backward and fell on his ass. He clutched his head, moaning.

"You're both banned from Howling Jack's for the next six months." As senior enforcer, nobody would challenge my call.

My gaze traveled around the bar, searching for any hint of dissent, any sign of more trouble. I saw none. The Garveys weren't popular. Their drinking buddies looked the other way. An all too familiar fear filled my packmates' eyes. I was the brute who kept them all in line. Few people dared to cross Medved's number one enforcer.

"Take your brother and get out," I ordered.

Jasper struggled to his feet. He grabbed his unconscious sibling under his arms and dragged him from the bar.

"A round of beers on the house," the bartender called. The crowd relaxed and a clamor of voices once again filled the room.

Her hand shaking, Liv downed her scotch in one giant swallow. "Can we go, please?"

Dammit. I'd scared her. My chest tightened. I'd intended this to be a fun excursion, a chance to catch our breaths and relax before the big meeting tomorrow. A moment, stolen in time, before Liv and I had to go our separate ways.

"Please, Viggo. Can we just go?"

Chapter Sixteen

Liv

The old-fashioned shopkeeper's bell over the door jingled. I looked up from the case of baby food I was unpacking.

The Garvey brothers stood in the doorway of the community store. Jasper sported a purple lump on his forehead. A bruise covered Hank's temple, and his eyes were bloodshot. Despite their beat-up appearances, both men looked positively giddy with excitement.

A warning chill ticked up my spine.

Owen plastered a welcoming smile on his face and rushed forward to greet the enforcers. "Can I help you gentlemen? We just got a new shipment in of that chewing tobacco you like, Hank. I can grab some for you from the back."

Hank waved a dismissive hand. "We're here to escort the prisoner to pack headquarters."

"Hold on a minute." Owen raised his voice. "Viggo didn't tell me anything about Liv being taken to HQ."

"That's because he didn't know. Medved decided this morning to put her in the Hole till the meeting. He sent us to retrieve her."

Viggo was out of town and incommunicado, flying one of the pack's planes to Fairbanks to pick up Adam's delegation. The Garveys were clearly taking advantage of his absence to move against me. They'd either talked Medved into sticking me in the Hole, or they were acting independently. Bad as the Hole might be, being taken God-knows-where by the Garveys was a far worse prospect.

No way would I allow Owen to put himself between me and the spiteful enforcers. Hallie had already lost her mother. I wouldn't allow her to lose her uncle, too. And I didn't want anything bad to happen to the kind young grizzly during some futile attempt to stop the Garveys.

"It's okay, Owen." My left foot had fallen asleep when I knelt on the floor. I wobbled to a standing position and leaned against a shelf while the feeling returned to my tingling tootsie. "The Garveys are just following Mr. Medved's orders."

Shut your mouth and cooperate before the dickheads hurt you.

"No." Owen slammed a hand on a shelf. "Something is fishy. I'm gonna close the store and walk over to HQ with you."

Jasper gave a half shrug, unconcerned by Owen's threat. "Suit yourself."

They *were* following Medved's orders to put me in the Hole. Five minutes ago, such a prospect wouldn't have filled me with so much relief. Proof positive that some calamities were worse than others.

Put one foot in front of the other and keep moving forward.

Owen flipped the open sign around in the window and locked the door. He stuck to my side during the short walk to pack headquarters.

When we entered the building, the secretary silently handed Jasper a set of keys. He led the way toward a metal door behind her desk.

"I'm sorry, Owen," the secretary said. "Only enforcers are allowed in the basement."

"Viggo didn't know anything about this," he said. "You sure it's on the up-and-up?"

"Yes. The alpha ordered the Garveys to bring her in."

"I don't appreciate your attitude, son." Hank scowled,

"Tough shit." Owen shook a finger at Hank. "Anything happens to her while she's in your custody, you'll answer to Viggo."

"Ohhh." Hank raised trembling hands into the air and fake-trembled. "I'm quaking in my boots."

Owen offered a mirthless smile. "After last night, you should be."

"Why you little—" Hank took a step toward Owen.

"None of that." The secretary's voice was sharp, and she shot the Garveys a stern look, then turned to Owen. "The prisoner will be fine."

"Owen, please go back to the store," I said in a low voice.

"All right." His reluctance to leave me warmed my heart, but I had this.

I turned my back on my friend and followed the Garveys through the door and down a staircase to the basement. To our left was a large storage room. Metal shelving units filled one wall. Old office furniture—chairs and desks—lined another. Next to a small window on the storage room's exterior wall, a rectangular iron hatch drew my eye. It was an old-fashioned coal chute, obviously long disused.

The Garveys hustled me past the storage room and through a door that led to a hallway. Two inadequate overhead lights illuminated a long narrow corridor. A cement floor and walls painted a dismal green hemmed me in and triggered an uncharacteristic wave of claustrophobia. I paused and laid a hand against a clammy wall, catching my balance.

Don't you dare swoon in front of these jerkwads.

I lurched forward before the Garveys could notice my rubbery legs.

Hank came to a stop next to an open door, angling his head toward the interior of the room. "Check this out. Your new boyfriend's playroom."

His glee gave me the heebie-jeebies. I reluctantly looked through the opening and immediately regretted it. What looked like a dentist chair with straps attached to the arms sat on one side of the room. Shackles hung from chains affixed to the ceiling, the chipped cement beneath stained a dark, ominous color. A workbench hugged a wall. I spied a hammer and pliers on its surface before I looked away.

Viggo's playroom?

Acid crawled up my throat. I stared wide-eyed at the Garveys.

Jasper bobbed his head. "Sometimes people need a little persuading before they spill the beans about fellow traitors. Viggo can be *very* persuasive."

I swallowed. Viggo had told me he was a lost soul, that he'd done horrible things in Medved's name. But this Spanish Inquisition shit?

"I don't believe you," I said through stiff lips.

Jasper gave an indifferent shrug. "Ask him."

"Keep moving," Hank barked.

We followed the corridor past two closed doors until the hallway dead-ended with a final door, a metal one Jasper unlocked with a key. The door swung open with an unsettling creak and revealed a black void. The Hole. An apt name. I saw nothing, no floor, no walls, only darkness. A musty smell rose from the space. I instinctively took a step backward.

"No you don't," Hank chuckled, grabbing my arm and yanking me closer to the gaping maw. He pulled on a string dangling from the Hole's ceiling. An old filament light bulb flickered to life, illuminating the interior. A rope fire-escape ladder was rolled up and attached to the inside of the metal door. Hank shook it out, dropped one end into the hole, and hooked the other over the doorsill.

"Down you go." Jasper sounded way too cheerful, like he was having the time of his life.

I looked down into the dimly lit cavern. They'd excavated a five-by-five-foot wide pit at least a dozen feet deep. I thought the corridor was claustrophobic? This was a freaking nightmare, a skinny shaft carved into the earth, leading straight to hell.

Get a hold of yourself, woman.

"There's a bucket down there if you need to take a dump," Hank said.

Lovely image.

"Move your ass," his brother added.

My limbs locked and I couldn't force myself to move.

"You climb down the ladder or we'll toss you in," Hank said.

That threat got my rear in gear. I dropped onto my knees and carefully lowered myself onto the flimsy rope ladder. It swung but held my weight as I slowly climbed down.

Put one foot in front of the other and keep moving forward. Never had Grandma's advice felt so appropriate.

My feet struck the packed dirt at the bottom of the hole. No sooner had I released the ropes than the ladder was snatched out of my hands. Hank hauled it to the top and hung it on the door, leaving me trapped in the pit. Dank dirt walls surrounded me, rising straight up toward the weak light emanating from the ancient bulb.

One of the Garveys yanked on the string. The light dimmed, then died.

"Buh-bye," he taunted.

The metal door clanged shut, leaving me alone in the dark at the bottom of the Hole.

"Shit. Shit. Shit." I turned in a circle, patting the cool earthen walls. My foot kicked against the bucket, which mercifully sat empty. Fumbling in the dark, I turned the bucket over and dropped down onto it. The rigid plastic rim poked into my thighs, but it was better than sitting on the cold, damp ground.

My thoughts spun out of control. How come they didn't leave me any water? As soon as I asked myself the question, a desperate thirst seized me. That's why I always smuggled a bottle of water into a movie theater. There was no better way to guarantee a parched throat than to find yourself without a handy drink. Another thought. Was there an air vent somewhere that I hadn't noticed? Would I run out of oxygen and suffocate?

"For fuck's sake," I hissed. Panicking wouldn't help.

I sucked in a deep, calming breath, and consciously stilled my rampaging thoughts.

Medved planned to trade me for the Black Rock. He needed me alive. The Garveys wouldn't leave me to die in this pit. They'd haul me out of here and show me to the wolves—to my people—in a few hours. At this very moment, Viggo was on his way to pick up Adam's delegation.

Viggo.

Images of the torture chamber flashed into my mind.

Viggo's playroom.

If it was true, how could I make peace with that knowledge?

Wrapping my arms around my waist, I rocked back and forth.

CHAPTER SEVENTEEN

VIGGO

Leaning against a wall, pretending a nonchalance I didn't feel, I eyeballed two men walking toward me from the security checkpoint at the entrance to the concourse. Wolves. The human sea around the men parted, creating distance between themselves and the shifters. On a subconscious level, folks recognized the men were dangerous and something other than strictly human. Stepping aside was a visceral, involuntary act.

I straightened, recognizing both men. Zane Hunter, the wolf alpha's cousin and one of his top lieutenants, had a backpack slung over one shoulder and a duffel in his hand. The tall, blond sentry was mated to Liv's sister, Annika. Next to him—stooped and frail—Matthew Strauss, the former alpha of the Black Rock Guardians pack, shuffled forward on unsteady feet.

What the hell? Landry sent his elderly grandfather to negotiate?

Hunter tensed as I strode toward the pair, clearly ready to do battle if I made a move against the old man. I halted and stuck out my hand, curious about how the wolves would handle this first meeting. If they scowled and ignored my proffered hand, it'd be a sign we were in for a long slog during the negotiations.

"Viggo Creed," I introduced myself, knowing full well they'd recognize the name. I'd mastered dominance games. Raising my chin and relaxing my shoulders, I telegraphed confidence and authority.

Hunter's eyes flashed and his jaw tightened. Oh yeah, the wolf lieutenant knew I was the man who took his mate's sister. Without question, if he had half a chance, he'd gut me where I stood.

"Mr. Creed, thank you for picking us up." The former alpha nodded politely and shook my hand. At the contact, vestiges of his alpha power zinged along my skin. I resisted the impulse to yank my hand away and shake off the tingles.

"No problem."

Despite the bad blood between our packs, maybe the negotiations would go off without a hitch. The wolves had already agreed to the essentials. Once they delivered the Black Rock, Liv would go home.

I'd never see her again.

At that thought, my bear roared a protest. *Ours.*

Slow your roll, I shot back.

Butting heads with my shadow brother in the presence of an alpha who could sense a shifter's internal struggle. Was I trying to trash my credibility?

I'd considered confiding in the wolves. Confessing that I wanted nothing more than to release Liv to their custody. Promising that I'd do everything within my power to make that happen. Such an admission might placate my conscience, but it'd do nothing to change the outcome or their opinion of me. I did what I did. I couldn't weasel out of my responsibility now.

"Follow me to the air-park, please."

As we walked past one of the airport's most famous sights—a tall taxidermied grizzly—Hunter snickered. I paid no heed to the provocative sound.

"Heard you crashed the Beaver," he said conversationally, holding a door open for his grandfather.

I lifted a shoulder. "Yeah, but we have two more."

He flashed his teeth in a humorless smile. "We know. My pack bought and paid for the planes before you stole them from us."

"Zane." A sharp rebuke from the former alpha, who apparently had taken on the role of peacekeeper.

"Sorry, Grandpa." He sounded anything but.

I sighed. It was going to be a long flight to the village.

We set down at the airstrip outside of town. I called Evelyn to give Medved a heads-up that we'd arrived. I'd left my truck at the airstrip. We climbed in for the short trip into town. Glancing into my rearview mirror, I saw Hunter rest a hand on his grandfather's shoulder. The old man leaned toward the window, eagerly watching the world go by.

This was a homecoming for the former alpha. He'd grown up in the village and had fled it with the rest of his pack when he was a teenager. Maybe that was why he'd accompanied Hunter on the mission—his last chance to see his old home. Or maybe Landry thought the elder statesman would provide the voice of reason if the negotiations soured.

I parked in front of grizzly HQ and led the way into the building. Evelyn eyed the wolves with curiosity as we passed the front desk on our way to the meeting room at the end of the hall. We walked into the room, a bland, inoffensive space without a single mounted wolf head. Instead of rising to greet his guests, Medved kept his seat at the head of the long conference table. Jasper and Hank flanked the alpha. He must have replaced two of the enforcers I'd assigned to the meeting with the Garveys. Three additional enforcers spread out behind him.

Overkill if you asked me, but Medved always liked to make an impression. He waited a beat before he spoke, leaving us standing awkwardly inside the door.

"Gentlemen." An oily smile creased Medved's face. His arm swept out in an extravagant gesture of welcome. "Please be seated." Matthew Strauss sat opposite Medved, with Zane Hunter on his right. I dropped onto a chair next to Medved.

The conventional niceties followed. Blah. Blah. Blah.

"You have my granddaughter," Strauss remarked without heat.

The designation surprised me. Liv shared no blood with the former alpha, although according to my research, her grandfather, Aleksandr, had been the old man's closest friend. Two of Strauss's grandsons had mated Hagen women. I guess he considered all of them as family.

"That's right." Medved inclined his head. "And I'd be happy to return her to you, just as soon as we reach a friendly agreement about the ownership of the Black Rock. I'd say it's past time for the meteorite to be returned to its home in Alaska."

"That's why we're here." Zane spoke through clenched teeth.

Medved twisted around in his chair and addressed Jasper Garvey. "Get the woman and bring her up here."

"Yes, sir." With a smug glance toward me, Jasper sauntered from the room.

My heart kicked. I'd left Liv safely with Owen. "What do you mean, *up here*?"

Medved smacked his forehead, like he'd forgotten something important. "That's right. You were gone so you don't know. I had the Garvey boys pick her up and put her in the Hole."

Shock made me forget caution. "Why the hell would you do that?"

Medved's eyes narrowed. He'd make me pay for my insubordination, maybe not now in front of the wolves, but I'd earned a spot high up on the alpha's shit list.

"You've had your fun. You deserved it after delivering Liv Hagen to me." The boss cheerfully dug my grave. "But it's time to take her outta your bed and treat her like a prisoner, not your little plaything."

I couldn't argue facts with him. I'd gone out of my way to make my alpha believe she *was* my little plaything.

Hunter made a choking sound. I cut a glance at him and saw my death reflected in his eyes. Strauss laid a warning hand on his grandson's arm. If Medved was trying to give the wolves a powerful motive to negotiate for her release, he'd achieved his goal.

I'd make sure not to turn my back on the wolf lieutenant.

Footsteps sounded in the corridor. The door swung open. Jasper frog-marched Liv into the room. He'd pulled her arms tight behind her back and held her wrists in one meaty fist as he shoved her inside.

I scanned her body from head to foot, searching for any sign of mistreatment. No bruises or contusions. Dirt smudged her hands—like she'd been pounding on the earthen walls of the Hole. Her clothes were intact, although her hair was mussed. She looked pissed off and undaunted. Good on her. She glanced at me, then at her family.

Hunter rose to his feet, the wrath of God stamped on his features. "Take your hands off her." The lack of inflection in his voice was more chilling than if he'd yelled.

"Sir?" Jasper glanced at Medved for instructions.

The alpha gave an indifferent shrug. "Sure. Let her go."

Jasper pushed her and she stumbled. I was closer to Liv than Hunter. Thanks to the chip of black rock I wore on my wrist, I beat him to her side and caught her elbow, steadying her.

"You all right?" I asked in a low voice.

"Yes." Her fingers closed around my forearm, clinging to me like I was her anchor. She met my eyes, then her gaze swung to the wolves. For a fraction of a second, her chin trembled. Pressing her lips together, she swallowed. Tears gathered in the corners of her eyes, tears she furiously blinked away as my woman fought to regain her composure.

My woman.

My chest clenched as the full import of that realization sunk in. This stubborn, defiant, spirited human called to me in a way no other woman ever had. My shadow brother was right all along. She was my other half, my fated mate.

And it didn't make a damned bit of difference. I couldn't keep her.

"Hey, Grandpa." She tossed a reassuring, I'm-okay smile to the old man then turned to her brother-in-law. "Zane, it's good to see you."

"Go ahead," Medved said magnanimously. "Hug your family."

She rushed into Zane's embrace. His arms wrapped protectively around her and she held on tight. Over her head, he glowered at me with murderous intent. She extracted herself from his hold and hugged the former wolf alpha.

"Heartwarming, isn't it?" Medved said. "Let's talk about how to make this little family reunion permanent, shall we gentlemen?"

Zane pulled Liv onto the chair next to Strauss and took a seat next to her, sandwiching her between the wolves. Fat lot of good it would do. Outnumbered, isolated, surrounded by grizzlies, her people couldn't keep her safe if Medved barked an order for his men to grab her.

For the next half hour, we talked the logistics of the exchange, which would take place in two days. A small team of wolf soldiers would bring the Black Rock to Alaska. Until then, Hunter and Strauss would stay in a small guest house close to downtown.

"You'll be our guests," Medved assured them. "Of course, since the war, our people aren't on the friendliest of terms. In case some hothead gets a notion to do violence, I'll assign grizzly guards to keep you two safe."

Assigning guards to ensure their safety? Why did he bother with a lie so blatantly untrue that a five-year-old could see right through it?

"You're too kind." Zane's lip curled, and his voice was heavy with sarcasm.

Medved dipped his head. "Not at all. Now, one last thing. I believe you brought a token of goodwill with you from your alpha." He rubbed his palms together, expectation on his face.

Zane dug in his pocket and extracted a small drawstring bag. He tossed it to Medved. The Garvey brothers and the other enforcers craned their necks and eagerly watched our alpha open the bag.

"Aren't you a thing of beauty?" Medved murmured, pinching the marble-sized chunk of meteorite between his fingers. He shivered as a jolt of power shot into him.

"Can I touch it, boss?" Jasper asked. The Garvey brothers weren't among the lucky few entrusted with slivers of the rock.

"Why not?" Medved held it out. "'Bout time you boys see what all the fuss is about."

"Thank you, sir."

The enforcers crowded around, taking turns laying a finger on the piece of rock. When they finished, Medved slipped it into the bag and pocketed it.

He turned to Strauss and Hunter. "I'm sure you're tired after your long trip. A couple of my men will walk you to the guest house. I'll have dinner sent over from Howling Jack's. They still make the best cheeseburgers in all of Alaska. Tomorrow, if you want to walk around town—see the old sights—I'll be happy to arrange for an escort."

"You're too kind," Hunter's voice held as much sincerity as the first time he said the words.

"Not at all." Medved resolutely refused to take offense at the wolf lieutenant's tone. He signaled for the Garveys to take the men to their quarters. Another hug for Liv, another homicidal glance sent my way, and the Black Rock Guardians departed the conference room.

"Get out," Medved barked to the other enforcers. They filed from the room, leaving Liv and me alone with the boss. He jabbed a finger at me. "Don't you ever disrespect me like that again."

Time to eat shit and try to get back in Medved's good graces. I arranged my features to appear contrite and chastened. "I'm sorry. I was dead wrong, sir. Don't know what got in to me."

Medved leaned back in his chair. "That's what happens when you think with your little head and not your big one."

"Yes, sir."

He turned to Liv. "Now what am I going to do with you? Put you back in the Hole, or send you home with Creed?"

"Do I get a vote?" she asked without an ounce of fear in her voice.

He laughed. "No."

I leaned forward, drawing the alpha's eye. "Did you see the look on Hunter's face when he heard I was fucking his mate's sister?" My crude choice of words was deliberate, negating any emotional bond between Liv and me.

"Wasn't that a sight to behold?" Medved cackled. "I thought he was going to have a stroke."

I lifted a shoulder. "Best way to keep the wolves on edge is to let 'em know I'm keeping their woman in my bed till we get the Black Rock."

"You might be right. The notion of a grizzly enforcer putting it to their precious little human is sure to keep them riled up." He steepled his hands, considering the matter. Thirty seconds later, decision made, he slapped his thigh. "Take her home with you and let the wolves stew."

"Yes, sir." My lewd grin hid my relief. I stood and held out a hand to Liv. "Come on."

"Asshole," she hissed, rising to her feet.

Medved chuckled, delighted by her apparent distaste and reluctance.

I stood between her and my alpha, so he couldn't see the relieved expression on her face when she took my hand, couldn't tell she was playacting for his benefit. Her fingers closed around mine, and I squeezed hers back.

We marched in silence down the corridor, past all the people going about their business in grizzly HQ. To my surprise, Owen waited for us on the sidewalk outside the building, pacing back and forth nervously. As soon as he spied us, he dashed to our side.

I frowned. "Where's Hallie?"

School got out more than two hours ago, and Hallie should've been with her uncle.

"I left her playing with one of her friends." He handed Liv her coat, a remorseful expression on his face. "I'm sorry I couldn't stop the Garveys from taking you. Did they hurt you?"

"That wasn't your fault, Owen. There was nothing you could do to stop the Garveys. They put me in the Hole without any food or water. I'm hungry and thirsty, but I'm okay. Viggo talked Medved into letting me go back home with him. It's all good."

Our woman was hungry and thirsty. Beneath my skin, my furious shadow brother pounded his front paws and clacked his teeth.

I tucked her hand into the crook of my arm, protective instincts riding me hard. "Let's get you home and get some food into you."

Chapter Eighteen

Liv

By the time Owen got home with Hallie, I'd wolfed down the grilled cheese sandwich Viggo made for me and was polishing off my second glass of water. Hallie didn't cue into the tension in the house and prattled on happily about her day.

Owen insisted that I rest rather than help him prepare dinner. Viggo lit a fire in the stone fireplace. Hallie and I occupied opposite ends of the sofa, our feet tangled together in the middle, one oversized fleece blanket covering us both. We each had our nose in a book. Bosco jumped onto the sofa and managed to straddle both my legs and Hallie's.

"Who's a good boy?" I patted his sleek head. He squinted happily at me and rolled onto his side.

From the kitchen, Viggo and Owen carried on a low, urgent conversation.

I kept lifting my gaze from my book and stealing glances at the little girl. Her eyes were round with excitement, and her lips moved as she sounded out difficult words. She'd twirled a strand of strawberry-blond hair around her pointer finger, a nervous habit I shared with her.

"I do that, too," I said

She glanced up. "What?"

"Play with my hair, especially when I'm tired."

She put down her book. "We have lots of things in common, you know. We both like outer space and reading and pancakes. We both love Bosco." The dog heard his name and thumped his tail. "And we both love Uncle Owen and Daddy." She looked at me expectantly, as if challenging me to agree or disagree.

The conversation in the kitchen abruptly cut off.

I knew the sweet kid liked me. She'd said she enjoyed having another girl in the house. Was she fantasizing about having a new mother? Did she think I'd stick around if I loved her father?

"Umm…" I hesitated. Owen was a great guy. And Viggo… Sexual attraction wasn't love. Admiration for his strength and skills wasn't love. Neither was sympathetic understanding for a man caught between a rock and a hard place. Respect for his devotion to his family? Nope, not love.

Well then, just what *was* love if not all that?

Love wasn't something that happened to you. You didn't trip and fall headfirst into it. Unlike shifters, I didn't believe in fated mates. Love was something you chose, at least that was what I'd always thought.

I didn't have a masochistic bone in my body. What would be the point in allowing myself to fall in love with a man I couldn't keep?

"Hey, peanut, dinner is almost ready." Owen stood in the opening to the living room. "Go wash up."

"Okay." She hopped up and headed for the bathroom.

I nodded my thanks to Owen for his timely rescue.

I joined Viggo, Owen, and Hallie at the kitchen table. After the grilled cheese sandwich, I didn't have much appetite. I picked at my salad.

I felt restless, twitchy, and uneasy. Events were coming to a head. Zane and Grandpa Matthew were less than a mile away—surrounded by enemies—at the mercy of a man I didn't trust. In two days, the Black Rock Guardians would turn the meteorite over to the grizzlies. If all went according to plan, I'd return home to my old life.

And I'd never see Viggo and Hallie and Owen again.

I pushed my salad plate away, my appetite gone.

After dinner, we cleared the table and played cards, old maid and go fish. Owen and Hallie carried the weight of the conversation, laughing and joking. Whenever I glanced his way, I found Viggo watching me with a thoughtful expression on his masculine face.

I needed some downtime to restore my equilibrium after being locked into the Hole and my far-too-brief reunion with Zane and Grandpa Matthew.

"I'm going to go take a long soak in Viggo's tub," I announced.

Hallie ran to the hall bathroom and returned clutching a pink plastic bottle. "You can use my bubble bath. It'll make you smell just like bubblegum."

"Cool beans, kiddo. Thank you." I slid an arm around her waist and pulled her close for a hug. I felt Viggo's gaze on us, sensed his pleasure that the little girl and I got along so well.

I lingered in the tub till the skin on my fingertips puckered, the bubbles subsided, and the water cooled. After drying off, I pulled one of Viggo's giant black tees over my head.

Walking into the bedroom, I found him sprawled in his overstuffed leather chair. Darkness shrouded the room, the only illumination coming from the floor lamp that threw a pool of light over the man in the chair. Wearing only gray sweatpants, Viggo swirled a glass of amber-colored liquid—probably his favorite scotch. When he saw me, he lifted the glass to his mouth and took a slow sip.

I padded across the room and held out my hand. "May I?"

Without a word, he handed me the glass. I turned it around and placed my lips on the exact same spot where he'd pressed his, probably as close to a kiss as we'd ever come. A sadness for what might have been swept over me as I took a small swallow.

Viggo took the glass from me and set it on the small side table. He held out a hand. "Come here."

I hesitated. Smart women didn't invite heartbreak.

"Please." He curled his fingers, inviting me in.

I sighed, torn.

Brave women didn't tremble at the prospect of loss. Loss was inevitable. Nothing and nobody lasted forever. Memories might endure, precious moments locked safely in your heart, a treasure you pulled out and relived. Maybe this was such a moment.

Before I could think better of it, I allowed him to pull me onto his lap. Curling onto my side, I tucked my head against his shoulder and splayed my fingers against his chest. He dragged his chin across the top of my head. The stubble raised goose bumps across my flesh. I shivered and pressed into his heat.

"I'm sorry," he said. His palm stroked up and down my back.

"For what?"

"That I wasn't here to stop the Garveys from putting you in the Hole."

I yielded to temptation and scratched my fingernails through the dark hairs sprinkled across his chest. He trembled and sucked in a breath. His arms tightened around me.

"Then it's a good thing you weren't here," I said. "If you tried to stop the Garveys when they were following Medved's orders, there would have been hell to pay."

He didn't argue with me. He couldn't.

"The thought of you trapped in the dark—"

"Shhh." I pressed a finger against his lips. "It wasn't so bad, and it's over."

"You'll never see that fucking hole in the ground again," he vowed.

I'd seen other things that troubled me far more than the pit.

"Viggo?"

"Yeah?"

"The Garveys showed me a torture chamber with shackles hanging from the ceiling, and a retrofitted dentist's chair, and a workbench full of… implements. They called it your playroom."

He stilled. For thirty seconds, he didn't take a breath. Finally, he spoke. "I told you I've done bad things."

"Yes." I nodded against his chest.

"I'm not a good man." His voice was flat and expressionless as he rattled off his sins. "I've put the fear of God in people. Kidnapped them. Blackmailed them. Threatened to take away everything they hold dear. Beat people up. Broke their bones. I've executed men Medved deemed traitors."

"The playroom?" I held my breath waiting for his answer.

"I've never had to tie someone down and torture them to get the information I want. Torture is unreliable. Folks will do anything, say anything, to make the pain stop. The combination of a little pain and a lot of fear works better, at least in my experience."

"The floor under the shackles was stained with blood." I shuddered at the memory.

"I didn't say nobody used the playroom. I said it wasn't me."

I turned my head to meet his eyes. "Then who?"

"Medved."

Of course it was Medved.

"The boss gets off on inflicting pain. He said it relaxes him and sets his mind right so he can focus on leading the pack."

A leader who got his jollies by torturing people, who inflicted pain to calm his nerves. A horrifying state of affairs.

"There's nothing right about that asshole's mind," I cried.

"Ain't that the truth."

"Why did the Garveys tell me it was your playroom? They had to know I'd ask you about it and find out the truth."

"They probably thought Medved would keep us separated and you'd never get the chance to ask. They figured out that I had feelings for you and wanted to poison your mind against me."

Despite the heat pouring off Viggo's skin, I shivered.

"You cold?" he asked.

"Ever since the Hole, I can't seem to get warm."

Still cradling me in his arms, he stood and strode across the room. He folded back the covers, gently placed me in his bed, then climbed in next to me. He pulled the blanket up to my chin. We spooned, his broad chest pressed against my back, his palm resting on my stomach. Welcome heat leached from his body into mine.

"That's nice," I breathed, feeling toasty warm, safe, and cherished.

At least for now.

"Go to sleep, Liv," Viggo's voice rumbled in my ear. "I got you."

Yes. He had me. But for how long?

CHAPTER NINETEEN

REMY

"Did you see Hunter's face when he heard I was fucking his mate's sister?"

The grizzly enforcer's vile words came in loud and clear through the bugging device Zane had planted under the table in the bears' conference room.

A sharp, furious intake of breath. The alpha of the Black Rock Guardians kicked at the snow that had sifted down through the branches of the black spruce we stood under.

"I'm gonna kill the fucker," Adam vowed.

He rarely swore and never made threats he didn't follow through on.

"Get in line," I muttered.

No matter who struck the fatal blow, Viggo Creed was a dead man.

"Asshole." Liv's defiant retort came through the speaker, her voice a knife to the heart.

"Dammit." I scrubbed my hands over my face. Liv was my friend. The thought of what she was enduring at the hands of the grizzly brute chilled my blood.

As the pack's tech guy, I'd brought listening devices, remote cameras, signal jammers, and drones. To my amazement, I discovered that the grizzlies hadn't installed security cameras on their land. Maybe they thought they were so powerful and their land so isolated that nobody would dare a preemptive strike.

Their arrogance and conceit would bite them in the ass. Come nightfall, we'd make our move.

I craned my neck, looking for Thomas Morrow, our new lynx ally from New Hampshire. Liv and Annika's parents owned a vacation house in Aldrich, New Hampshire. Thomas had known the Hagen sisters since they were all children. Until recently, Liv and Annika had no idea that the Morrow family were lynx shifters. Thomas Morrow was fully committed to Liv's rescue. Hell, we couldn't have kept him away if we tried.

Alaska was crawling with lynx, both natural and shifters. Three separate packs—all of them allied with the Morrows—called the state home. Thomas served as the very willing liaison between the Black Rock Guardians and the Alaskan cats. Thanks to his help, we were staying in a cabin in lynx territory. From there, we could sneak onto grizzly land.

"Thomas." I whistled. No response. "Here, kitty, kitty."

Three Canadian lynx loped out from between the trees. Their huge paws slapped against the ground, and their black ear tufts stood out against the white snow. The one in the middle shifted back to human form. The other two ran into the woods to patrol.

Thomas Morrow rolled his shoulders and arched his back, working out the kinks from his second shift of the day. He hiked a pair of jeans up over his hips and shoved his bare feet into boots.

"What did you see?" I asked.

The grizzlies tended to ignore the cats, who stood absolutely no chance against the huge bears in a one-on-one fight. Medved's cocky indifference gave the lynx free rein to roam up to the very outskirts of the village.

"I saw two enforcers on the grounds of the guest house." Thomas pulled a sweatshirt over his head. "I couldn't get close enough to look into a window, so I don't know if there are any in the house."

"If there are, Zane will take care of them."

We knew the locations of all our people. I'd personally deployed the drones that tracked Zane and Grandpa's movements after their meeting with Medved. Another drone had followed Liv, Viggo, and a young man to a house at the end of a quiet residential street.

Adam walked over and joined us. "Let's go over the plans one more time," he said.

Chapter Twenty

Viggo

Restless melancholy kept sleep at bay. Even as I held Liv in my arms, I knew down to my bones that our time together was slipping away. Careful not to wake her, I nuzzled the pulse point below her ear, breathing in her orange-peel scent and consigning it to my memory. In fifty years' time, if we passed each other on opposite sides of the street, that distinctive fragrance would draw me irresistibly to her side. I memorized the small sounds she made in her sleep, the distinctive timbre of her breathing, the patter of her heart.

Ours, my bear sighed.

Yes, brother. Ours.

She was it for me. My shadow brother would accept no other mate.

Why the hell had fate brought me my perfect match if there was no possible way for us to stay together? It was too cruel, but perhaps no less than I deserved after the harm I'd done in the world. Liv merited none of the blame for my actions, but she'd suffer for my sins. If she was my predestined mate, I was hers. Capricious fate worked that way.

I carefully swept the dark hair that feathered against her nape aside, baring her fragile skin. There—where her neck curved to meet her shoulder—there was the spot where I'd mark her with a claiming bite. If only I could. At the thought, my canines punched out. One fang punctured my bottom lip. I tasted blood and saliva flooded my mouth. Once I broke her skin, sinking my teeth through muscle and bone, I'd lick the wound to heal the worst of it.

I clenched my fists, willing my canines to retract.

She hummed in her sleep, a soft sound that wove itself around my heart.

Maybe even this small slice of heaven was more than I had coming.

Slowly, inexorably, a deep, dreamless sleep claimed me.

Sometime in the middle of the night, I jerked awake, my heart racing. My hand shot out. I slapped at the lamp on the nightstand. The light revealed two men standing at the foot of the bed. The wolves—Adam Landry and Remy Hunter—both pointed pistols with silencers straight at me.

Cool air from the open window whispered across my skin. How the hell had they broken into my house and caught me unawares?

"You shift, you die," the wolf alpha warned me in a cool, emotionless voice.

From the look in their eyes, something told me they intended me to die whether I complied or not.

Even with the power of the black rock I wore on my wrist, no way could I shift and attack them before they got off a shot. I had a pistol in my nightstand. With a curious child in the house, the pistol was locked down tight. Which meant I couldn't get to it before the wolves fired.

Liv stirred. Her eyes fluttered open. Spying the wolves, she sat up in bed, gasping.

Adam held out his free hand. "Come to me, sweetheart."

Her head whipped toward me, as if she doubted her eyes and wanted to be sure I saw her packmates, too.

I jerked my head in confirmation.

She turned back to face the wolves. "Adam—"

"We'll talk later." He cut her off. "We gotta go. Come on."

She hesitated.

"Go," I told her. Surely the wolves had a plan to get her safely away from the village. If I survived this, I'd deal with the fallout from Medved.

"Remy, take Liv and get out of here." The voice held no heat, but a vein in Landry's forehead pulsed. "I'll be right behind you."

He intended to shoot me once Liv was gone. Clear as day, I saw the intent stamped on his face. Guess I'd have to rush him once she was safely away.

A thump, then footsteps sounded from the hallway. Landry and Hunter swung their pistols toward the bedroom door. Hallie stumbled into the room, Bosco on her heels.

"Daddy," she sobbed, tears streaming down her face. Dammit. She must've had another bad dream and had come looking for me.

I vaulted out of bed and threw myself at the wolves, desperate to put my body between them and my child. They wouldn't shoot her. I saw the horrified look on Landry's face when he realized he was pointing a weapon at a little girl. Still, with my daughter in harm's way, my urge to protect overrode reason. I tackled the wolf alpha to the floor, dragging his lieutenant down with us.

I was dimly aware of Liv lunging off the bed and wrapping her arms around Hallie, who screamed loud enough to wake the dead. Bosco's frenzied barks added to the racket. Owen's footsteps thundered up the hall, and he burst into the room. He thrust Hallie and Liv behind him and started to shift. The air around him shimmered and hummed with power. His big body blocked the bedroom door and prevented the wolves from getting to Liv.

From the bedside table, my cell phone rang. Outside the house, the village's emergency siren blared, calling all grizzlies to arms.

What the hell was happening?

I grabbed Landry's shoulders and brought my face close to his. "Go. Get out while you can. I'll keep Liv safe, I promise."

"What?" Stunned disbelief stamped the wolf alpha's face.

Somebody pounded on my front door.

"I'll protect Liv and get her back to you, but you gotta go now." I rolled to my feet, praying the wolves wouldn't shoot my brother midshift in order to get past him to Liv.

I saw the second Landry decided to believe me. "Let's go," he barked to his lieutenant. They backed up to the open window and slipped away into the night. With grizzly soldiers pouring from their houses and filling the streets, the odds of the wolves escaping the village undetected weren't good, but if anybody could pull it off, I suspected it was Landry.

I turned to my brother. We needed to talk—to get our story straight—before we faced Medved. Without the advantage of the meteorite's power, it was almost impossible for a shifter to reverse course halfway through the change.

"You gotta stop the shift and revert to human."

It took several seconds for the words to register in Owen's brain. His body stilled. Half-human eyes swung my way.

I slowly approached my brother's nebulous form, a body caught between human and animal shape. I unfastened my leather bracelet and held the black rock out till it made contact with skin half covered with the grizzly's golden-brown fur.

He hissed and his eyes flashed.

"Stop the shift," I repeated.

Owen trembled as the fur receded and his limbs reshaped themselves into human legs and arms. He fell back against the door frame, breathing hard.

"You okay?" I asked, sliding the bracelet onto my wrist.

"Yeah," he gasped and pointed at the stone. "That thing has amazing power. No wonder Medved wants more."

I slipped past him and dropped to my knees next to Hallie and Liv, who huddled together on the hallway floor.

"Daddy." Hallie flung herself into my arms. Over her head, my eyes met Liv's. She bobbed her head, letting me know she was all right. Holding out an arm, I pulled her into our embrace.

Liv's actions had surprised me. The woman could've ignored Hallie's cries and dashed straight toward her wolf rescuers. Instead, she instinctively ran to comfort my hysterical daughter.

See? Satisfaction tinged my bear's voice. *She knows where she belongs.*

The pounding on the front door took on greater urgency. If I didn't open it, somebody might break it down.

Owen staggered into the hall, sweat trickling down his bare chest.

"Armed wolves broke in through my bedroom window," I told him. "We secured the prisoner and ran them off."

"Got it," he said.

Leaving Hallie and Liv with Owen, I marched toward the front door.

My stomach clenched at the sight of the Garvey brothers standing on the stoop. "Medved sent us," Hank said. "Zane Hunter and the old alpha are gone. Boss thinks the wolves are gonna try to rescue the prisoner."

"They did try." I laid both hands on the door frame, preventing the Garveys from pushing their way into the house. "Owen and I ran 'em off."

"Can't believe those fuckers thought they could pull this kind of shit on us," Jasper cried. "Medved is fit to be tied. He wants all enforcers at headquarters stat."

"Gonna grab my boots and a shirt. Be right there." I shut the door in their faces and jogged down the hall.

"What's going on?" Owen asked.

"Emergency meeting at HQ."

I touched Liv's arm. My gaze searched her face for any sign that she regretted her mad dash to Hallie's side, that she was sorry she'd forfeited her chance to escape. Trepidation shone in her pretty eyes, but not remorse. Liv Hagen didn't waste time or energy wringing her hands over what couldn't be undone.

"Medved will be furious," she said.

"Yeah, he will. The wolves played him for a fool. But don't you worry. I'll handle it."

I saw a million questions in her eyes, but all she said was, "Be careful."

I grazed my knuckles across the petal-soft skin on her cheek. Capturing her chin between my thumb and forefinger, I tilted her face up. The small smile that curved her lips let me know that she'd welcome my kiss. With Hallie clinging to Liv's side, this was not the time to go hot and heavy. I brushed my mouth gently across hers, savoring the softness of her lips. We broke apart far too soon.

"I gotta go." I ran into the bedroom and threw on my boots and hoodie, the same one I wore when I kidnapped Liv five days ago.

Five days. My life turned on its head in just a handful of days.

I paused in the hall once again, dropping to my knees to hug my daughter. "I'll be home soon. Uncle Owen and Liv will take good care of you while I'm gone."

The Garveys had waited for me on the porch. We walked to headquarters through streets filled with agitated bears in both human and animal form. Inside headquarters we found Medved pacing back and forth in his office.

"Damned wolves played us," he spat as soon as we entered the room. His eyes narrowed on me. "The prisoner?"

"Still in custody. They tried to break in and take her, but I stopped them." I infused just the right note of cockiness in my voice, implying that of course, a grizzly enforcer could handle a couple of measly wolves.

"Good. Good." He turned to the Garveys. "Take two snowmobiles and join the soldiers searching the woods for intruders."

"Yes, sir." Jasper and Hank dashed from the room.

Medved dropped onto his chair, scrubbed his hands over his face, then focused his furious eyes on me. "We'll show those bastards what happens when you try to pull a fast one on grizzlies."

Alarm ticked up my spine. What the hell was Medved planning?

"Yes, sir. We will," I agreed.

"I'm gonna make an example of the Hagen woman. A public execution—right in the middle of the village square—as soon as the sun comes up. My bear will rip the bitch to pieces then I'll send the parts to Landry." He gave a low, malicious laugh.

I bit back my revulsion. "That's a fine plan, sir."

"Bring her in," he ordered. "We'll keep her in the Hole till first light."

A half-formed notion solidified in my mind. "Happy to, sir, although—" I paused.

"Although?"

I scratched the back of my head. "Would you mind if I take an hour for one more go at her before I bring her in?"

"You devil." He slapped his thigh, clearly tickled by my request. "Sure. Let the bitch go out with a bang." He glanced at a clock. "It's two thirty. I want her in the Hole by five."

"You got it, boss. Anything else?"

"Nah. I got a hundred men combing the town and the woods. Go have your fun."

I touched my fingers to my head in a salute and sauntered from the room like I had all the time in the world. Once I exited the building, I broke into a jog. When I got home, I found Owen waiting for me in the living room.

"Hallie finally fell asleep," he said. "Liv's lying down in your room. What happened with Medved?"

"He's spitting mad and vowing revenge on the wolves. He plans to kill Liv at first light."

Owen paled. "How are we gonna save her?"

The *we* warmed my heart. "Don't worry, brother. I have a plan."

"Can I help?" he asked.

Despite the dire situation, I grinned. "I appreciate the offer. I truly do, but you can't help with this. It's a one-man job."

His eyebrows slanted down and he frowned, confused. "What do you mean?"

I clapped him on the shoulder and walked from the room without answering. Slipping into my bedroom, I found Liv leaning against the headboard, her knees drawn up to her chest.

I locked the door.

"Adam and Remy came for me," she said.

I sat down next to her and tucked a strand of wayward dark hair behind her ear. "You surprised?"

"No. I told them not to risk it, but I can't say I'm surprised." She threaded her fingers through mine.

"You were right," I admitted. "Landry never intended to give Medved the Black Rock. It was all a ruse to get his people in position for a rescue."

"I knew Adam was too smart to give his enemy that kind of an advantage," she said with satisfaction.

I squeezed her hand. "You should've gone with them when you had the chance."

"Could've, would've, should've," she recited. "What happened, happened. None of us has the power to change the past. The only thing we can control is the present." She nodded toward the nightstand. "Epictetus teaches us that."

"Damn, woman. You're a fan of the Stoics, too?"

"Yep."

"You really are perfect for me."

Laughter exploded from her throat. "Nobody—in my entire life—has ever accused me of being perfect. Even people who love me call me a pain in the ass." She tilted her head and made a face. "Except for my sister. Annika doesn't have it in her to verbally abuse anybody."

At the mention of her sister, she sobered. Sadness ghosted across her face.

"Hey." I caught her eye. "I promised Landry I'd keep you safe and get you back to your people, to your sister."

She studied my face. "How are you going to do that? Medved must be beyond angry. What does he plan to do with me? Put me back in the Hole?"

The moment of truth had arrived. I raised her hand to my mouth and kissed her knuckles, a promise that everything would be all right.

"Medved intends to put you to death as payback for the wolves double-crossing him." She jerked and tried to pull her hand out of mine. I held on tight. "I won't let that happen. I swear it."

She paled and her lips trembled, then she sat up straight, clearly rallying her courage. "You can't do anything that will put Hallie in harm's way."

Her concern for my daughter's safety touched something deep inside me.

"Don't worry. I won't."

"Then what are you planning to do?" she asked.

"Remember how I told you that Medved had changed pack law so men can't be healers and women can't be soldiers?"

She nodded. "I called it sexist bullshit."

"Sometimes there's an upside to sexist bullshit. According to the new law, a mated female—a potential mother to a cub—can no longer be put to death. Her mate is responsible for keeping her in line and curbing her bad behavior."

As expected, that went over like a ton of bricks.

"Keeping her in line?" Scorn curled Liv's lip. "And just how would that law help me anyway? I'm not mated."

My canines descended and I flashed a predatory smile. "I can change that."

CHAPTER TWENTY-ONE

LIV

From the time my cousin Marit mated with Adam, I'd shamelessly pestered her for details about the claiming bite and sex with a shifter.

Sex with a supernatural being was the stuff of mythology. I'd always wondered about the mechanics. It defied imagination. I mean, just how was it supposed to work with Leda and the swan?

Come on. Who could blame a girl for her curiosity?

Marit—the wench—turned surprisingly prim and skimped on the details, even when I plied her with tequila. Best sex ever, she offered. Strength and stamina out the wazoo. Other than that, she left it to my imagination.

My sister was slightly more forthcoming. Shifters retained their human form during sex, except that their canines come out during the bite. And Zane did something with his claws that made Annika blush and squirm when she mentioned it.

In order to save my life, Viggo had offered to mate me. Sex and a good bite, that's all it took to create a lifelong attachment.

I stared—transfixed—at his fangs. Almost three inches long, slightly curved, and tapering to a blunt point, they were designed by nature to tear into flesh. I tried to visualize holding still and allowing him to sink those teeth into my shoulder. It would require a supreme level of trust. Deeply ingrained survival instincts might compel a woman to resist baring her vulnerable neck to a predator. Only deep love and a desire for a happily ever after would give someone the strength to bear it.

My fingers floated to my neck.

Viggo's lips quirked.

I pointed at his fangs. "Can you put those things away so we can talk?"

He sheathed his canines. "Better?"

"Yes, thanks." A pause while I gathered my thoughts. "Mating is a big deal for shifters."

"It is."

"If we mate, we'll be stuck with each other forever."

He winced.

Crap. I'd done it again, spoken before I considered my words. Embarrassment tore through me, as if I'd inadvertently mocked someone's deeply held faith. I laid my free hand on his knee. "Bad choice of words. I'm sorry. Listen, it's very noble of you to offer to mate me—"

He raised a hand and interrupted me. "In my entire life, nobody has *ever* accused me of being noble."

I shook my head. "Seriously? To give up your chance of finding true love—a real soulmate—in order to save my life, that's noble. Devoting your life to keeping your brother and daughter safe, that's noble, too. Not to mention how how you've treated me."

He made a face. "I kidnapped and drugged you."

"True, but you didn't hurt me. You gave me food and water. You kept me warm. You made sure I could breathe. If Medved had sent the Garveys instead of you, how do you think they would've treated me?"

"Yeah, I'm a prince," he scoffed. "Dammit, woman. Even you have to admit that there's nothing noble about the things I've done for my alpha."

Maybe not, but I refused to judge. Right or wrong, I'd torch the world to protect the people I loved, too.

"That's on him, not you."

He snorted, rejecting my assertion.

"I don't want to die, but mating isn't the answer," I continued. "Tell Medved you got home and found me missing. Say I climbed out the window and took off while you were at headquarters."

"Wouldn't work. The streets and woods are crawling with bears. You'd never get away. Besides, he'd blame Owen for not keeping an eye on you."

"Shit. You're right." I scrubbed my hands over my face, my brain scrambling for another solution.

His big hands closed around my shoulders. "There's no other way to save your life."

"But we're not in love," I burst out. "Under different circumstances, maybe we could be, but—"

"My bear chose you," he said.

"What?" Shock broadsided me.

He nodded. "You *are* my fated mate, Liv Hagen. My one and only. My bear will never claim another." His fingers tightened on my shoulders. "Mating you won't keep me from finding true love. You're it."

I rubbed my hand over my heart. "I feel a connection, too, but I've been fighting it. What's the point of falling in love if it's impossible to stay together? I can't live here under Medved's rule. I *can't*, and my people would never stop trying to bring me home."

"Don't expect you to stay." Sadness and resolve glowed in his honey-brown eyes. "I promised Landry I'd help you escape, remember?"

"So your solution is that we mate then go our separate ways?"

Pain flickered across his face. "Yeah."

"Your bear won't like that," I said.

"My bear will fucking hate it."

"*I* hate it," I said emphatically. "A mating bite is a promise. It's cruel to give your bear hope for a future that will never be. He'll fight you."

"I'm strong enough to handle him," he assured me.

"That's what you want? To spend the rest of your life at war with your other half?"

His eyes flashed. "What I want doesn't matter. Keeping you safe—making sure you have a good life—does. Over time, my bear will come to understand and accept that."

"This sucks," I bit out.

"It does." He heaved a deep sigh. "Despite your shifter blood, you aren't one of us. You aren't bound by our rules. Maybe someday you'll fall in love with somebody else."

Abandon Viggo, Hallie, and Owen to their fates, then go my merry way and fall in love with somebody else? Not likely.

There had to be a door number three. "Are you sure you and Hallie and Owen can't run? Remy can use his high-tech gear to find the trackers hidden in their bodies. Our healers can remove them. You'd be safe taking refuge with the wolves."

With one hand, he massaged the back of his neck. "No. I can't run. Trust me, it's impossible. But I can save your life if we mate. Give me that win, please, Liv… I need it." An unexpected vulnerability showed in the face of the dangerous enforcer.

My resistance crumbled.

God. We were going to break our hearts, weren't we?

I shifted positions and knelt facing him. If we were going to do this, we had to push past any awkwardness. We had to ignore the knowledge that we were temporary. This wasn't my first one and done, but it was the first time I went into it knowing I wanted more, knowing that it would cost me to walk away.

Viggo held perfectly still and watched me with the unwavering focus of an apex predator tracking his prey. Was he waiting to see if I'd change my mind and bolt?

I wouldn't bolt. Instead, I drew in a slow, steadying breath and reached for him.

"I like your face." My thumb traced the outline of his full lower lip.

"You do, huh?" He wrapped both hands over my hips, holding me in place while my fingers explored his rough-hewn features. "Nobody ever mistook me for a pretty boy."

I laughed softly. "Then it's a good thing I don't want a pretty boy."

He tracked my movements with avid eyes, his thick dark brows angling down like a raven's wings.

I scraped the pads of my fingers through his short beard. "I love your stubble," I murmured.

"Yeah?" His voice was a harsh whisper.

"Yeah. Whisker burn is one of my very favorite things." My fingers twitching with eagerness, I seized Viggo's shaved head and pulled it toward my mouth. Unresisting, he came, raking the short bristles across my cheek and mouth. With a stunned half smile, I lifted a finger to my lips, gently touching my tingling skin.

I hadn't been with a man since last spring, and that was an only marginally-satisfactory hookup with a guy from my gym. Now, my dormant nerve endings woke up and clamored for sensation. Touch, taste, smell, all my senses cried out for stimulation. I pressed my palm against Viggo's chin, angling back his head and exposing his throat.

I nuzzled his neck and tasted his skin. Inhaling deeply, I fixed in my memory the provocative fragrance of cypress, black pepper, and man. It was intoxicating, as essential a part of the grizzly enforcer as the aura of strength and danger he wore.

"Strip," I ordered.

"You first," he growled. Without waiting for me to react, he seized the hem of my sleep tee, pulled it over my head, and threw it across the room. His heated gaze fell on my breasts. My nipples puckered and hardened, and I swayed toward him. Even through the thick cotton of his hoodie, I felt the heat pouring off his body.

"Your turn." Was that sexy rasp mine?

The mattress compressed and almost threw me off-balance when he knelt facing me. He pulled down the zipper on his hoodie and tossed it across the room to join my shirt.

I moaned—I actually moaned—at the sight of his formidable chest and arms. Call me shallow, but muscles do it for me, and Viggo had been blessed with a magnificent physique. If ever a man's body invited an admiring caress, it was his. My hands trembled as I explored the curves and hollows of his heavily muscled shoulders and biceps.

"Ho-ly shit, you're beautiful," I breathed.

"Beautiful?" He chuckled. "That's a first, but I gotta admit, I kinda like the way you… uh… stroke my ego."

I slow-blinked. "If you think your ego is the only thing I want to stroke, big guy, you're in for a surprise."

I trailed my fingers along the deep clefts in his perfectly carved six pack.

His hands cupped my ass. Frowning, he plucked at the thin cotton of my boy shorts. A claw slid out—a real claw—and sliced through the fabric. "That's better," he said, tossing the scrap aside, leaving me naked.

Tilting his head, he pulled in a slow, deep breath, scenting the arousal that already swirled through me. His lips peeled back and his tongue tasted the air. The primitive, animalistic action drove my heart rate into the stratosphere. My pulse pounded in my throat, and a whooshing sound filled my ears. I gave a small whimper, and his raptor eyes swung to my face.

I swallowed and pointed at his jeans. "Fair is fair."

"You're right," he said, his voice thick. He worked the button fly and within seconds his jeans joined the rest of our clothes on the floor. I checked him out. Of course I checked him out. My gaze dropped to a spectacularly erect cock.

"Wow," I muttered.

"*Not* the first time I heard that," he conceded with a small shrug.

"I'll bet," I laughed, but my happiness faded as reality once again intruded.

"What do you need?" he asked gently.

"I need—" I paused and gathered my thoughts. "I don't want to think about death threats or forever. I don't want to think about *anything*. Can you make the world go away, please Viggo?"

"Yeah, I can do that," he said with a slow smile.

He reached for me. Calloused fingertips delicately sketched the contours of my mouth, following the curve of my plump bottom lip and tracing the small notch in the top one. Eyes darkening, he spread his fingers. His entire body thrummed with strength and purpose. One powerful hand skimmed down my neck and spanned my throat, the pad of his thumb resting over my carotid artery, the blood vessel that carried oxygen to my brain.

An exhilarating mixture of fear and certainty swept over me. This man whom Adam called a stone-cold killer could snap me like a twig. Not so many days ago, he'd threatened to choke me out. I knew now that he never would.

Shifting his weight, he nuzzled the pulse point in my neck. Warm breath danced across my skin when he brought his mouth to my ear. He nipped the lobe, and I jerked. His fingers tightened on my throat, just enough to compel my attention.

"You want slow and gentle or fast and hard?"

Slow and gentle would give me too much time to think, to preemptively mourn what we were losing.

I pushed my hands up his torso and reached for his head, irresistibly drawn to his shaved crown. The stubble rasped along my fingertips as I pressed against the grain, a delicious friction that ignited my senses. Desperation lent urgency to my actions. I wanted to be consumed by this man, swept up in a carnal firestorm that left no room for thought.

"Give me fast and hard," I demanded.

His eyelids closed to half-mast. Through the slits, his pupils glittered golden-brown. "You got it."

Before I had time to draw another breath, Viggo *moved*. The hand on my throat propelled me backward, flattening me against the mattress. He straddled my hips, his cock heavy against my stomach. A glistening drop of pre-cum beaded its tip.

I licked my lips. Heat pooled in my sex and my breasts ached with need. My greedy fingers reached for his cock.

He captured my wrist, dropped a kiss on my knuckles, and pressed my hand flat against the mattress.

"Hands down," he ordered.

Balancing his weight on one palm, he kneed my thighs apart. Cool air kissed my exposed sex. His strong fingers clamped my skin and pushed my leg up, leaving me wide open and vulnerable. Vulnerable and I weren't usually on speaking terms, but instead of shying away from the sensation, I welcomed it and spread my legs even more.

He dragged the tip of his cock through my slick folds and positioned himself at my entrance. He paused and locked eyes with me, a man on the ragged edge of self-control. "Fast and hard?" he confirmed.

I'm usually a gimme-half-an-hour-of-foreplay kind of woman, but not this time. I groaned and arched my hips, desperation making my voice hoarse.

"Do it."

With one explosive thrust, he breached my core. My mouth flew open in a silent scream, and pain curled my fingers into claws. Never had a man filled me so entirely.

"You're big," I groaned, willing my muscles to relax, my body to stop fighting his incursion. I refused to live in a world where fucking Viggo Creed was a physical impossibility.

"You need me to pull out?" he asked, panting. A bead of sweat trickled across his temple, and his biceps quivered from the strain of holding still.

Give the man points—mega points—for asking.

"No way," I gasped.

Shifting his weight to one elbow, he slipped a hand between our bodies. Clever, clever fingers found my clit. Pleasure spiraled through my core, and my tight muscles relaxed. Pain loosened its grip on me, slid away, and sensual passion filtered in to fill the void. I sank into the mattress, my body pliant and eager.

Viggo's feral eyes honed in on my face, tracking my every twitch, my every reaction.

I locked my heels around the small of his back. "Hard and fast," I urged.

All the encouragement he needed. Bracing his weight on both hands, he rammed his cock into me, pulled out, then powered back in. Striking a brutal pace—exactly what I asked for—he pounded into me.

He'd ordered me to keep my hands down, and I'd obeyed. What was I thinking? My fingers flew up and clamped onto Viggo's shoulders. Digging my nails into his skin, I clung to him.

We were temporary, our time together finite. My future promised endless lonely days and nights, eons to get through without seeing Viggo, without hearing his voice, without savoring his touch. If I could, I'd dip this moment in amber and secure it in place in my memory. Drag it out and crack it open whenever I missed him.

If this was all we got, I was going to enjoy every damn second of it. I was going to touch and taste and *feel.*

I lifted my head and sought his mouth with mine. Gasping, we swallowed each other's breaths. I dragged my tongue across his still-human teeth. Instantly, his canines dropped. I tasted blood on the tip of my tongue. The coppery tang left me half-mad with need, propelling the act toward its inevitable culmination.

"Bite me," I whispered.

Not the first time I said those words, but the first time I meant them literally.

With startling abruptness, Viggo jerked out. He flipped me over onto my stomach, yanked my hips up, and shoved inside. A hand tangled in my hair and tugged my head to one side, exposing the crook of my neck. His head descended. Hot breath tickled the spot, and his broad tongue swiped across my skin, leaving a trail of goose bumps in its wake. The blunt tips of his fangs pressed into my flesh.

Panic flared, a mindless fight-or-flight reaction that had me attempting to roll to one side.

His fist tightened in my hair.

"Hold still." The guttural rasp was barely human, a man holding on to self-control, to civility, by the thinnest of threads.

Calloused fingers cupped my breast. He scraped the pad of his thumb back and forth across my nipple then roughly pinched the supersensitive nub, rolling it between his fingers.

"Eep," I gasped, reduced to blithering incoherence by the electricity that zinged from my nipple to my sex. My thighs trembled, barely able to support my weight. My fingers clawed at the sheets as lust blazed through me.

All the while Viggo pistoned into me, propelling me closer and closer to the edge. He gave a final tweak to my chafed nipple then slid his hand down my quivering stomach to my clit. One, two, three featherlight strokes across the hypersensitive bud.

I sucked in a breath and held it. My mind fuzzed as I tumbled headfirst into brain-numbing orgasm. Spasms rocked my entire body.

One arm banded around my waist, he struck. Powerful fangs lanced my skin, drilled through tendon and muscle, and buried in bone. The world blanked white as shock and pain pummeled me. In some dim corner of my mind, I remembered not to scream. Sweat pooled between our bodies and trickled down my sides. My hands scrabbled against the bed, and I tried to buck him off.

Impossibly large, his cock jerked inside me. Heat flooded my core. Viggo's fangs withdrew and his rough tongue licked across my broken flesh. Instantly, the pain in my shoulder faded to almost nothing. Arching his hips, he pulled out, leaving something hot and slick coating my upper thighs.

Comes like a geyser.

Marit had said that, too. Guess it was true for bears as well as wolves.

Viggo kissed the mating bite. "You okay?"

"Yes."

The arm pinning me in place slid away. I face-planted on the sheets, too limp, too spent to do more than grunt.

Laughing softly, Viggo rolled onto his side and pulled me against his chest.

"Too hot," I moaned, wriggling away from the sticky skin-on-skin contact.

He deliberately misinterpreted my comment. "Not the first time I've been called that," he said, his voice smug.

I lifted one feeble hand and batted at him. "Seriously, I feel like I'm marinating in sweat and cum."

A low, contented growl rumbled from his chest. "Everyone will scent me on you and know that you're mine."

I glanced at his face. His eyes glittered with the grizzly's joy and triumph. For the moment, the bear was ascendant over the man. He believed he'd won, that he claimed his prize, that I was his forever.

Dammit. Guilt and sorrow swirled together in a toxic stew. When I'd agreed to mate with Viggo, I'd made a promise to his bear that I couldn't keep. Viggo would handle the aftermath—Medved's anger—his bear's sense of betrayal—the same way he handled everything else, the same way he took every burden on himself. A lesser man would've crumbled under the weight.

I want to stay with him.

The realization came out of nowhere, a dagger to my heart.

The mating bite tingled, reminding me of the bond we'd forged. I'd assumed I could ignore it, that as a human the connection wouldn't call to me the same way it would for a shifter. I was wrong. I wanted to build a life with this strong and capable man. To share his burdens. To be his shield and support. To love and help raise his daughter. To claim his brother as my own.

"I can't do that," I whispered.

"Can't what?" Drowsy and at peace, the bear's satisfaction still filled Viggo's voice.

An inch of space lay between our bodies, just enough distance to allow my overheated skin to cool. A chasm separated our spirits, the elated bear, the selfless man, and me, the lost and conflicted human.

No need to say aloud what the man already knew, that I couldn't stay and make a life with him, no matter how much I wanted to.

"Never mind," I murmured.

He let it go.

His eyes had drifted shut. Peace and contentment stamped his features. His left hand stroked lazily up and down my arm. I wished I could give this to him forever, what Grandma Freya called a "God's in his heaven, all's right with the world" moment.

A few more minutes, I told myself, my gaze lingering on his brutally handsome face.

Mine, the small voice inside my head declared.

If only…

Five minutes later, his eyelids opened and he turned to me. "How about a shower before we head over to headquarters?"

At the mention of headquarters, I repressed a shiver. Despite Viggo's assurances, I wasn't confident that Medved would heed the constraints of the law, that he wouldn't kill me anyway or punish Viggo for mating me.

"Sounds good." I forced cheerfulness into my voice.

Viggo stilled. His nostrils flared. "My mate is frightened."

I couldn't lie to a man who could scent an untruth. "A little."

Sliding a hand around my nape, he lowered his forehead to mine. "I have a plan. You're gonna be fine."

I nodded. "I know."

Hand in hand, we walked into his bathroom. The shower stall was small for two people, but we squeezed in together. Viggo picked up a bar of soap, lathered up his hands, and washed me from head to toes. When he was done, I took the bar and returned the favor. My fingers skimmed over his soap-slicked skin, shaping beautifully defined muscles. When my hand slid down and stroked along his shaft, he groaned.

"No time for round two. We need to get moving."

"Okay." I reluctantly let go of his cock and placed a quick kiss above his left nipple. "Turn around so I can wash your back."

He complied, bracing his elbows against the shower wall while my soapy hands glided across his broad back. Indulging myself for just a minute, I massaged his shoulders and neck. He groaned with pleasure, and I smiled to myself. When my thumb brushed across a raised ridge, I paused. I directed the showerhead to the spot, rinsing off the suds so I could see better.

A white welt an inch long—a scar—hidden under a bony protrusion at the base of his skull. If I hadn't felt it, I doubt I would've noticed it. Tracing over it with a fingertip, I frowned.

"How did you get this scar?"

Viggo's massive body jerked and his shoulders tightened. He dropped his head then slowly turned around to face me, blinking against the water that struck his face.

"You know that Hallie and Owen have trackers planted somewhere in their bodies?" he asked.

I nodded. "Did Medved put a tracker in you, too?"

He shook his head, scattering water droplets. "No. Not a tracker."

Dread squeezed my chest. "Then what is it?"

Strong hands gripped my upper arms.

Goose bumps skittered across my shoulders as dread transformed into sheer terror. "Viggo? What is it?"

The powerful muscles in his neck worked. He swallowed.

"A kill chip."

CHAPTER TWENTY-TWO

VIGGO

A little before five a.m., Liv and I walked through the entrance to grizzly headquarters. Despite the early hour, Evelyn sat at her desk. Sympathy shone in blue eyes that flicked from Liv to me. Apparently she knew of the alpha's plans to execute Liv.

"Mr. Medved is waiting for you. Go on back," she said, not unkindly.

Holding Liv's elbow, I strode down the hall to the alpha's office.

"Come in," he called when I rapped against the closed door.

We stepped into the room. There was no need to offer an explanation. He smelled the mating the second we crossed the threshold.

"What the fuck have you done?" He leapt to his feet, eyes blazing.

I took a step forward and shoved Liv behind my back. The stubborn woman immediately scooted around me, planting herself at my side.

I lifted a hand. "Let me explain."

He stomped toward us. I braced, ready to intervene if he tried to hurt her. He pulled her collar aside, exposing the still-fresh mating bite. Her broken skin had sealed shut, but an angry red bite mark remained. It would fade over time—turning from red to pink to white—but she'd wear the scar for the rest of her life.

"You stupid son of a bitch." His eyes swung from the bite mark to my face. "You'd better have a damned good explanation for this."

I lowered my eyes, feigning a respect I didn't feel. "Yes, sir. I do. When I was… um... saying my goodbyes to the woman, my bear gave me the idea. He said he was willing to mate her if it helped us gain the advantage over the wolves. I acted on it and claimed her."

True enough. Mating *was* my bear's idea, and because it was true, Medved couldn't possibly smell a lie in his words. At the best of times, his olfactory senses weren't particularly keen. Maybe nature short-changed him. Maybe he was so arrogant, so sure of his judgment that he didn't rely on his senses. Luckily, I was better than most shifters at concealing mine. But still, caution ruled the day.

Medved waved his hand impatiently. "Get to your explanation."

I cleared my throat and deliberately played into his misconceptions about the new wolf alpha. "If we kill Liv, the wolves will mourn. Hell, Landry's woman will probably make him sleep on the couch for a month—"

As I expected, Medved snickered, delighted by the thought of a weak-willed wolf alpha browbeaten by his human mate.

"They'll be angry and sad," I continued, "but in time they'll get over it. And in the future, we can be damned sure they'll be doubly on guard against any new move we make against them. We'll probably never have another good shot at getting our hands on the Black Rock."

Medved's eyes narrowed as he imagined the unhappy scenario I described.

"How does mating the bitch make anything better?" he asked.

Next to me, Liv's body hummed with rage, but she wisely kept her mouth shut. Not even Medved could miss the potent fury that poured off her, but he'd likely think it was directed at me—the man who mated her against her will—and not at him.

"Think about it, sir. The humans have a saying, 'Death before dishonor.' What could be worse for a wolf alpha than knowing that a female relative—a vulnerable and defenseless human—was forced to live as a mate to one of Maxim Medved's enforcers?"

The boss liked the way I said his name, like he was the undoubted big bad who put the fear of God in the wolves and everybody else. He preened, a smirk curving his lip. "Go on," he said, more willing to listen.

"Well, sir, that knowledge would get under Landry's skin and burrow in deep. Guilt would poison his every thought. Make him reckless. Drive him to commit a deadly mistake."

"You're saying our best shot at bringing down Landry and securing the Black Rock was for you to mate the Hagen woman?"

"That's right. Wolves have a fatal flaw. They're soft and sentimental, especially about family. They don't put the needs of the pack above everything else, the way you taught us to do."

"What's in it for you?" he asked slyly.

"She's mouthy and stubborn," I conceded with a small shrug. "But she's a good lay. It'll be fun to break her spirit and teach her to obey. And like you pointed out the first time you saw her, sir, she's got shifter blood. If I knock her up, she'll give me feisty, strong-willed grizzly cubs."

Liv shot me a disgusted sideways glance. I wasn't entirely sure it was for show. She was going to make me pay for the line of bullshit I just spun. I clenched my jaw against the grin that threatened to bust out across my face.

The prospect of being reamed out by my scrappy mate elated me.

"A good lay, huh." He studied her. "Too bad you sealed the deal before I got a chance to sample the goods."

In Medved's pack, the alpha had the right to sleep with any unmated woman. He didn't often assert that right. Why stir up a potential hornets nest, he'd told me. But sometimes, he did.

"Yes, sir." Took everything I had to smile and nod, as if I agreed it was too bad the bastard lost his chance.

"Still." His voice took on an edge that set off warning klaxons in my mind. "You disobeyed a direct order."

"I did."

"Glad to see we're in agreement." He strolled over to his desk, sat down in his big chair, and opened the top drawer. He pulled out a black object that looked like a fancy remote key fob. Spinning it around a finger, he asked. "What am I gonna do about that?"

Shit. I knew exactly what he was going to do. I braced for it, but there was no preparing myself for the agonizing jolt of pain that blasted through my head. I dropped heavily to my knees, a deadweight that rattled the pictures hanging on the walls.

The gizmo Medved's surgeon planted at the base of my skull had three levels. The first, the one he hit whenever he was pissed off—like when he found out I crashed the Beaver—shot an eye-watering spear of pain through my head.

I was used to level one.

The third level was programmed to set off a small charge that would blow out the back of my brain. He'd never used it—obviously—but I lived with the knowledge that a sadist with poor impulse could control could kill me at any moment, even from a distance.

Liv had asked why I didn't steal a plane and fly Hallie and Owen to freedom. The chip was why. If Medved got word of our escape and pushed the third setting, I'd die and the plane would crash, killing my daughter and brother. No way could I risk that. No way would I leave the people I loved unprotected, so I minded my Ps and Qs.

He rarely resorted to the second level, the one he used now to punish me for mating Liv. The pain was unreal. If I didn't know better, I'd swear somebody had sunk a pickax into my skull. My ears rang. My vision blurred. Bile crawled up my throat, and I fought the urge to puke. Blood dripped from my nose onto the carpet. If I looked into a mirror, I'd see that the small blood vessels in my eyes had ruptured.

As abruptly as it started, the pain stopped. I swayed, still fighting nausea. Medved was saying something I couldn't make out. Squinting up at him, I saw him gesturing impatiently for me to stand. I struggled to my feet, wiping all signs of pain from my face, so he wouldn't see how much he'd hurt me.

My ears popped and suddenly I could hear again.

"… never again." I caught only the last words of Medved's sentence but nodded like I'd heard the whole thing. The gist was clear enough.

"Yes, sir," I agreed. "Lesson learned. Never again."

He nodded with satisfaction.

Liv had stumbled backward and was leaning against the doorjamb. Her cheeks had gone pale, and she'd wrapped her arms around her waist, as if she was holding herself together. Her gaze swept over me. When she saw I was fine, she visibly relaxed, then turned to the alpha.

"Did your people find Zane and Grandpa Matthew?" she asked Medved.

I shot her a warning look. Of course she was curious about whether her family got away, but Medved was in no mood to humor her question.

He made a face. "Control your mate, Creed."

Putting my back to Medved and blocking his view, I banded my hands around her upper arms. "Unless he asks you a question, don't speak to *our* alpha." The words were harsh, but I kept my grip on her arms gentle, and my expression conveyed a genuine warning.

She jerked her head, acknowledging my silent message.

"I apologize," she said through gritted teeth.

Medved pressed the intercom button on his desk.

"Yes, sir?" Evelyn asked.

"Come escort Creed's new mate to the lobby. You'll need to keep an eye on her while my enforcer and I have a little chat."

"I'll be right there."

As soon as Liv and Evelyn exited the room, Medved signaled for me to shut the door and take a seat. I folded my hands over my lap, waiting for him to speak. He spun the key fob around and around, a clear reminder that I was at his mercy. Took all my willpower to tear my eyes away from it and focus on the alpha's face.

"You said wolves came to your house and tried the take the woman?"

"Yes, sir."

"Did you recognize them?"

I controlled my breathing and willed my pulse to remain steady. "One of 'em. Remy Hunter, one of Landry's lieutenants. Didn't know the other man," I lied. Medved would lose his shit if he realized that the alpha of the Black Rock Guardians was in Alaska. He'd tear the state apart to get his hands on our old enemy.

"Any idea where they are now?" he asked.

"None," I said honestly. "If they're smart, they burnt rubber hightailing it out of the state."

"They're wolves." Medved snorted. "Brains aren't their strong suit. We have to assume they're gonna stick around and try again."

"Where the hell are they?" I asked.

"No fucking clue." Medved shook his head. "I've had soldiers combing through the woods. No sign of them."

"Maybe it's time to consider installing security cameras around the village and in the woods," I suggested.

I'd been after Medved to do just that for years, but the boss didn't want to spend money on something he deemed unnecessary. Not when he had a heated pool to install at his house. The bastard's short-sighted selfishness had turned out to be a very good thing.

"You could be right," he conceded. "But that's a problem for another day. Today, I want you to take over the search."

Exactly what I was hoping for. My bland expression hid my excitement. "I'll set up a search grid and assign soldiers to scour the woods. If the wolves are out there, I'll find them. You can count on it."

His fingers fondled the key fob, and he shot me a look filled with both glee and malice. "Oh, I *am* counting on it." He angled his head to one side. "By the way, how's that sweet little girl of yours?"

"She's fine." My voice betrayed no hint of the anxiety his question provoked.

"And your brother?"

The less Medved thought about Hallie and Owen, the better. I lifted a nonchalant shoulder. "Keeping busy running the store."

"Good. Good." He slapped his thighs and rose to his feet. "You might've mated the Hagen woman, but her allegiance is still to the wolves. You can't trust her not to try something stupid. I don't want her wandering around town without a guard. Tell her to stick with Owen today."

I stood, too. "Exactly what I was planning to do, sir."

"I'm depending on you to keep your mate in line, Creed."

I flashed my teeth. "It will be my absolute pleasure to keep my mate in line."

Medved chuckled.

Good thing Liv wasn't around to overhear the conversation.

"Report in the minute you find any sign of the wolves," he ordered.

"Will do." I touched my fingers to my head in a salute then strode from the room.

I had a role to play, a reputation to protect. Liv sat in a chair across the lobby from Evelyn's desk. Without breaking stride, I snapped my fingers and pointed at the door, silently ordering her to follow me outside.

She caught up with me on the sidewalk and matched her step to mine. "You enjoy taking your life in your hands, don't you, big guy."

I bit back a grin, both my bear and I delighted by her defiant spirit. "Whatever do you mean?"

She snapped her fingers in my face. "This snap-your-fingers, do-as-you're-told shit won't fly with me."

I stopped in my tracks and turned to face her. "We're playing a part. Just till I can track down the wolves and hand you over to your people."

"But still—"

"I'm a big bad enforcer," I reminded her. "Every member of the pack shakes in their boots when they see me coming."

Her mouth pulled down. "Interesting. I don't recall shaking in my boots when I saw you coming."

It took a good thirty seconds for her meaning to sink in. She watched me work it out, a smug smirk on her face.

Duh.

"If I recall correctly," I said slowly. "You had your back to me when I was coming. You couldn't see a thing."

She touched my face. "I was trembling, all right, but not from fear. I'm not afraid of you, remember?"

"Yeah, I remember." From the first, Liv had refused to be intimidated by me, one of the many things I loved about her.

My chest tightened. Who would have guessed that the woman I kidnapped and dragged kicking and screaming to Alaska would be my one true mate? A mate was a gift I didn't deserve and never expected to find. Now that she was mine, I'd do anything to keep her safe.

Beneath my skin, my shadow brother huffed in agreement.

Fate had reshuffled the deck. For the first time in a long time, hope took root in my heart. The chip in my head sealed my destiny, but if I played my cards right—if I was lucky—I might be able to save everyone I loved.

Chapter Twenty-Three

Liv

Bears gossiped. Big-time.

By the time Owen and I opened the community store, word had gotten out that Viggo and I had mated. Maybe Evelyn blabbed, or maybe somebody who walked past me when I sat in the lobby had caught a whiff and called a friend. Over the course of the morning, dozens of people crossed the store's threshold. They called out a greeting to Owen, but their inquisitive eyes locked on me. The chief enforcer's mate. A human. An enemy. The reason wolves had infiltrated their village the night before. Curiosity burned bright in their eyes, but they kept a wary distance.

A little before noon, the flow of customers reduced to a trickle then petered out. The lull wouldn't last, but it gave us a chance to catch our breaths. Owen tossed me a bag of spicy chips. I tore into the package and leaned against the counter, munching away.

"My new sister," he said, his voice thoughtful.

My hand paused halfway to my mouth.

I'd always wanted a brother. When I was a little kid, I created an imaginary one—Charlie—who lived in the woods.

Annika didn't give our parents one ounce of trouble. Charlie was my partner in crime, spurring me on to all sorts of mischief.

"I wasn't *playing* with the matches, Mommy. I was *using* them. Charlie and I wanted to roast marshmallows in the fire pit."

When I got into trouble and named names, my folks commended me on my imagination but refused to cut me any slack. They were all about accepting responsibility for your actions and logical consequences. I outgrew Charlie and came to embrace my parents' no-nonsense attitude, but the wistful longing for a male sibling had remained.

If I could pick any man to be my brother, it would be Owen.

"I wish… I wish…" For once, I found myself at an absolute loss for words.

"I know," he sighed.

Early that morning, when Viggo and I returned home after our meeting with Medved, we'd found Owen in the kitchen mixing up a batch of blueberry muffins. As soon as we walked into the room, he'd whirled around, dropped the whisk into the bowl, and rushed me. He pushed my collar aside, exposing my neck, and gently touched the bite mark. His nostrils flared, his golden-brown eyes sparkled, and he inhaled a deep breath.

His gaze snapped to Viggo. "What did you do?"

"The law forbids killing a mate, so I mated her."

Owen had shot me a concerned look. I nodded, reassuring him that I'd been willing.

"*That* was your plan? No wonder you called it a one-man job." He dropped heavily onto a kitchen chair. "Holy hell, brother. I know you care for her and your bear wants her, but how is this going to work? How can Liv stay with us?"

"She can't. I'm gonna reach out to the wolves and help her escape."

"You can't do anything that will put Hallie in danger," Owen said.

"I won't. I swear to God I have a plan that won't endanger Hallie or you."

Listening to the brothers talk, I squeezed my hands into fists. "If not for that damned kill chip, you could all escape with me."

The atmosphere in the room shifted, the air charged with tension.

"What did you say?" Owen's face paled. "A kill chip?"

Oh, crap. Owen didn't know.

Why had Viggo kept the kill chip a secret from his brother? No sooner had I formed the question than the answer came to me. Viggo was determined to shoulder every burden by himself and give his family as normal a life as possible.

"Yeah. Implanted here." Viggo touched the small scar at the base of his skull. "Medved keeps the control fob with him all the time." He offered his brother a reassuring smile. "It's all right, Owen. I've been living with it for years."

"Fuck." Owen shoved his hands through his hair and rocked back and forth in the chair. "Fuck. Fuck. Fuck." After a moment, he lifted his head, hope in his eyes. "When you're away on a mission, could you find a sympathetic shifter healer and have the chip removed?"

"Only if I'd first deactivated the fob. Otherwise, the chip would blow if somebody tampered with it. As long as Medved has the fob, I can't touch the chip."

"Damn," Owen signed.

"What's your game plan, Viggo?" I asked. "Because Owen is right. If my escaping puts Owen and Hallie at risk, I won't do it."

Viggo clapped his distraught brother's shoulder, then walked over and pulled me into a hug. "I need to work out the details before I explain it to you, but trust me that I have a plan."

Hallie skipped into the kitchen and skidded to a stop when she saw me in her father's arms. "Are you sad?" she asked.

"I'm fine, kiddo, but I'll always take a Hallie hug." I held out an arm, and she ran to my side, joining us in a three-way embrace.

"Uncle Owen, too," she declared. He hopped up and our embrace turned into a four-way hug, just like the kind I used to share with Annika and our parents when we were little.

Our conversation left me wistful and disgruntled, my mind full of what-ifs.

Mating changed shifters at a profound level and created a compulsion to keep their mates close and safe. By promising to send me back to the wolves, Viggo was going against deeply ingrained instincts.

As a human, mating Viggo hadn't rewired my system. But my desire to stay with him—to explore our budding relationship—had morphed into a deeper connection to both him and his family.

What do they say? *To thine own self be true.* I half wished I could survive living under Medved's autocratic regime, but I knew better. Sooner or later I'd snap and mouth off to the dickhead, and the Creeds would pay for my disrespect.

And the Black Rock Guardians? They'd never abandon me to their oldest enemy or accept I'd willingly mated a grizzly enforcer. I could image Marit and Annika muttering about Stockholm syndrome, or Adam and Zane talking about saving me from myself.

For a whole host of reasons, I couldn't stay in Alaska.

After breakfast, Owen and I walked Hallie to school before opening the community store. Viggo went to grizzly headquarters to coordinate "the search" for the wolves.

The shopkeeper's bell over the door rang again, signaling the end of our break from customers. Owen headed to the front of the store to greet the young mother and small child, pausing only to give my hand a reassuring squeeze as he passed by. He dropped down on his haunches and spoke to the shy little boy. Owen did a magic trick—pulling a Dum Dum out from behind the kid's ear—and reduced the child to giggles.

"Dammit," I said under my breath.

Owen was a good man, and he deserved a good life.

Without conscious intent, I reached up and touched my still-tender mating bite. It throbbed. Even if I went away and never saw Owen or Hallie or Viggo again, I'd feel connected to them forever.

I sighed. Viggo's plan better be a good one.

CHAPTER TWENTY-FOUR

VIGGO

I knew the woods surrounding the village like the back of my hand, but I had no clue where to find the wolves. They could've hunkered down and set up a campsite anywhere.

If I were them, I'd steer clear of the shelter cabins. In November, four sturdy walls, a solid roof, and a wood stove would tempt anybody, but they had to realize that we'd search the cabins first.

Impossible to know for sure, but my money was on one of the small caves that dotted the hilly forestland northwest of town. Matthew Strauss had grown up here and doubtless had explored the underground chambers as a kid. The elderly wolf could direct his people to a good hiding place close to his former home.

I sent the Garveys to check out the remote cabins within a day's travel from the village, a fool's errand that would keep them out of my hair. I assigned another team to comb once again through the forest east of the village, land where the caves were few and far between.

Carrying a specially designed pack, I hiked northwest into the woods. I'd cover more ground on four legs than on two. I stripped and shoved my clothing and boots and leather bracelet into the pack, then hung its extra-long strap over a branch. Sucking in a deep breath, I settled my stance and shifted.

Familiar pain washed over me. My spine elongated. Every bone cracked and reshaped itself as my limbs took on a new configuration. A large hump formed over my shoulders. My jaw unhinged, a snout took shape, and my face lost all human features. Tawny fur erupted from my skin and crawled across my entire body.

Shuddering, I threw back my head and roared. I shuffled flat-footed over to the branch where I'd hung my pack and slipped my head through the strap. The pack dangled beneath my short neck. A grizzly wearing a pack around his neck, a ridiculous sight, but efficient. When I shifted back to human, I wouldn't find myself buck-ass naked and knee-deep in snow without recourse to warm clothing.

I threw back my head again and took short, shallow sniffs of the frigid air. Smells bombarded me. The woody perfume of evergreens. A porcupine carcass. The pungent stink left behind by a black-tailed deer who marked his territory by rubbing his antlers against a tree. Owl scat. A snowshoe hare. Lynx.

No wolves, at least not nearby.

Lumbering between tall trees, I began my search. An hour later I spied a pair of lynx shadowing me. No grizzly would think twice about encountering a wildcat. One swipe of a bear's massive paw would disembowel a lynx. They usually kept a safe distance from bears, but these two stuck to my tail.

Odd.

I reared up on my hind legs and sniffed the air again, honing in on their scent. Nostrils flaring, I wheeled around and faced the cats. They plopped down on their haunches, their short tails swishing back and forth. A low growl rolled from their throats.

They were shifters, not natural lynx.

What the hell was going on?

A high-pitched buzzing sounded directly overhead. I looked up. A small, fixed-wing drone hovered in the air a few feet above me. The drone operator was making absolutely no attempt at stealth. It was as if they wanted me to take notice of the device, a notion that was confirmed when the drone bobbed up and down in a way sure to draw the eye.

The Black Rock Guardians owned a fleet of drones. Remy Hunter—their tech expert—had showed up in my bedroom last night.

I hadn't found the wolves, but it looked like they'd found me.

I dropped to all fours. The drone dived down to my eye level then zoomed forward, leading me deeper into the woods. I followed, with the lynx shifters trotting behind.

The wolves and cats were allies. Who would've seen that coming? Not Medved, who considered the lynx beneath his notice. Once again, arrogance had led him astray. Lynx territory butted up against grizzly pack land. We paid no attention to the cats who crossed daily into our terrain. The wolves couldn't have asked for a better positioned ally.

I tagged after the drone for a good mile before it led me into a small clearing then flew straight up and disappeared from sight. Lowering my head, I dropped the pack onto the ground and started to shift. By the time I completed the change, wolf shifters surrounded me: Adam Landry, Matthew Strauss, Zane and Remy Hunter, as well as a sandy-haired man who smelled like cat.

The wolves were big, powerfully built men, but I stood taller and broader than any of them by a good couple of inches. The added height and muscles wouldn't make a damned bit of difference if they decided to attack. Wolves were excellent fighters, and Landry was an alpha born and bred. At five against one, the odds wouldn't be in my favor if they jumped me. From the looks on their faces, ripping me apart was exactly what they had in mind.

Snagging my pack from the ground, I grabbed my clothes and hastily dressed. When I fastened the leather bracelet with its chunk of black rock around my wrist, their expressions grew positively feral.

"Where the hell did you get that?" Zane snarled.

"Medved's father took it off a dead wolf during the Great War." A simple fact, no gloating on my part.

Landry's eyes flashed. He took a step toward me, then paused. His head tilted and he sniffed the air. Once. Twice. Lowering his chin, he fixed steely eyes on mine.

"What did you do?" he demanded.

Of course an alpha would smell a mating before anyone else. Zane and Remy exchanged confused glances.

I braced myself.

"Did you force her?" Landry asked in a low voice that held the promise of death and pain.

This meeting was going sideways fast. I held up my hand. "It was the only way."

Zane's bewildered gaze flicked from his cousin's face to mine. "What? What's going on?"

"He mated Liv." The lack of heat in Landry's voice made it all the more chilling.

For a fraction of a second, Zane stood frozen in horror, and the next, he blasted toward me like a runaway locomotive. His fist slammed against my chin. I saw stars. The force of the blow knocked me off-balance. I recovered and lunged, using the advantage my height and weight gave me to put the wolf lieutenant in a hammerlock.

"Let the man speak." The authority of an alpha still rang in Matthew Strauss's voice.

I shoved Zane away. He stumbled then whirled to face me, clearly ready for another go.

"I mated Liv," I acknowledged. "She was under a death sentence after the failed rescue attempt, and it was the only way to save her life."

Zane jabbed a finger in my direction. "Don't try to pull that altruistic crap with us. I planted a bug in Medved's office. We all heard what you said to him." His voice took on a mocking intonation. "'Did you see the look on Hunter's face when he heard I was fucking his mate's sister?' Your words, exactly. And then we heard Liv call you an asshole."

I groaned. The wolves couldn't have eavesdropped on a more damning conversation.

"Yeah, I said that." My hand wandered automatically to the back of my skull. I massaged the spot right above the kill switch. "But it was a giant fake out. Liv and I were telling a lie for Medved's benefit."

"Bullshit," Zane spat.

Matthew Strauss held up a hand, silencing his grandson's protests. He walked toward me on halting feet. Landry leapt forward to steady him, but the elder waved him away. He came to a stop within arm's length, close enough that if I intended him harm, I could reach out and snap his neck before the wolves could stop me.

No fear shone in Strauss's intelligent, compassionate eyes. Decades of experience as a leader had left their mark on the man. Traces of alpha power still coursed through his veins. He laid a hand on my chest. Even through the thick fabric of my shirt, I felt that power, and I gasped. He studied me, his sharp gaze probing to the depths of my soul and laying me bare.

"Did you force my granddaughter to mate you?"

"No, sir. I'd never claim a woman without her consent."

A moment's pause while he weighed my words. "True." He nodded, satisfied by my answer. "And do you love her?"

His question startled me into momentary silence. "I… I—"

Zane barked out a contemptuous laugh. "For fuck's sake, Grandpa. Of course he doesn't love her. Even if what he said about mating her to save her life is true, do you think Maxim Medved's most ruthless enforcer is capable of love?"

"Zane." A single word from Strauss silenced the young lieutenant's tirade.

Ignoring Zane, I spoke what was in my heart. "My bear knew first."

"Our shadow brothers often do," Strauss murmured.

I forced the words out. "But I'm more than halfway in love with her myself."

"No fucking way," Zane burst out.

Glancing over the old man's shoulder, I saw Landry grip his cousin's arm, holding him back.

"I knew Maxim Medved's father," Strauss said. "A brutal, capricious alpha who ruled with an iron fist."

I nodded. "Like father, like son."

"Then why do you serve him?" Landry spoke up. "Why do you do his dirty work?"

I shot a furious look at the wolf leader. "He's my alpha, asshole. You're surprised I follow his orders?"

Landry cocked his head to one side, studying me with an intensity I felt to my bones. I had to force myself not to shuffle my feet or look away.

"No." He twisted his lips into a skeptical line. "There's more to the story than that."

Shit. The wolf saw right through me. "How do you get your packmates to obey you?" I asked defensively.

Remy took a step forward. "We obey Adam because he's earned our trust and our respect. He'd die for any one of us, and we know it. Like our grandpa before him, he embodies everything we hope for in a good alpha."

"Well, hell," I muttered. "Wouldn't that be nice?"

"Why do you serve Maxim Medved?" Landry asked again, carefully enunciating each word.

Time to speak the truth. "I have an eight-year-old daughter and a younger brother. If I don't follow Medved's orders—if I don't do exactly what that bastard tells me to do—they'll pay the price."

"Your alpha threatens your family to keep you in line?" Genuine shock crossed Landry's face, as if he couldn't wrap his head around such despicable behavior.

A tight knot inside my chest eased, a tension I'd been holding for years. Hallie and Owen would be safe under Landry's care. I knew it, and that knowledge gave me the strength to ask for our enemy's help.

"Hallie is a sweet little girl, bright and curious. Owen is a natural healer, not a killer like me. Medved put trackers in their bodies. He said if I try to take my family away to someplace safe, he'll turn the world upside down to find them and bring them back. He said he'd…" My voice faltered, but I pushed the next words out. "He said he'd make examples of them. Listen, I know I've got no right to ask you for anything. I'm the very last man you'd want to help, but—"

Landry lifted a hand, cutting off my plea. "As alpha of the Black Rock Guardians, I offer sanctuary to your brother and daughter. We'll find a way to remove the trackers. We'll give your family a home, and my wolves will keep them safe."

"Thank you." Relief robbed the strength from my limbs. I bent over, bracing my hands on my knees. After a moment I regained my composure and straightened to my full height. Back to business. "Medved put me in charge of the hunt for you."

"That's damned convenient." Landry offered a small smile.

"For once, luck's on my side." I returned the weak smile. "I can bring Liv and Hallie and Owen to you, and make sure you get away safely."

"What about you, son?" Strauss asked. "Why don't you come, too?"

If only I could.

If I disappeared with my family, Medved would activate the kill chip. Watching her father die a violent and bloody death would scar my little girl forever. Owen and Liv would be traumatized, too. And as Medved's number one enforcer, I was in the best position to facilitate the escape. If I stayed in place and covered their tracks, they'd get away before Medved figured out what was up.

Self-sacrifice—what Liv called nobility—played no part in my plan. I was a hard-nosed realist with a simple set of priorities. Once the people I loved were safe, I'd do my level best to survive. I'd confront Medved and try to get my hands on the control fob before he could activate level three. The odds weren't in my favor. Taking down an alpha in a one-on-

one battle was nearly impossible. But if I died, I'd go out knowing my family was safe.

Good enough.

"I can't come with you. I need to stay in place in order to misdirect Medved's soldiers, to make sure you get away clean."

"You'll follow afterwards?" Strauss frowned.

"I'll try."

"You've been gone for a couple of hours. We don't want to arouse any suspicions." Landry took charge of the conversation. "Remy, give Creed one of our sat phones, then let's nail down our plans."

Chapter Twenty-Five

Liv

A venison pot pie baked in the oven, filling the house with the savory aroma of meat, onions, carrots, and sage. I still might have reservations about the venison, but the pie crust—made with Grandma Freya's recipe—was going to be killer.

While we waited for Viggo to return home, Hallie took an early bath and donned her favorite flannel pajamas. Owen built a roaring fire then retired to one end of the sofa with his laptop and earbuds. Hallie curled up in the opposite corner of the sofa and read a book out loud to an indifferent Bosco, who sprawled sleepily across her lap. I sat cross-legged on the flokati rug, warming my fingers and watching the dancing flames.

A tickle on the back of my neck told me that Viggo had returned home. I turned around and found him leaning against the arched opening to the living room, his hands shoved into his pockets. His gaze traveled from one of us to the next, melancholy etched across his rugged face.

He lifted a finger to his lips and jerked his head toward the rear of the house. I silently stood and followed him to his bedroom. Once inside the room, he shut the door with a quiet *snick*. Gripping my waist, he walked me backward till my shoulders struck the rigid surface. Cool wood pressed against my back. Even as a shiver ran across my shoulders, Viggo's heat warmed my breasts and abdomen. Hot and cold converged deep inside me. Everywhere I was surrounded by strength and solidity, unyielding wood at my back and rock-solid muscles at my front.

His hands tangled in my hair. I rose up on my tiptoes and lifted my mouth to meet his, anticipating our third kiss. That quick brush of lips in Hallie's presence barely counted. It was more of a promise of a kiss than the real deal. During our fast and hard mating—when the man fucked me into oblivion—our mouths had touched only once.

"We're doing this backassward," I murmured.

He stilled, his mouth an inch from mine. "What?"

"Usually kissing comes first. A *lot* of kissing."

"Is that right?" The vibrations from his deep rumble penetrated my core.

"Yes," I whispered, trembling.

So much for my vow that Liv Hagen trembles before no man.

My tongue darted out, and I licked my lower lip.

Viggo followed the movement through half-closed eyes. His fingers tightened in my hair. "Then we better make up for lost time."

I've kissed dozens of men over the course of my adult life. Never before had the prospect of a kiss rendered me weak-kneed and breathless. My stubborn lungs went on strike, refusing to suck in air.

With exquisite slowness, he closed the distance between our mouths and nipped my lower lip. The small bite of pain obliterated both self-control and rational thought. Whimpering from need, I rose higher on my toes.

Seconds ticked by. My lips tingled and anticipation spiraled out of control.

"Viggo, please," I whispered against his mouth.

He unchained the beast and claimed my mouth with devastating ferocity. One hand slid to my nape, the other seized my thigh and hoisted me into the air. Locking my legs around his waist, I gyrated against him.

A small corner of my consciousness registered the distant ding of the kitchen timer going off. Moaning, I yanked my mouth away from his and mentally kicked myself. We should have known better than to start something when Hallie was awake and dinner almost ready.

"What is it?" he asked on a pant.

"The pot pie is done. Hallie is going to be at the door in three, two, one." I counted down and sure enough, her light footsteps tapped down the hall, followed by a knock on the bedroom door.

"Dinner is ready," she piped.

"Your daddy and I will be right out," I said. "Will you ask Uncle Owen to take the pot pie out of the oven, please?"

"Okey doke." She skipped down the hall.

Viggo dropped his forehead against mine. "Rain check?"

"Count on it." I shimmied down his legs and pointed at the bulge in his pants. "You'll need a minute to... uh… deflate that bad boy."

"Yeah, tell Hallie I had to wash my hands and change my shirt before dinner."

"Try imagining Jasper Garvey in a speedo," I suggested helpfully.

"Dear God." He made a pained face. "Talk about a boner killer."

"My work here is done." I blew him a kiss and headed toward the door.

"Liv," he called.

I glanced over my shoulder. "Yeah?"

Beneath hooded lids, Viggo's brown eyes glittered. "Tonight, let's try slow and gentle."

A core of absolute sweetness lived inside the scary enforcer. Coupled with his strength of character, it was a sweetness I couldn't resist. Turning on my heel, I walked to his side and touched his stubble-covered chin. "I'd love that, big guy."

"Good." He took my hand and pressed a kiss to my palm. "It's a date."

By the time Viggo emerged from the bedroom, Hallie and I had filled water glasses and taken our seats. Owen set the venison pot pie and a salad in the middle of the table. We dished up and dug in. Hallie carried most of the conversation. Owen appeared preoccupied and Viggo contentedly listened to his daughter's happy chatter, a small smile on his face.

When she paused to take a breath, Viggo spoke up. "Tomorrow is going to be a special day."

That got her attention. Hallie set down her fork and turned wide eyes to her father. "What's happening tomorrow?"

Viggo set his fork down, too, and leaned back in his chair. "Tomorrow, you, and Uncle Owen, and Liv are going to go on a little trip."

My pulse kicked into overdrive.

Owen shot me a quizzical look. I shook my head, silently answering his question. I hadn't heard about this either, but I could guess what happened. Viggo had contacted the wolves. Adam had offered safe refuge to Hallie and Owen. How Viggo managed to pull that off I had no idea, but the prospect of Hallie and Owen with the Black Rock Guardians was the answer to a prayer.

But what about Viggo?

"Where are we going?" Hallie asked. Viggo held out an arm. She hopped up and took a seat on his lap.

"It's a surprise," he said.

Hallie thought about it. "Are you coming, too?"

"No, sweetheart. I can't get away from work."

My stomach cramped at this proof Viggo intended to stay in place. He didn't have a choice though, did he? Running wasn't an option. What would Medved do to my mate when he discovered Hallie and Owen and me gone? The memory of Viggo dropping like a ton of bricks—his entire body contorted in agony—flashed through my mind. If Medved discovered that Viggo had orchestrated the escape, with the push of a button he could torture him forever or end his life.

"Tomorrow is a school day," Hallie said.

A pink barrette had slid to the bottom of Hallie's silky hair. Viggo unfastened it, then clipped it in place above her ear, a simple, loving gesture that got me in my feels.

God, I'm turning into as much of a softy as Annika.

"You're going to miss school tomorrow, and Uncle Owen will miss work."

"How long will we be gone?" Hallie's brow puckered.

Viggo lifted a noncommittal shoulder.

She frowned. "What about Bosco?"

"Bosco is family. He's coming with you," Viggo assured her.

"Okay." The knowledge that Bosco would accompany her on their little trip assuaged her concerns, and she perked up. "Will you help me pack my suitcase after dinner?"

"Of course." Viggo stroked a hand through her strawberry-blond locks. His smile didn't falter, but I saw past the smile to the sorrow he tried so hard to hide. He thought this was it, his last night with his daughter and brother and me. He was saying goodbye to all of us.

Fuck that.

No way would I run home to Washington and leave Viggo to meet his fate. He was my mate, dammit. There had to be a way for us to either disable the kill chip or wrest the control fob away from Medved.

The adults picked at our food, then we retired to the living room for what Hallie called a Creed family music night. Viggo played the piano, Owen the guitar, while Hallie and I sang. Hallie had a sweet voice. Unlike my cousin Marit, I could more-or-less carry a tune, so I didn't spoil the sound.

Afterward, Owen went to his room to pack a bag while Viggo and I helped Hallie with hers. Clothes were easy to replace, souvenirs of her life weren't. Luckily, Hallie didn't question why in addition to some clothing, we filled her suitcase with sentimental stuff—her baby blanket, her jewelry box, her favorite knickknacks and books, her pillow, the framed photo of Rosalie.

Leaving Viggo to read his daughter to sleep, I went in search of Owen. I found him in the kitchen loading the dishwasher. As soon as he saw me, he abandoned the task and pulled me into a corner for a huddled conversation.

"What do you know?" he asked in a low voice.

"Nothing more than you do. Viggo must have gotten ahold of Adam, and it looks like Adam offered sanctuary to you and Hallie."

Owen scrubbed his hands over his face, then fixed worried eyes on me. "If we run, Medved will activate that damned kill chip. I'm not going to gain my freedom at the cost of my brother's life."

I understood. I couldn't imagine ever running away and leaving Annika to face likely death, but I got where Viggo was coming from, too. He'd exchange his life for his daughter's in a heartbeat. And if he could ensure that Hallie had somebody who loved her at her side—someone who'd watch over her, tell her stories about her family, teach her what it meant to be a grizzly—he'd consider his death an acceptable tradeoff.

Resolve filled me. If Hallie fled, Owen was going with her.

I threw an arm around his shoulders. "We need to trust that Viggo has a plan to outsmart Medved and get away."

"You think?" Hope filled his eyes.

"I bet he does."

Not a lie, not exactly, but a wish cast out to the universe. Tossing positive thoughts out to the universe? I wasn't usually given to such woo-woo behavior, but I was like the atheist in the foxhole. Desperate times and all.

"We'll find out soon enough." Owen sighed. Craning his neck, he glanced from the kitchen toward the living room. "I've never lived anywhere other than this house. I've grown up hearing stories about how weak and incompetent the Black Rock Guardians are. How grizzlies are superior to wolves. And now I'm supposed to abandon my home and everything I know and go live with the pack's oldest enemy. It doesn't feel real."

"Change can be hard," I commiserated. "Remember, you've only heard one side of the story. From the wolves' point of view, grizzlies are the bad guys who attacked without provocation and stole their land and homes."

"I suppose so," he admitted.

"Wolves aren't weak or incompetent, I promise. They're smart and strong. They cherish children. I can't imagine a better, safer place for a kid to grow up than with the Black Rock Guardians."

His cheeks puffed out in an exhale. "Yeah. You're right. Nothing matters more than Hallie having a shot at a good life."

"She will." I touched his arm. "And so will you. Give the wolves a chance. I bet you'll like them."

"And at least we'll have one friend there to help ease the transition." He bumped shoulders with me.

From his mouth to God's ears, like Grandma used to say.

While Viggo continued settling Hallie for the night, I whipped up a batch of sweet dough and set it to slow rise overnight in the refrigerator. In the morning, I'd get up early and make cinnamon rolls for breakfast. Owen stacked a metal dish, a toy, and a few of cans of dog food on the counter to bring for Bosco.

A subdued Viggo finally emerged from Hallie's room. He angled his head, inviting Owen to join him in the living room. I kept busy in the kitchen while the brothers had a private talk. As I was wiping down the counters, Bosco trotted up to me and nudged my leg. He whimpered and raced to the front door.

"I can take a hint," I told him. We came back inside after his potty break and found that Owen had gone to bed and Viggo was waiting for me in the kitchen.

"Come here." He held out a hand.

Sliding both arms around his waist, I pressed my cheek against his muscled heat. The familiar scent of cypress and black pepper surrounded me. I gave myself a full minute to bask in the warmth before pulling away and lifting my face to meet his eyes.

"So, spill," I said. "What's the plan?"

"Tomorrow morning, we'll meet Landry and his wolves in the woods northwest of the village. Then you, Owen, and Hallie will travel with them to the lodge on Shooting Star Lake. You'll all be safe."

Not so long ago, I would've assumed that anybody living in the lodge was safe. Personal experience had taught me otherwise.

"Even if our healers take out Hallie and Owen's trackers, Medved will know where they are and might try something."

Viggo rubbed a soothing hand up and down my back. "You can be damned sure the wolves have stepped up their security after I snuck past their defenses. It's all good."

"It's all good?" Disbelief made my voice harsh. "Even if the lodge is secure, what about you? What will Medved do to *you* when he figures out we're gone?"

"Don't worry. I've got it handled."

I waited for an explanation. When none came, I poked his chest. "You can't just tell me you've got it handled and expect me to drop the subject."

"You know, life would be easier if you were a sweet, compliant woman who'd take me at my word."

Laughter bubbled up from my throat. "If you wanted sweet and compliant, you mated the wrong woman, buddy."

He massaged the back of his neck. If touching the skin above the kill chip would activate it, he would've died years ago. Still, watching him palpate the spot made me wince. I tugged his hand away from his skull.

"Talk," I urged.

"Medved has no clue I've turned on him. Before he figures it out, I'll find an opportunity and make my move."

"Make your move, what does that mean?" I persisted.

"I'll jump him. Take the control fob."

"You intend to kill him?" I asked.

"Yeah. If I leave him alive and try to run, he'll sic my packmates on me before I could get away. Last thing I want is to kill a grizzly who's just following orders."

Panic raised goose bumps across my shoulders. "Your plan consists of a fight to the death with an *alpha*?"

"Yes." From his tone, you'd think challenging an alpha was no big deal. I knew better.

An alpha's power was a tangible thing, an irresistible force of nature.

A few weeks ago, I watched Adam break up a bloody fistfight between two adolescents.

"Stop," he'd barked.

The single word instantly halted the brawl. Both boys fell to their knees and angled their necks to the side, exposing their throats. Watching from the sidelines, I felt the force of Adam's power wash over me. It freaked me out. I loved and trusted my cousin's mate, but the compulsion to yield to his authority—however fleeting—left me reeling.

Remy had witnessed my reaction and pulled me aside. He explained how shifters were wired to obey their alpha and assured me that it wasn't a bad thing. Folks who spent their lives balancing their human and animal sides sometimes required a firm hand to maintain their equilibrium, he said. A good alpha—like Adam—wielded his power wisely.

Which begged the question, what about a bad one, like Medved? Did unhappy packmates ever try to replace their leader, I'd asked.

Now, Remy's answer sprang ominously to mind. "The only way to remove a leader is to challenge them to hand-to-hand combat, a fight to the death that an alpha rarely loses. Only a contender with alpha blood stands a chance."

Viggo wore a shard of the black rock on his wrist, making him stronger and faster than the average shifter. Unfortunately, Medved wore an even bigger chunk of the meteorite on a leather cord around his neck.

The odds were stacked against Viggo surviving a battle with his alpha. Epictetus said to take things as they come and make the best of what's in your power. Wishful thinking wouldn't cut it. I needed a viable plan, but at this moment, I had no clue how to help him.

Chills slithered up my spine, and I clutched at his shirt. "I don't want you to die."

Smiling gently, he brushed the hair from my forehead then wrapped his big hands around my head. "Don't count me out. If there's a way to get back to you, and Hallie, and Owen, I'll find it."

No fear shone in his honey-brown eyes, only calm determination and an odd serenity. He'd made peace with his fate.

Not me. Epictetus would disapprove, but I wanted to shake my fist and hurl abuse at the bad luck that put a good man in such an unwinnable situation. I bit back the angry words that could only undermine his confidence.

Instead, I lifted my chin. "I know you'll do your damnedest to get back to us."

His nostrils flared, but if he scented my doubts, he chose to ignore them.

We stood in silence for a moment, our gazes locked on each other. If this truly was our last night together, I didn't want to spend it in premature mourning, counting down the seconds as they ticked by.

"I need to get out of my head," I muttered, my voice louder than I intended.

Viggo tenderly brushed his knuckles over my cheek. "Let's go to bed, mate."

My heart flip-flopped. I finally understood why Annika and Marit gave a happy wriggle when their men called them *mate.*

Okay. Get your head right.

Instead of taking the hand he held out, I smacked him on the ass and took off down the hall. "Race you," I called over my shoulder.

I didn't make it three steps before Viggo swooped me up into his arms and carried me the rest of the way. He locked the door then deposited me across the bed. I sat up on my elbows, ogling him expectantly.

He grabbed the hem of his shirt and yanked it over his head, exposing chiseled abs and a wide, sculpted chest.

"So damned beautiful," I sighed. Sitting up, I reached for the hem of my shirt.

"No." He touched my hand. "Let me."

Maybe undressing me was part of the slow and gentle he promised.

Resting one knee on the bed, he unzipped my boots and tugged them from my feet. My shirt came next. He paused, his heated gaze admiring either my cleavage or my fancy red mesh balconette bra, the same bra I wore under my party dress the night he kidnapped me.

"Up," he ordered.

I lifted my butt an inch off the mattress. He slid his fingers into the waistband of my black yoga pants, peeled them off my legs, and tossed them aside, leaving behind a red mesh thong that matched my bra.

Viggo pointed. "Pretty."

I batted my lashes, playing coy. "Me or my undies?"

"Both." His gaze swept up and down my body then honed in on the raised pink welt on my right flank, a scar left behind by the bullet that grazed my side last month. His smile faltered. "You could've died when that damned coyote shot you."

My *brilliant* plan to get information from Vilhauer's son had gone off the rails. I'd held a gun on the young coyote. He'd rushed me and the pistol accidentally discharged. Two inches to the left and I would've suffered a penetrating abdominal wound. I'd been damned lucky.

Was anything more unpredictable—less reliable—than luck?

My lighthearted mood dissolved and slipped away, as inexorably as a retreating tide. Fear pushed in from every side. My pulse accelerated. My greedy little heart wanted *more. M*ore time with this man. More experiences. I wanted everything he had to offer.

Stop thinking. Don't wreck this.

"Liv?" Viggo frowned, plainly sensing my distress.

"I need—" My voice choked. Sitting up, I shook my head, beyond frustrated with myself.

"Tell me."

"Same thing as last time. I need you to take me away from reality." I balled my hand and smacked it twice against my head. "Make my damned brain shut up."

He seized my fist and gently pried my fingers apart, then pressed a kiss to each knuckle. "I'll give you whatever you need."

Lifting my chin, I rallied my spirits. "How about you start by cutting off my underwear."

A dark eyebrow lifted. He held up a hand and flexed his fingers. Claws shot out from every fingertip. He pointed at my bra. "You want me to—" He mimed slicing through the fabric.

Trash my expensive Italian lingerie? Why not? I usually wore a soft stretchy bra anyway, or let the girls fly free. The mental image of my grizzly mate shredding my fancy bra and panties shot liquid desire into my sex.

"Yes, please."

The tip of a curved, reddish-brown claw touched the corner of my eye then traced a line from my cheek to my jaw, down my neck, to the valley between my breasts. One sudden flick of his wrist and the center of my bra split apart. I knew it was coming, still, a shocked laugh burst from my throat. Before my laughter died away, he cut the straps, and my bra fell onto the bed.

Viggo lightly dragged his hand down my stomach and over my navel. He slipped three fingers under my thong. The sharp points of his claws pierced the thin mesh. He tugged and sliced the fabric into ribbons.

"My beautiful mate," he murmured, gliding a palm over my inner thigh. He curved both hands under my hips and pulled me to the edge of the bed. Dropping onto his knees, he shouldered my legs apart and nuzzled the strip of dark hair over my mons. With a broad, flat tongue, he slowly licked across my sex. I whimpered and he did it again. He took his time, licking and gently biting my flesh. Strong hands held me firmly in place, his fingers pressing divots into my hips and ass.

I scraped my hands over his shaved head, savoring the rasp of stubble against my fingertips. As if they had a mind of their own, my hips rose and fell, and I ground against his mouth.

Releasing my hips, he pushed a finger inside me, then groaned. "So wet and hot." A second digit followed the first, sliding in and out as his mouth laid waste to my slick and swollen sex.

"Viggo," I gasped, teetering on the edge of orgasm.

He lifted his face, his mouth glistening with my juices as he shoved his fingers deep into my pussy. "Come for me."

I splintered and came, convulsing around his clever fingers. Before my heart rate slowed or my breathing returned to normal, he climbed on top of me and nudged my legs apart. The broad head of his cock found my entrance. With one powerful thrust, he slid home.

His body stilled, giving me time to relax and accept the incursion. I wrapped my arms around his neck and clung to him, gasping. My thumb brushed across the welt above the kill chip.

"No," I moaned, pulled out of the moment by this reminder that with the push of a button, I could lose Viggo.

"Shh," he murmured. "Stay in the here and now, darlin'." Slowly rocking his hips, he set a leisurely rhythm, as if we had all the time in the world. Gentle kisses rained down on my face.

If only I could prolong this moment, hold on to it forever, hold onto Viggo forever. But I was powerless to stave off the inescapable passage of time.

Stay in the here and now.

I shoved away all my fears for what tomorrow would bring and wallowed in the joy I found in my mate's arms.

Chapter Twenty-Six

Viggo

I woke up on what might be the last day of my life and reached for Liv. Instead of the warm, pliant body of my mate, I found her side of the bed empty. The cool sheets held not a hint of body heat. If I didn't know better, I'd swear I'd slept alone in the big bed.

For a few seconds, irrational panic flooded my half-awake mind. What if finding my mate was a dream, and Liv no more than a figment of my imagination? What if time had reset—if I'd never kidnapped her—and I was waking up to a world where I had no mate and little hope of saving my brother and daughter?

Fate wouldn't be that cruel, would it?

Ha.

Lifting my head, I squinted at the alarm clock. 5:18 a.m. I focused my senses and listened hard. From the kitchen came the faint reassuring sound of the refrigerator door opening and closing.

You're off the hook, fate.

I swung out of bed, snatched my jeans from the floor, and yanked them up over my hips. The furnace wouldn't come on till six, but I was plenty warm as I padded barefoot to the kitchen. I sniffed, catching an enticing whiff of spices and coffee. A tray of unbaked cinnamon rolls sat rising on top of the stove. Liv leaned against a counter, sipping a mug of coffee. Once again, she'd appropriated my black robe. It dragged on the floor, and she'd rolled up the sleeves several times to free her hands. On her feet she wore a pair of my heavy winter socks.

"You look warm," I observed.

She lifted a foot swathed in a thick gray-and-black striped field sock.

"The word you're searching for is fetching." She wiggled her toes. "I look fetching."

God, she was cute.

"That you do, darlin'."

I took the mug of coffee from her hands, set it on the counter then untied the terry cloth belt. The robe fell open, exposing breasts and thighs that still bore the faint pink marks of whisker burn.

Humming with satisfaction, I touched the light scratches on her breasts, then traced my thumb along the edges of her mating bite.

She shivered. "I see the grizzly in your eyes."

I felt my shadow brother close to the surface. "Does he frighten you?" My hand stilled as I waited for her answer. It would break my bear's heart if our mate was frightened of him.

"How could he scare me? He's *you.*"

Beneath my skin, my bear huffed in satisfaction.

From the back of the house, a door slammed.

I jerked the sides of Liv's robe together and knotted the belt.

Owen staggered into the room, yawning.

"Coffee is ready." Liv pointed at the thermal carafe.

He groaned. "You're the best."

Half an hour later, Liv put the cinnamon rolls in the oven then went to take a shower and get dressed.

I put my truck in the garage every night, out of sight of the neighbors or any passersby. When we drove out of town a few hours from now, my family would ride in the back with the truck bed cover hiding them from prying eyes.

While Liv showered, I put Hallie's suitcase and Owen's duffel in the bed of the truck, and laid out a thick quilt and a few pillows on the floor. On impulse, I packed Owen's guitar, too. Sure, he could buy a new one, but he loved playing Grandpa's guitar. It would be a comfort for him to have a familiar object in his new life.

The smell of freshly baked cinnamon rolls woke Hallie. She skipped to the kitchen, buzzing with excitement about the trip.

At seven a.m., when the school office opened, I called in. "Hallie's going to be absent today," I told the secretary.

"Oh, no. Is she sick?"

"We opened a bottle of unpasteurized apple cider last night. It'd been refrigerated, so we thought it was fine. Apparently not."

"Ohhh," she moaned in sympathy. "Food poisoning is the worst."

"Yeah," I agreed. "Owen and my new mate are sick as a dog, too."

"And you?" the kindly woman asked.

"I drank beer. I'm fine."

"That was lucky," she said with a laugh. "I'll let Hallie's teacher know that she's home sick. Tell your little girl I hope she feels better soon."

"I will. Thanks."

If everyone in the village was a bastard, wrenching Hallie away from her familiar life would be a lot easier.

At eight a.m., I called Evelyn to tell her that Owen had food poisoning, and to ask her to have somebody else man the community store for the day. By nine a.m., most of the inhabitants of town were either at school or work. The streets would be as empty as they were likely to get.

Owen took a last walk around the house, saying goodbye to the only home he'd ever known. He ran his fingers over the piano keys and crouched down and touched the wolf andirons. When he was finished, he held out a hand to Hallie and opened the door between the laundry room and the garage. "Come on, peanut. How would you like to play a game of make believe?"

"Can I play, too?" Liv followed close on their heels.

Owen winked at her. "Sure. Let's pretend we're running away from an evil troll. We have to hide because he wants to steal all the…" He glanced around, clearly looking for something the troll might want to steal.

Liv held up a plastic container holding the leftover cinnamon rolls.

"He wants to steal our cinnamon rolls," Owen finished.

Liv mock gasped and climbed into the bed of the pickup. "Come on, kiddo. Let's hide here from the greedy troll."

"You guys are silly." Hallie giggled as Owen lifted her into the truck. She lay down on the quilt flanked by Liv and her uncle.

"Bosco is riding in the front with me," I told her. "I'm going to pull the cover over you now, okay? You'll need to stay quiet so the… uh… troll won't find you." I'd been worried that hiding in the bed of the truck might frighten her, but Hallie seemed happy to play along with the charade.

Bosco's legs weren't long enough to jump onto the front seat. I lifted him into the truck then rolled out of our driveway, possibly for the last time. Didn't allow myself a backward glance as I drove out of the neighborhood and turned left onto the village's main street. Only a handful of folks were out and about. I spied Hank Garvey on the steps of headquarters. Wearing a scowl, he craned his neck and eyeballed me as I passed.

On the outskirts of town, instead of turning south toward the airstrip, I headed north. I followed an old logging road into the woods for half a mile until a fallen tree blocked the way. I parked and quickly rolled up the pickup bed cover. Hallie sat up and held out her arms. Lifting her up and out of the truck, I held on for a few seconds longer than necessary before depositing her on the ground.

She glanced around in confusion at the forestland. "I thought we were going on a trip."

"We are, peanut," Owen assured her. "We're going to take a little hike then meet up with some friends."

I checked my watch. 9:22. Good. We were supposed to rendezvous with the wolves at 10:30. In case something went awry during our trip out of town, we'd left early. The early departure gave me more precious minutes to spend with my family before they fled and I faced down Medved.

Shit just got real. I gulped and swung my eyes from Hallie, to Owen, to Liv.

A concerned expression crossed Liv's pretty face. She walked up and snaked her arms around my waist. I held her tight. A slight tremble racked my mate's body. Liv had put on a brave face, but I tasted her worry.

Capturing her chin between my fingers, I tilted her face up to meet mine. I lowered my mouth on hers, going deep with a lingering kiss. I pulled back. Tears had gathered in the corners of her eyes. Mine were soggy, too.

"I love you." I hadn't intended to say the words, to burden her with the knowledge of how deep my feelings ran. I'd told myself that if the worst happened, she'd find it easier to move on if she didn't know that I loved her. Hell, maybe I was being selfish, but I needed to say the words.

"Aren't we a pair?" She sniffed. "Right back at you, big guy. I love you, too."

Hallie hurled herself on us, wrapping her arms around our legs. "How about me?"

Liv laughed and ruffled Hallie's hair. "And I love you, kiddo."

Gratitude for my mate hit me hard. No matter what happened to me, Hallie would grow up with people who loved her.

Light snow began to sift down between the tree branches.

Owen cleared his throat. "Viggo, do you want to start walking to the meeting place or wait for a bit inside the truck?"

The rest of us were bears—untroubled by cold—but I didn't want Liv standing in the snow any longer than necessary. "Let's wait in the cab."

For the next half hour we sat inside the truck. Owen steered the conversation to a discussion of happy family times. We laughed at Bosco, who stood up on his hind legs and licked the condensation off the window. Hallie was so excited about the upcoming trip that any tension in the air went right over her head.

At precisely ten a.m., I opened the driver's-side-door. "We ought to get going."

"Come on, Bosco. It's vacation time." Hallie couldn't contain her excitement.

Holding hands with my mate and my daughter, I took the lead. With her free hand, Liv carried Hallie's suitcase. With hers, Hallie held the handle of Bosco's leash. Owen marched through the snow with a duffel in one hand and the guitar case in the other.

The land gradually sloped uphill. We rounded a large boulder and had just ducked under the branches of a black spruce when I felt it, a prickle on my neck, a warning sign from my primitive back brain.

"Stop." I let go of Liv and Hallie's hands and took three steps forward, pivoting to scan the woods. Owen dropped the duffel and guitar case and took a position next to me.

"Daddy? What's happening?" Hallie asked in a small voice.

"Come here, kiddo." Liv pulled Hallie to her side.

On our left, a tall figure stepped out from behind a tree.

"Well, well, well. What do we have here?" A smirking Jasper Garvey pointed a pistol at me.

Hank Garvey strode from behind an elderberry bush. "Looks like Creed's turned traitor." He pulled a phone from his pocket. "We should call the boss and let him know, don't you think?"

CHAPTER TWENTY-SEVEN

LIV

While Hallie and I stood frozen in stunned silence, a frantically barking Bosco lunged forward and pulled the leash handle right out of the little girl's hand.

"Shit." I snatched at it, but the dog was too fast for me.

"Damned mutt," Jasper Garvey snarled. The barrel of his gun swung from Viggo to Bosco.

In a blur of motion, Viggo sprang at Jasper and tackled him to the ground.

Hallie shrieked, pulled away from me, and tore off her coat. She began to shift into her bear form, shredding her jeans and tee. The air shimmered and clogged with the pungent scent of ozone. I stumbled backward, putting a necessary distance between my human body and the supernatural shift.

Bosco shrank back and hunkered down on his belly.

Owen charged at Hank and batted at the phone the brawny enforcer held in his hand. Hank had longer arms and at least fifty pounds of heft on the younger man, and he used both to keep the phone away from Owen.

Panic flared inside me. If Hank got a call in to Medved, it would be game over for our escape plan. The alpha would send every soldier at his disposal into the woods, jeopardizing not only our lives, but the lives of our wolf rescuers, too. And I had absolutely no doubt a vengeful Medved would activate Viggo's kill chip.

My options narrowed down to a pinpoint. I launched myself at Hank, throwing myself onto his back and clenching my legs around his waist. Grunting, I grabbed his chin with both hands and yanked with all my might. If I could throw him off-balance, maybe Owen could gain the advantage.

Bang.

A gunshot shattered the morning.

My body reacted before my brain registered the sound. I jerked as unwelcome memories of being shot bombarded me. The acrid smell of gunpowder. The burning sting of a bullet grazing my side. Cold water soaking into my coat and chilling my back as I lay face up on a rain-drenched highway. Blood. Shock. Fear.

I shook my head, forcing my thoughts back to the present.

Who… who fired a gun?

Oh, God.

Viggo. I craned my neck, looking for my mate. My heart stuttered.

Viggo lay atop Jasper on the ground.

Hank stood stock-still, staring slack-jawed at his motionless brother.

Owen recovered his wits first. He knocked the phone from the grizzly enforcer's hand and stomped on it. Growling, Hank turned away from the sight of his brother and focused his malevolent attention on Owen.

Nope.

Still riding piggyback, I dug my heels hard into Hank's gut, locked an elbow around his beefy neck, and squeezed with all my might. Out of the corner of my eye, I spied Viggo slowly lift up onto his knees, the gun in his hand. Jasper stayed down, a bloody hole in his chest, his eyes glazed over in death.

Thank God. Relief almost weakened my grasp on Hank's neck, but I remembered in time to hold on tight when he looked over to his brother.

"Jasper?" Hank croaked.

He grabbed my forearm. On his wrist, he wore a chunk of black rock.

Crap.

That was new. Kissing up to Medved had paid off big-time for the Garvey brothers.

Hank yanked my arm away from his throat then roughly shook me off his back.

I hit the ground and landed on my ass. Drawing back my leg, I shot a hard kick to the back of his knee. I possessed only a fraction of a grizzly's strength, but a joint was a vulnerable spot for anyone in human form. His leg buckled out from under him.

I crab-walked backward, scrambling to get out of reach before he recovered.

From under a nearby bush, the Hallie cub whimpered, her honey-brown eyes wild with fright.

"Stay down, kiddo," I whispered.

Viggo jumped to his feet and whirled around. His gaze slashed from Hallie to Hank.

Hank recognized the real threat. Ignoring me, he hopped up and lowered his head, facing Viggo. "To the death," he snarled.

"Agreed." Ice filled Viggo's voice.

Owen rushed to my side and hauled me to my feet. We clung to each other as Hank peeled off his coat and clothes. The air around him grew thick and sparkled with a wavy light. Viggo threw the gun into the woods, tore off his clothes, and started to shift.

"Why didn't Viggo just shoot him?" I whispered in Owen's ear.

Owen shot me a startled look. "Honor. When one shifter challenges another to battle, pulling a gun would be dishonorable."

Honor? As far as the Garveys were concerned, I'd say they'd forfeited any expectation of honorable behavior, but Viggo clearly felt otherwise.

I watched through a glimmering haze as their bodies contorted, their limbs elongated, and fur sprouted over their skin. If I lived for a thousand years, I'd never get used to the sight of humans morphing into beasts.

Transformation complete, the two huge grizzlies lowered their heads and grunted, swaying as they shifted their weight from one foot to the other. Without warning, both reared up on their hind legs. Growling, they slapped at each other with massive paws. Their lips peeled back, revealing long, sharp fangs.

"Ho-ly shit." My fingers dug into Owen's arm.

Viggo charged. He clamped his teeth around Hank's muzzle and held on as his enemy struggled to escape. Hank gained momentum, shoved forward, and pushed Viggo down onto the ground. Viggo landed flat on his back. Before Hank could go for his throat, Viggo rolled over onto all fours. As he rose up on his feet, Hank sank his teeth into Viggo's back and tossed his head from side to side, sending tufts of fur flying.

I whirled on Owen. "What can we do to help?"

He shook his head, his expression bitter. "Not a damned thing. It's a fight to the death. I can't interfere. Besides, without the black rock, I couldn't shift in time to help."

The black rock.

If Medved gave Hank a black rock bracelet, maybe he'd done the same for Jasper.

Giving a wide berth to the grappling bears, I ran over to Jasper's body. Bright-red blood stained the snow around him as I knelt and pushed up the sleeve of his coat. Nothing on his right wrist, but a familiar-looking leather bracelet was fastened around his left.

My hands shook so much it took a good thirty seconds for my clumsy fingers to unfasten the clasp. I leapt to my feet and dashed to Owen's side and held out the bracelet.

"Even if you won't intervene, you should be ready to fight in bear form to protect Hallie in case Hank wins."

"You're right." Owen closed his fist around the chunk of meteorite, shuddering as its power zinged into him. He peeled off his coat and started his supercharged shift.

I turned my eyes to the battle.

Viggo had wrenched free of Hank's grip. Now, the two bears stood on their hind legs, grappling like titans. Growls rumbled from deep in their chests. Claws slashed. Jaws snapped. Fur rippled over powerful muscles.

Between one blink and the next, Viggo wrestled Hank to the ground. His teeth locked around Hank's throat.

I held my breath, waiting to see what would happen. A few months ago, I watched a nature documentary about grizzlies. They said that in the wild, a victorious grizzly usually walked away from a fight without delivering a fatal blow.

But Viggo and Hank weren't natural bears, and this was a fight to the death.

Viggo's jaw jerked back and forth. A sickening ripping sound filled the air. Finally, Viggo lifted his head. Rivulets of blood dripped from his mouth, and he panted from exhaustion.

A halo of shimmering light surrounded the fallen bear. Fur melted away and the corpse reconfigured itself. Human once again, Hank lay sprawled on the forest floor, blood gushing from his throat.

Beside me, Owen shifted back to human and pulled on his clothes.

Raising up on his hind legs, Viggo lingered in his grizzly form. The beast's golden-brown eyes sought mine. He held perfectly still, as if locked in place.

Was he afraid that he'd frightened me? That I'd reject him?

Refusing to look away from the blood-splattered fur on his face, I met the grizzly's gaze. My mate's shadow brother—the other half of his soul—needed my reassurance.

I straightened my spine and walked to the bear. He towered over me. I slowly stretched out my hand and touched the fur on his chest. It felt coarse and bristly beneath my fingers.

"You did good, big guy. You saved us."

Unmistakable love and relief shone in his eyes. He lowered his head. I gently touched the fur at the base of his ears. He made a happy, snuffling sound, so I scritched the softer fur for a full minute before speaking again.

"We need to get to our rendezvous with the wolves. Can you change back to human?"

The mighty grizzly bobbed his head. I shuffled backward away from the shift.

I looked around for Hallie. Her hiding place under the bush was vacant, and the cub nowhere to be seen. I clutched at Owen's arm. "Where's Hallie?"

"Shit," he hissed. "She must've run into the woods."

Bosco was missing, too.

Viggo completed his shift, yanked on his clothes, and slid his feet into his boots. He glanced at the corpses of his fellow enforcers. "No point in hiding the bodies. Any shifter would smell them as soon as they got close."

"Hallie ran away," I said quickly.

Alarm flared in his eyes. Without another word, Viggo charged after his daughter, Owen and I on his heels. Viggo followed Hallie's scent trail for half a mile then burst into a small clearing in the woods. He skidded to a stop.

Adam sat on the snow-covered ground, murmuring soft, comforting words to the frightened bear cub he cradled in his arms. She curled against his chest while he stroked her shoulders. Bosco crouched a few feet away, his wary gaze on the wolf alpha.

Zane, Remy, Grandpa Matthew, and Thomas stood nearby in the dappled shade of tall trees.

"The cub sensed Adam's alpha power," Grandpa spoke up. "And recognized that he would protect her."

Viggo sank to his knees next to the pair and gently touched the cub's head. "Thank you."

Adam nodded. "I'll keep your child safe. You can count on it."

The cub reacted instantly to her father's voice. Wriggling out of Adam's arms, she threw herself at Viggo.

"Daddy's got you," he said, his voice thick. She snuggled in his arms for a minute then scooted away and began her shift back to human.

Adam stood and took a position next to his grandfather.

"I'm gonna run and get our stuff." Owen pointed to the way we'd come.

Viggo stripped out of his coat. As soon as Hallie finished her change, he wrapped it around her and held her close.

A few minutes later, a breathless Owen ran into the clearing and dumped the bags and guitar case onto the ground. He walked up to Adam, holding Jasper and Hank Garveys' leather bracelets in his hand.

"I believe these rightly belong to your people."

Seventy-odd years after the end of the Great War, the bracelets of fallen wolf soldiers were once again in the hands of the Black Rock Guardians.

Adam smiled at the young grizzly and inclined his head. "Thank you, Owen. Once we're home in Washington, you'll get your own chunk of black rock. But these—" He slipped the bracelets into his pocket. "These, I'll pass on to our new lynx allies."

Owen returned to the center of the clearing and opened Hallie's suitcase. "Come on, peanut. Let's get you dressed."

Silence descended as the longtime enemies took stock of each other. I tore my gaze away from Viggo and looked toward the wolves. Adam held out a hand. Without hesitation, I rushed to his side. Strong arms enfolded me. I closed my eyes and let his alpha power—rife with the sense of family, home, and protection—wash over me.

He brought his mouth to my ear. "Are you okay?"

How to answer that question? I was unhurt, glad to be reunited with my family, and terrified that Medved would kill the man I loved.

"Yes." I opted for a simple reply.

The one word answer didn't satisfy Adam. He pushed my collar aside, exposing the still-pink bite mark. His eyes darkened with the threat of violence. "Creed said he didn't force you to mate, that you were willing. Is that true?"

"It's one hundred percent true." I pulled back, laid both hands on his chest, and lifted my face to meet his eyes, willing him to see the sincerity in mine. "Listen to me. I know it happened fast and that under the circumstances, it sounds crazy, but the mating is genuine. It's not Stockholm syndrome or anything else you might be telling yourself. Viggo is a good man doing his best in an absolutely shitty, no-win situation." I hesitated for a few seconds, then the truth fell out of my mouth. "I love him, Adam, and I couldn't stand to lose him."

A myriad of conflicting emotions danced across Adam's face. Surprise. Dismay. A grudging acceptance of reality. And finally, resolve. "All right." Nodding, he squeezed my shoulders. "Creed can come with us. I'll offer him sanctuary, too."

Viggo appeared by my side, holding hands with a now-dressed Hallie. "I appreciate the offer, Landry, but I gotta stay behind."

Hallie tugged on his hand. "I want you to come with us, Daddy."

He dropped into a squat, tucked a strand of strawberry-blond hair behind her ear, then tapped the tip of her nose. "I've got some things to take care of, but as soon as I'm finished, I'll come find you."

"You promise?" Hallie's lower lip trembled.

Viggo hesitated. "There's nothing I want more than to be with you and Uncle Owen and Liv. I promise to do my very best to make it happen."

"Okay." Taking him at his word, she threw her arms around his neck.

The answer that satisfied Hallie left Adam confused. Glancing at me, he cocked a quizzical brow. I gave a slight shake of my head. My lips shaped the word *later*. I couldn't explain Viggo's decision in front of Hallie. The very last thing he'd want would be to frighten his little girl with knowledge of the kill chip.

Inhaling a slow breath, Viggo stood and extended a hand to Adam. "Thank you for offering shelter to my family."

Adam inclined his head. "Your invitation stands. When you finish your… uh… business, you're welcome to join them."

Viggo glanced at the ground, clearly struggling to maintain his composure. I pressed a hand against his lower back, offering my mate the comfort of touch. He swallowed then lifted his head, once again in control of himself. "You'll need to move fast, before Medved figures out that Hallie and Owen are gone."

"We will. Straight to the airport, then home. We'll scan for the—" Adam hesitated, glancing at Hallie, probably wondering if she knew about the trackers Medved had implanted in their bodies. "For the *devices*, and our healers will take care of them."

"Good." Viggo adopted a businesslike tone. I felt him emotionally disconnecting from us all, putting on the stiff upper lip that would allow him to say goodbye to his family and move forward alone to meet his fate.

Not going to happen.

"Owen has access to my bank accounts, so my brother and daughter won't be showing up empty-handed."

"You sure you can't come with us?" Adam asked.

"Yep." One clipped word. Viggo swung Hallie up into his arms and rubbed the tip of his nose across hers. "I love you with all my heart, sweet girl, and I always will."

She flung her arms around his neck and held on till he gently untangled her limbs and set her on the ground. Owen stepped forward. Viggo pulled him into a bear hug. The brothers clapped each other on the back in a wordless farewell. They broke apart. Owen reached for Hallie and tugged her to his side. Viggo turned to me, a man holding on to his equilibrium by a thread. His gaze swept over my body then lingered on my face, as if he were memorizing every line, every curve, as if he was certain he'd never see me again.

No.

Two quick steps brought me to his side. I laid my hands on his shoulders and felt the slight tremor in his muscles. I rose up on my tiptoes and spoke in his ear. "We're not done, Viggo Creed. Not by a long shot. We're going to get our happily ever after."

Strong hands cupped my face. "You've already given me a helluva lot more happiness than I expected or deserve. Never forget that."

His mouth descended on mine in a kiss that held equal parts tenderness, sorrow, and love. My big scary grizzly enforcer—my captor—loved me. Tears swam in my eyes and resolve filled my heart. Screw fatalism or any stoic acceptance of the inevitable. I'd be damned if I let him go to his death without a fight.

We broke apart. An unconvincing smile touched his lips as he glanced from me, to Owen, to Hallie. He straightened his shoulders and set his chin, his hard-ass mask firmly in place. "I gotta go."

He pivoted on his heel and strode away from us, leaving silence in his wake.

Time to take control of the situation. I glanced at Owen. "Could you and Hallie walk ahead of us for a few minutes, please?"

He understood instantly that I needed to talk to the wolves.

"No problem. Come on, peanut. I'll race you."

As soon as Hallie and Owen disappeared from sight, I turned to Adam.

"I'm not leaving Alaska without my mate."

CHAPTER TWENTY-EIGHT

VIGGO

B*lank. Go blank. Shut down your emotions and do the damned job.*

Not the first time I told myself that, but the first time when the stakes were so high.

Eyes fixed straight ahead, I marched through the snow. Every instinct shrieked at me to turn around and snatch one last look at Liv, and Hallie, and Owen, but I resisted. My battered heart couldn't take another hit.

I made my way to the truck, sparing only a quick glance at Jasper and Hank's bodies as I passed. Killing my fellow enforcers didn't trouble my conscience one bit. They'd always been jealous of my position and authority, but when they crossed the line from rivals to enemies—when they threatened my family—they'd sealed their fates. Their blood stained my hands and my clothes, but not my soul.

I glanced down at my pants. A shower and a fresh pair of jeans and shirt were called for before I ventured into grizzly headquarters and confronted Medved.

I drove straight to the house, parked my truck in the garage, and walked inside. Without my family's presence, it felt eerily empty. Familiar, but fundamentally altered, no longer home. I wandered into the kitchen and poured a mug of coffee, emptying the thermal carafe. It was still warm. My mind flashed back to the image of Liv leaning against the counter, wearing my robe, sipping the coffee she'd poured from the same carafe.

I drank down the java, rinsed the mug, and put it in the dishwasher. On my way to the shower, I stuck my head in Owen's messy bedroom and Hallie's tidy one. In each room, I sucked in a deep breath and immersed myself one more time in their familiar scents.

Be safe. Be well. Build a good life.

I shoved thoughts of my loved ones into the darkest recess of my mind.

Time to get on with it.

A quick shower scrubbed away all evidence of my bloody encounter with the Garveys. I threw on clean clothes and dry boots. After a final look around my bedroom, I walked down the hall and out the front door. I marched past the thorny, leafless Nootka rosebushes Rosalie had planted. At the reminder of Hallie's mother, my heart pinched. She deserved better than the hand fate had dealt her. We hadn't been in love, but I'd cared deeply about her and would always mourn her death.

If the afterlife exists, odds are good you'll be seeing her again very soon, a small voice in my head warned.

"No," I said out loud, rejecting the voice of doom and gloom and startling a neighbor I passed on the sidewalk. "Sorry." I raised a hand in apology. The elderly woman shot a sideways glance and shuffled away.

Five minutes later, I jogged up the steps to grizzly headquarters.

Evelyn looked up from her desk, a welcoming smile on her face. "How's your family?"

I almost jerked back, startled by the question, but stopped the reaction in the nick of time. Food poisoning. She was asking about their supposed food poisoning, not their escape.

"They'll live." My answer held an entirely different and far more satisfying meaning.

"I told Hank about the bad apple cider, and he offered to pick up some ginger ale and bring it to your house." She made a face. "Surprised the heck out of me. I didn't think you were friends."

The puzzle pieces slotted together. *That* was how the Garveys figured out something was up. After talking to Evelyn, a suspicious Hank had gone to my house and found it empty.

I forced out a laugh. "Friends? I wouldn't go that far, but even the Garveys like Owen and Hallie."

"We all like Owen and Hallie."

"Is the boss in?" I asked.

Her smile faltered. "Mr. Medved is in his thinking spot."

His thinking spot, a deceptively benign name for the alpha's favorite place.

"I'll head on down."

She handed me the keys. I unlocked the door to the basement. Standing on the top step, I closed the heavy door and twisted the deadbolt. Evelyn wouldn't worry that I didn't immediately return the keys. She'd give me the benefit of the doubt and assume that I'd absentmindedly stuck them in my pocket. Now nobody would get past the locked barrier and interfere.

I jogged down the steps then forced myself to slow down and stroll to Medved's "thinking spot." I leaned against the doorframe.

Medved sat on the former dentist's chair inside his torture chamber. One foot swung idly back and forth. His fingers tapped against the armrests, armrests where he'd installed straps for securing victims in place. Only Medved would find such a spot conducive to deep thinking.

"Hey, boss."

Medved grunted a greeting.

Stepping inside, I nonchalantly closed the door behind me. It didn't have a lock—nobody would dare interrupt Medved when he was "playing"—but with the door closed, not a peep could be heard from inside the soundproof room.

"I sent the Garveys to search the caves northwest of town," I lied, hoping to hell the alpha was too preoccupied to attempt to hone in on my scent.

"The search is taking too long." He reached into his pocket, extracted the key fob, and swung it back and forth. It glinted in the bright overhead light.

He'd brought the remote activator with him.

Excitement blasted through me, an elation I did my best to suppress. I'd been half-afraid he'd left it in his desk. In that case, even if I killed him, I'd have to get to his office and grab the fob before I fled town with every nearby grizzly on my tail.

Sigh.

"Yes, sir." I kept my voice level. "It's taking way too long. Guess the wolves are better at hiding than we thought."

"Or they have allies," he suggested blandly.

The skin on the back of my neck prickled, but I managed a derisive snort. I forced my gaze away from the swinging key fob. "Who? None of the local shifter packs would dare make a move against you, sir."

"Probably not. But maybe we have a traitor in our midst, you know, a fox in the hen house."

The accusation hit far too close to home. An awful suspicion took root. Had the Garveys spoken to Medved before they came after me?

I lounged against the closed door, my posture deliberately relaxed. Thanks to the black rock strapped to my wrist, I could shift lightning fast. But in the handful of seconds it took to complete the transformation, I'd be as helpless as a baby, giving Medved more than enough time to activate the kill chip.

Shifting was out.

My best bet? The element of surprise.

Making sure my expressionless face telegraphed none of my intent, I sprang at him. I knocked the fob out of his hand and reached for the bastard's throat.

"Stop." As my fingers touched his neck, he choked out a single word, a command imbued with the age-old authority of an alpha.

His power washed over me. For a fraction of a second, deeply ingrained instincts—the compulsion to obey my alpha—trounced my intent. I froze, fighting the urge to drop to my knees and bare my throat.

By the time I shook off the stupor, it was too late. Medved's fist slammed into my temple. I stumbled backward, seeing stars. He struck again, a blow to the exact same spot. I blinked and shook my head from side to side, trying to clear my vision. I was only barely aware of him seizing my arm and hauling my body across the room.

Clank.

The cold bite of metal touching my skin shocked my senses. I tugged against the restraint. Too late. He'd already locked my right wrist into one of the shackles that hung from the ceiling. I stood on bloodstained cement in the exact spot where Medved tortured his victims.

Damn it all to hell.

I yanked with all my might on the metal cuff. The shackles designed to withstand the strength of shifters didn't give.

"Hold out your left arm so I can put on the other cuff." Authority filled Medved's voice. He licked his lips, his eyes bright with happy anticipation. "I've never played with someone as strong as you."

Fuck. He wanted to *play*.

Alpha power rolled over me once again. Summoning every ounce of determination I possessed, I pushed back against the impulse to obey.

"No."

"No?" Medved marveled. "Really? You said no? Well, hell. I always suspected your smidge of alpha blood might assert itself someday."

My head jerked back. "*My* alpha blood?"

"Yep. From your mama's side, six or seven generations back. Before the Medveds took over the pack. Another reason why I put the chip in your head. Added insurance in case you get any ideas about challenging me."

Why hadn't my parents told me we had an alpha ancestor? I'd never know the answer for sure, but maybe they intended to tell me once I came of age. Since they died when I was still a teenager, could be they never got the chance to reveal the family secret.

Regardless, Medved knew.

"Why didn't you just kill me?" I asked.

He tapped a finger against his head. "I'm too smart to waste a valuable resource. No need to kill you when I have other ways to keep you in line." His smile chilled my blood. "Where were we? Ah, yes. You're gonna hold out your left arm so I can put on the other cuff."

I was so fucking tired of dealing with this asshole. "No."

He crossed the room and picked up the key fob. "Let's see how long your disobedience lasts when I do this."

Level two pain blasted through my head. I convulsed and the world sheeted white. Thirty seconds later, the pain disappeared as quickly as it had come. I slumped forward, retching. Blood dripped from my nose and ears. Saliva pooled in my mouth.

"Where are the Garveys?" Medved asked mildly.

I shook my head from side to side, clearing my vision. "Told you. Searching the caves northwest of town."

"Liar."

Agony exploded once again then abruptly cut off, leaving me gasping for air.

"You think they didn't tell me your family is missing?" he asked. "You think I didn't put two and two together? Figure out you're helping the damned wolves?"

I wiped my expression clean, lifted my chin, and met my alpha's eyes.

"I guess the real question is, where's your family right now?" he continued. "Your mate, your brother, that sweet little girl of yours?"

Safe. I almost said the word—surely Landry had whisked them away by now—but I stopped myself. I'd give the fucker absolutely nothing.

"I can track Owen and Hallie down, remember?"

At the threat, panic reared its head.

Pull yourself together.

Medved had no clue the wolves had allied with our lynx neighbors. The cats would help the wolves smuggle my family to safety. And Landry had promised that his healers would remove the trackers. My family *would* be safe.

"You've always been a piss-poor excuse for an alpha," I said conversationally.

Pain—not unexpected—staggered me. It cut off as quickly as it started. I lifted my head and pulled my lips into a contemptuous smile.

Medved's eyes sparkled with malice. "And you've always done a piss-poor job of protecting your own."

What the hell did that mean?

He tilted his head. "You didn't really buy the story that Rosalie slipped and fell off a cliff, did you?"

Every muscle in my body tensed. "What did you say?"

"You knocked up that pretty little thing, then your bear refused to mate her." He made a *tsk-tsk* sound. "You left her vulnerable, son. You know the law. You know I was within my rights when I followed her up that hiking trail."

I couldn't breathe. Horror carved out a hole in my chest.

"Rosalie," I whispered.

"I always liked redheads," he continued. "The little spitfire put up a fight. I lost my temper and threw her over the side."

I saw it. In my mind's eye I saw Rosalie fight back against a brute who overpowered her in size and strength, but was no match for her spirit.

Medved was right about one thing. My failure to protect her cost a good woman her life, cost Hallie her mother.

He hit the button again. Pain nearly split my skull in two. My vision wavered. I retched. Darkness reached out its arms and pulled me under.

Chapter Twenty-Nine

Remy

I wrinkled my nose. "You smell like pussy."

The alpha of the Black Rock Guardians swiveled his head and tossed a reproachful look my way. "That was the whole idea, wasn't it? To throw the bears off our scent?"

I tugged at the collar of the too-tight black shirt I'd borrowed from a lynx soldier, a shirt the man had dug out of his laundry pile, complete with a mustard stain on the sleeve and God-knows-what dribbled down the front. "I'm not complaining. I smell like pussy, too."

Adam lifted his head above the fallen log and peeked at the back of the grizzly headquarters building. "You need a woman to keep you in line, cousin."

I studied the screen on the mounted-to-controls phone that displayed the camera feed from the drone. "Like Marit keeps you in line?"

Adam grinned. "Exactly."

"Nobody in sight." I touched the knife and pistol in the holster strapped to my thigh then tapped the pocket holding Grandpa's hastily sketched map of the building's interior. We were good to go, assuming the inside of the building hadn't changed since Grandpa last saw it seventy-some years ago.

Adam and I dashed across the open ground between the woods and the back of the two-story building. We crept along the foundation till we came to a rectangular cast-iron door emblazoned with the words Majestic Coal Chute.

"Shit," I hissed. "This thing's gotta be a hundred years old, probably rusted shut."

"One way to find out." Adam grabbed the handle and tugged. It resisted at first. Adam braced a foot against the brick foundation and put more muscle into the endeavor. I winced as the chute slowly creaked open. Anybody nearby in basement would hear the sound.

This rescue operation was fraught with danger and uncertainty. I still had a hard time wrapping my head around the notion of risking our lives to save the grizzly enforcer who'd kidnapped Liv, but she flat-out refused to flee without him.

A few seconds after Owen and Hallie had walked away, Liv had planted her feet in the middle of the forest clearing and crossed her arms over her chest, the picture of stubborn determination. "I'm not leaving Alaska without my mate."

Zane had shoved a hand through his hair, clearly exasperated. "You heard what Creed said. He's got something to take care of, then he'll follow us to Washington."

Zane was nowhere near ready to let the grizzly off the hook for kidnapping Liv and frightening Annika. When it came to causing his mate pain, my brother was an unforgiving son of a bitch. If Creed didn't manage to escape, I doubt if Zane would lose any sleep.

Liv had turned to Adam. "Medved had a chip implanted in Viggo's head. When he pushes a button on a remote control key fob, it causes debilitating pain. The highest setting would blow apart his skull."

I'd rocked back on my heels. Threatening his family. A fucking kill chip. No wonder Creed toed the line.

"He's going to confront his alpha?" Adam asked.

Liv nodded. "To fight him and take the fob. It's the only way to stop Medved from activating the kill chip."

Adam laid a hand on her shoulder, pity filling his expression. "Sounds like a long shot, sweetheart."

I'd never seen Liv cry, but tears filled her eyes. "I can't lose my mate, and I can't save him by myself. Will you help me, please?"

"Oh, hell," Zane groaned. My brother might not like the grizzly enforcer, but Liv's pain cut him to the quick.

Adam scrubbed a hand over his chin, his expression thoughtful. "We'll have to move fast."

With absolutely no time to waste, the plan came together quickly.

Thomas led Hallie, Owen, and Bosco into lynx territory. From there, they'd borrow a car and immediately set off for the Fairbanks Airport where they'd buy three tickets on the next flight to Seattle.

True to her vow, Liv refused to accompany them to safety, and Grandpa refused to leave without her. Zane, Grandpa, and Liv would take refuge in the lynx alpha's cabin, surrounded by a dozen cat soldiers. Adam and I would sneak into the village and attempt to rescue Viggo, a plan that gave my brother fits.

"You're the alpha of the Black Rock Guardians, for fucks sake," Zane argued before we went our separate ways. "You can't risk being captured or killed by the grizzlies. Let me go instead."

"I'm going in." Adam slipped a pistol and a knife into the holster strapped to his thigh. "I'm trusting you to keep Grandpa and Liv safe. If we don't make it back, the pack is yours."

"Don't be stupid. I'm no alpha," Zane burst out. "Send me in."

Adam's chin jerked up and he locked eyes with his top lieutenant. "You've got your orders."

The alpha voice worked its magic. Zane grumbled but shut up.

As soon as Adam decided that we'd go after Creed, I sent three drones over the town trying to locate him. One followed his truck to his house. Twenty minutes later, a camera captured him walking into grizzly headquarters.

The bug Zane planted in Medved's office was silent, the room presumably empty.

Where was Creed?

Grandpa drew a map of the building, then Zane reluctantly escorted Grandpa and Liv to the cabin on lynx land. And now Adam and I were crawling through a damned coal chute into the basement of grizzly headquarters.

What could go wrong, short of everything?

We landed on the floor of a storage room. No grizzlies in sight. To our right—just like Grandpa's sketch showed—I spied the steps leading upstairs. To our left, stretched a long corridor lined with small rooms. I snuck to the top of the stairs and put my ear to the door. No sound penetrated the metal. I tried the knob and found it locked.

Great. We were stuck in the basement. After searching the place, we'd have to climb out the coal chute and break into the building via the old fire escape on the second floor.

As an alpha, Adam's senses were more acute than mine. Cocking his head to one side, he listened for any signs of grizzly presence.

"Nothing," he mouthed.

We edged along the corridor, peering into each open doorway. Halfway down the hall, we came across our second closed door. Adam pressed his ear to the surface and frowned, sensing something inside. He drew his pistol and I followed suit. Opening the door, he swept high and I went low.

Maxim Medved—the grizzly alpha himself—whirled around to face us. My stunned eyes took in a scene straight out of a nightmare, a torture chamber filled with the tools of the trade. A dentist's chair with freaking straps to hold down victims sat to one side of the room. A table covered with hammers and saws. Behind Medved, Viggo Creed dangled from shackles suspended from the ceiling. Blood stained the floor at his feet, and its coppery taint polluted the air. The enforcer's body hung limp and still, blood dripping from his nose and ears.

Fuck. Were we too late? Was Liv's mate dead?

Alpha power times two charged the atmosphere in the small, enclosed space.

"Landry," Medved growled, a hectic light in his eyes. He touched the black rock he wore on his throat and started to shift. His clothes split apart. In grizzly form, even two against one, he'd be hard to beat. A simple, undeniable fact of nature. Grizzly shifters were bigger and stronger than wolves. Not necessarily smarter, though.

In the background, Creed groaned, regaining consciousness.

I pointed my pistol at the center of the glittering mass. Shooting a shifter midchange violated every precept of honorable behavior, but hell, my alpha's life was at risk, and that trumped everything else.

"No." Adam grabbed my wrist. "We can't kill him. You want every bear in town on our asses?"

Dammit. He was right. Medved's death would sever the connection between him and his pack, sending out a ripple effect that would alert them all to his passing. We couldn't kill him without bringing every nearby grizzly down on our heads.

If we couldn't kill him, how could we stop him?

"Should we shift?" I asked quickly. We had seconds to make a plan. Whether in human or wolf form, I didn't like our odds against a rampaging bear.

"I will." Adam touched his alpha stone, shuddering as power slammed into him. He tore off his clothes. "I'll keep Medved busy while you and Creed escape."

Abandon my cousin to fight a grizzly by himself? Adam could singlehandedly take on almost any shifter—wolf, cougar, coyote—but not a beast twice his size.

"What? No."

"You heard me." The command in Adam's voice almost drove me to my knees.

He sucked in air and lost the ability to speak as the shift consumed him.

I wavered, torn between the compulsion to obey my alpha and my reluctance to leave my cousin to his fate. The pack needed Adam, and I couldn't imagine returning home and telling Marit that Medved had killed her mate.

Creed groaned again, lifted his head, and squinted at us.

Now a bear, Medved reared up on his hind legs and snapped his teeth at Adam, who'd almost finished his shift.

I took a step back and raised my pistol. Some people said grizzlies were bulletproof, that it was almost impossible to get off a kill shot. Not true, but it was hella difficult to stop him in his tracks. He'd likely tear into the shooter before the injury took him down. We didn't want him dead, anyway. But maybe I could wound him. Slow him down. Give Adam the advantage. Disobeying my alpha cost me. My body rebelled; my hand shook violently as I took aim at the bear.

The shot went wide, dammit.

The bear turned his head toward me, pure malevolence gleaming in his eyes.

Creed swung both legs in the air and locked them around the grizzly's neck. "Get out of here."

Adam's wolf launched himself at the enemy, sinking his canines deep into the bear's leg.

No way was I turning tail now.

Creed's powerful thighs choked out the grizzly alpha, and Adam's fangs tore into his right leg. I edged closer to the beast then jumped back when he slashed at me with his giant paw.

Maybe I couldn't kill Medved, but no reason I couldn't hurt him.

"Fuck this." Raising the pistol again, I shot twice into Medved's left leg.

The bear's blood dripped onto the cement, joining that of Creed and countless other victims. Pain and shock from the triple assault—the lack of oxygen—finally stilled Medved's struggles. Adam's wolf fell back, his sides heaving. Creed loosened his grip on the bear's neck. Medved dropped to the floor. At losing consciousness, he reverted to his human form.

I kicked him in the head. "Gotta make sure he stays down."

While Adam shifted back to human and threw on his clothes, I unshackled Creed, who wobbled but kept his feet.

"My family?"

I slid a shoulder under his arm to steady him. "Owen and Hallie are on their way to the Fairbanks Airport. Liv's waiting for you in lynx territory."

Creed's brow furrowed and he swung startled eyes toward Adam. "You didn't make her go with them?"

Adam snorted and clapped a hand on the enforcer's shoulder. "Have you met Liv? Good luck making that woman do anything she doesn't want to do."

"Yep," I agreed. "You're gonna have your hands full, buddy."

Creed flashed a grin. "Can't wait."

Adam stretched, cracking his back. "Help me string up Medved."

We hoisted up the unconscious grizzly alpha and secured his wrists with the shackles.

"The room's soundproof. He can shout his fool head off when he comes to, but nobody will hear him." Creed shoved at Medved's chest, making his big body spin. "Wish I could gut him."

"Not now." My voice was firm. "Not when my alpha is surrounded by our pack's oldest enemies. Not when Medved's death would make them all come running. You owe Adam a clean escape."

"You're right," Creed said. "I'm grateful to you both. I owe your alpha everything. Doesn't mean I can't come back someday and settle the score."

"Or maybe challenge Medved and take over the pack yourself," Adam suggested. "It's something to consider."

"That's a subject for another time," I interrupted, ready to be gone. "Now we gotta haul ass." I bent over and picked up a key fob that had fallen out of Medved's pocket when his clothes ripped apart during his shift. I shot a glance to Creed. "This is it?"

Creed touched the back of his neck. "Yeah, that's it."

I turned the fob over in my hand, studying it. "I'll deactivate the device. When we get to the lodge, our healers can cut the chip out of your head."

Creed's expression went blank as he took in everything that had happened. "After all these years, after everything I've done in service to that bastard, it's over."

"And now it's time to build a new life with your mate and the Black Rock Guardians," Adam said. He opened the door and peered into the corridor. "Coast is clear. Let's go."

Chapter Thirty

Liv

"If you keep pacing like that, you're gonna wear a rut into the floor," Zane warned.

Zane was no more patient than I was, but instead of marching back and forth across the lynx alpha's front room, he stood in front of the fireplace, arms crossed over his chest and glowering at the universe.

Grandpa Matthew patted the seat next to him on the lynx alpha's corduroy sofa. "Sit with me, Liv."

It was a request rather than an order, but antsy or not, I couldn't refuse.

Dropping down next to the former alpha, I took his hand. I'd been so preoccupied worrying about Viggo that I hadn't given a thought to how Grandpa was handling the trip to his former pack land. It had to stir up a lot of mixed emotions.

"How are you doing, Grandpa?"

His lips curved in a small smile. "I never expected to see my old home again. Everywhere I look, memories haunt me. Of happy times. Of my parents and friends. Of the Great War." He squeezed my fingers. "It's bittersweet, but I'm fine and more than ready to go home."

"This waiting is killing me," I said.

He patted my hand. "You know, if anything happened to either Adam or Remy, I'd sense it."

I leapt at that reassurance. If Adam and Remy were okay, maybe the rescue mission was on track. "That's good."

"Creed is your mate. If he were gone, you should be able to sense it, too."

"How?"

"Here." He touched the still-healing mating bite on my shoulder then pointed at my heart. "And there. Sit quietly, center your thoughts, and open yourself to the connection you share with your mate."

Open myself up to a mystical connection? A year ago, I would have laughed my ass off at such a notion, but I'd learned since then that reality was more miraculous, more full of wonders than I ever expected.

I slumped against the cushions and closed my eyes.

Where are you, Viggo?

Holding my breath, I shoved aside my rational assumptions about how the universe functioned and opened my mind.

Viggo.

At first, I sensed nothing. No reassuring voice in my head. No zap along an invisible mating bond. Only when my fingers drifted to my shoulder and scratched idly over the welt did I realize that my claiming bite tingled.

Viggo?

I felt the thumping of a heartbeat, heard the *whosh-whosh* of blood rushing through veins. Not mine, but my mate's.

My eyes flew open. I turned to Grandpa. "I feel his heart beating."

He smiled. "Well, now. I'd call that a very promising sign."

The sat phone in Zane's pocket rang. "Yeah?" he answered.

I jumped up and rushed to his side. "What is it?"

He held up a hand, silencing my questions, then nodded. "We'll rendezvous in fifteen."

Grandpa stood. "Son?"

"Adam and Remy got Creed and the key fob. They left Medved trussed up in the basement of grizzly HQ."

I clutched Zane's arm, giddy with relief.

"Where are we meeting them?" I asked.

"At the airstrip. Creed wants to fly out in one of the bush planes. If we hurry, we should get away before Medved is discovered and alerts the pack."

After a quick goodbye and thank you to the lynx alpha, we hitched a ride with one of his soldiers, who deposited us on the side of the road a quarter mile from the airstrip. We cut through the woods on the back side of the facility. Hiding behind trees, we scanned the small airport for any signs of activity. The place appeared empty.

Two minutes later, Viggo, Adam, and Remy jogged into view. I sprinted toward my man, biting back a shriek of joy. His long strides closed the distance between us. I jumped at him and wrapped my legs around his waist. Strong arms enfolded me. He buried his face in the crook of my neck, breathing in my scent.

After a few seconds, I reared back and gave him the once-over. His eyes were red, crisscrossed with burst capillaries. Blood had trickled from his ears and dried on his skin.

"He hurt you." I moaned, patting his cheeks.

"Nah." He shook his head. "I'm fine, darlin', thanks to your alpha and Remy."

"Viggo," Adam interrupted. "Time to get gone."

"Yeah." A quick kiss, then he gently deposited me on my feet.

Adam, Zane, and Remy kept watch while Viggo prepped the pack's second Beaver for takeoff. Once ready, we climbed aboard.

Grandpa Matthew sat in the co-pilot's seat to the right of Viggo. As the plane taxied toward the runway, he laid a reverent hand on the dashboard instrument panel. "Never thought I'd see the old girl again."

"The universe set things right," Remy called from the rear of the plane. "The Beaver was ours first, and now she's ours again."

We flew to the Fairbanks Airport. Owen, Hallie, and Thomas had a head start on us, but since they were traveling by car, they arrived after we touched down. The excitement and stress finally got to the little girl. Hallie flung herself on her father and tearfully refused to leave his sight. Viggo had planned to put Hallie on a commercial flight to Seattle then to fly the Beaver to Washington state. Instead, he put in a call to a pilot buddy—a moose shifter—who agreed to stow the plane in his private hangar and to fly it to Seattle himself at a later date.

We were in a hurry to get out of the state and far away from Medved's reach, but we stopped to buy a TSA-approved crate for Bosco. Nine of us—well, ten if you count the dog—caught an evening flight to Seattle. We'd phoned ahead. Annika, Marit, and Xander drove two vans to Seattle to pick us up. We'd caravan to Belle Reve.

I was both tired and elated when I walked hand-in-hand with Viggo into the baggage claim area at SeaTac. As soon as my gaze fell on my sister and cousins, fatigue fled. Xander rushed forward to greet Grandpa and Remy. I bolted toward Annika and Marit. Viggo would've held back and allowed me a private reunion with them, but I clung to his hand and pulled him forward.

Throwing ourselves on each other, we jumped up and down in an emotional three-way hug. We broke apart and they stared at the big, scary grizzly enforcer who'd kidnapped me, both at a loss for words.

I tackled their hesitation head-on. "Annika, Marit, meet Viggo Creed, my mate, and the man I love."

Their eyes widened and they exchanged a glance. Who could blame them for their confusion? In a short period of time, he'd gone from enemy bogeyman to family.

"Glad to meet you," he said, without offering to shake hands.

Adam walked over and slid an arm around Marit. "I missed you, kitten."

Zane swept Annika into his arms. Happy tears filled her eyes. "Thank God you're home safe," she said.

An awkward silence. Looking around, I spied Owen in conversation with Xander and Remy. I waved to Hallie, who skipped over to join us. She smiled broadly and extended her hand to Marit, then Annika, demonstrating the same good manners she'd shown when we first met.

"I'm Hallie Rosalie Creed. It's nice to meet you."

Marit and Annika relaxed in the presence of the charming little girl and introduced themselves.

Hallie slipped her hand into mine. "Liv is my daddy's mate. If she's my new mama, does that mean you're my aunts?"

Viggo and I both stiffened.

Viggo and I were endgame. I had no doubt we'd stay together forever. I already loved his daughter and brother, but with everything that had happened since our mating, we hadn't discussed my role as Hallie's stepmother. Yet another thing we did backassward. I didn't want to step on anybody's toes or Rosalie's memory. I didn't expect Hallie to call me her mother, but now that she had, my insides went all gooey. Me, the Hagen woman least smitten with the idea of babies and motherhood, going misty-eyed because a little girl called me mama.

I wanted more than anything to do right by this child.

At the prospect of being an aunt, Annika melted. She dropped to her knees and held out her arms. "I'd love to be your Auntie Annika, sweetheart."

She elbowed her mate's leg.

He cleared his throat. "And you can call me Uncle Zane."

Hallie looked expectantly at the alpha and his mate.

"Auntie Marit." Marit pointed at herself then at Adam. "And Uncle Adam."

Marit was my cousin, not my sister, so technically she wasn't Hallie's aunt, but why get hung up on technicalities? I called Matthew Grandpa and we didn't share a drop of blood. Family was family.

Hallie hugged Marit then turned to Adam. "Are you really the alpha?"

He crouched down so they were eye to eye. "I am."

"But you're nice." She looked confused. "Our alpha back home is mean. All the kids are afraid of him."

Viggo placed a hand on his daughter's shoulder. "A good alpha—like your Uncle Adam—protects the children in his pack."

Hallie studied Adam, her expression serious. "You promise?"

He sketched an X on his chest. "Cross my heart. I'll never hurt or scare you, I promise."

His vow satisfied Hallie, who gave a little hop. "Are there other kids in the pack?"

"Lots," Marit said. "There are two little girls—Emma and Tory—who are especially eager to meet you."

"I'm going to go tell Bosco we have three uncles and two aunties now," Hallie cried.

"Four, not three," I corrected her with a laugh. "Don't forget your Uncle Zane's brother, Remy."

Hallie blinked. "Wow. Four uncles. Does Uncle Remy have a mate?"

"Not yet," I answered.

Hallie ran over to Owen, who stood next to Bosco's crate.

"Cute kid," Zane said. "You think she'd like me to build her a pint-sized rocking chair for her new room?"

Beside me, Viggo relaxed, as if it finally sank in that the nightmare was over and that the Creeds would be okay. "I'm sure she'd love a rocking chair, especially one her *Uncle Zane* made for her," he said.

Viggo and Zane exchanged measured looks. They'd come a long way. Zane no longer despised Viggo, or shot homicidal scowls his way, but I suspected it would be a while before they developed anything close to brotherly feelings.

That was all right. They had time. We all had time. To get to know each other. To build meaningful relationships. To cement the bonds of family.

Gratitude brought fresh tears to my eyes.

Marit's brows pulled together, as if she wondered who I was and what had happened to her snarky, unsentimental cousin.

Annika beamed at me and took my arm. "I want you to sit next to me on the ride home and tell me all about Viggo."

I smiled at my sister. "I can't wait."

Chapter Thirty-One

Viggo

By nature, grizzlies were solitary and territorial creatures. We shared close family bonds, but we valued our space and privacy. We weren't pack animals. Communal living—sharing a lodge with more than a hundred wolves—took some getting used to.

Marit assigned us family quarters on the third floor of the lodge. The wolves had knocked out a wall between two old guest suites, creating a three-bedroom space, with two bathrooms and a kitchenette. We ate most of our meals in the communal dining hall, but it was good to have the option to eat a quiet dinner in our quarters.

Remy used one of his high-tech gizmos to locate the trackers in Hallie and Owen's bodies. Adam's parents—Leigh and Jason Landry—removed them. The healers took the kill chip out of my head. When I told them that my brother was by nature a healer, they took him on as a trainee. He and Remy and Xander became fast friends. I've never seen Owen happier.

Hallie, too, was happy as a clam. She quickly made friends with Emma, Tory, and the other kids. The only rough moment came the first time she walked into the pack's party room and laid eyes on the giant taxidermied grizzly that stood in the middle of the space.

The humans who built the rustic lodge in the 1920s had placed the stuffed and mounted bear next to the reception desk in the lobby. When the wolves purchased the place, they named him Igor and moved him to their party room. They decked him out for every celebration. When Hallie saw him, the teenagers had put a party hat on his head and stuck a noisemaker in his mouth.

"He's dead." She'd shrieked in horror and burst into tears.

Adam ordered Igor put into storage.

After that small setback, Hallie settled in nicely. She loved her new friends, her aunts and uncles, her cousin Xander, and her Grandpa Matthew.

And she loved Liv with her whole heart. Watching them bond warmed all the dark, cold places in my soul. They read stories together and went for long rambles in the woods. Liv taught her how to pipe frosting on fancy cupcakes. We bought a new telescope to replace the one left behind in Alaska. On clear evenings, Liv and Hallie would set up the telescope and study the night sky. Sometimes they'd sit together on the lodge's stone patio, wrapped in thick quilts and watching for shooting stars.

"Make a wish before it disappears," I heard Liv tell Hallie when they spotted a meteor streaking across the heavens.

Hallie had hesitated. "But all my wishes have already come true."

Sometimes I had to pinch myself, unable to believe that a brute like me deserved such a happy ending.

I wasn't the only one. Wolves gossiped as much as bears. When word of my history with Medved made the rounds, most of them decided to cut me some slack. Most, but not all. Those with long memories—those who suffered at the hands of my old pack—still had reservations about a former grizzly enforcer in their midst.

Couldn't blame them. I watched my manners, kept my head down, and did my job. Inactivity made me restless and agitated. Adam assigned me to run patrols with his soldiers, a task I gladly took on. No doubt Medved was spitting nails, determined to wreak vengeance on me and the wolves. Lance Vilhauer and his coyotes still posed a threat, too.

A few hours before dawn in early December, I returned to the lodge after a night spent patrolling the woods. I stopped off in the communal dining hall to grab a banana, and spied a solitary figure sitting at a table next to a window overlooking the lake.

Matthew Strauss raised a hand and waved me over. "Have a seat."

Taking a chair opposite him, I glanced at the wall clock. 4:32 a.m. "What are you doing up in the middle of the night?"

He smiled and the wrinkles around his eyes deepened. "Story of my life. Woke up. Had to take a piss. Couldn't get back to sleep. Came down to the kitchen to brew a cup of chamomile tea."

I pointed at his tea and tried to keep the skepticism out of my voice. "You like the stuff?"

"No. My daughters say chamomile is good for me, so I drink it, but I prefer black coffee or a single-malt scotch."

Had to agree with him on both counts. "I'm a scotch man, myself." I sighed, thinking of the bottle of Knockando I left behind in Alaska. I should have the liquor store in Belle Reve order a couple of bottles for me and invite the old man over to give my favorite whisky a try.

"You missing your home?" he guessed.

"No, sir." I shook my head. "As long as I'm with Liv, Hallie, and Owen, I'm home. And I'm grateful for everything the Black Rock Guardians have done for us."

"Still, it must be hard to uproot your life and start fresh someplace new."

The eagle-eyed former alpha sensed that something was troubling me, had been troubling me since my last encounter with Medved in the basement of grizzly HQ.

I opened my mouth to reply, but the words stuck in my throat.

"What is it, son? What's upsetting you? Are folks here making you feel unwelcome?"

Out of habit, my hand traveled to the back of my neck. I rubbed the spot above where the kill chip used to reside.

I couldn't let him think that his packmates were giving me grief. "No, sir. Folks have been fine."

"Then what's bothering you?" he asked gently.

Damn. The sharp old man saw right through my denials. I squirmed, feeling about five years old.

He waited patiently for me to answer.

Clearly my suck-it-up-and-deal policy wasn't working. I'd caught Liv watching me a couple of times with a concerned frown on her face, but she was the very last person I wanted to talk to about this. I know… I know. You're not supposed to keep secrets from your mate, but this wasn't something I could share with the woman I loved. At least not till I worked it out in my own mind.

Fuck it.

"Last time I spoke with Medved, he told me something that knocked me for a loop."

"Yes?" Strauss took a sip of tea, made a face, and put the cup down.

"About Hallie's mother, Rosalie. She died when Hallie was just three months old. All these years, I thought it was an accident, that she slipped and fell off a cliff when she was hiking…" I paused, a knot forming in my stomach.

"What really happened to her?"

My voice choking with rage and regret, I told him everything Medved had said.

"I cared about her. We were friends, but I wasn't in love with her. My bear refused to accept her as his mate. Like Medved said, I failed her. I left her vulnerable. If I'd figured out a way to make my bear accept her, she'd be alive today."

"And you never would have found your true mate," he said.

"And that makes it all right?" I burst out. "Rosalie died, but it's okay because I found true love?"

"You're happy and guilt is eating you up?"

I nodded in silent agreement.

Strauss blew out a long breath. "As an alpha, I can promise you that there's nothing you could have done to make your animal accept the mating. *Nothing*. You can't beg, browbeat, or bribe your shadow brother into taking a mate he doesn't want. A shifter can build a good life with someone without a mating, but it will always be something… less."

He frowned and a cloud passed over his face.

"Rosalie deserved to be mated to a man who loved her. I took that away from her."

"Maybe, but what about Hallie? If you hadn't had a relationship with Rosalie, Hallie would never have been born. Would you choose that?"

Dismay smacked me upside the head. I bit down on my jaw so hard I thought my teeth might crack.

"It's a real damned-if-you-do-damned-if-you-don't situation," Strauss continued. "It wasn't your fault Medved killed Rosalie. The outcome can't be changed. He's the villain here. He took an innocent woman's life. Don't let regret poison your soul. Don't let it tarnish the joy you've found with Hallie and Liv."

Groaning, I scrubbed my hands over my face. What would it have been like to grow up in a pack led by an alpha with as much compassion and wisdom as Matthew Strauss or Adam Landry?

"Damn Medveds," I muttered. "The grizzlies deserve better."

"They do," Strauss agreed. He took another small sip of his herbal tea, frowned, and pushed the cup away. "Someday you might want to do something about that."

"Maybe." Since Adam suggested it, the idea had been percolating in my brain. In my last encounter with Medved, a single barked "stop" shut me down long enough for him to gain the advantage. If I were ever to best him in a battle, I'd need to learn how to overcome his alpha power and tap into my own. Even before Medved taunted me with the knowledge, I'd long suspected that I possessed alpha blood. I felt it stir within me, an incipient power, not yet fully formed.

Maybe Adam could help me tap into it, hone it into a weapon I could use against Medved.

"In the meantime, would you have any interest in becoming one of Adam's lieutenants?"

"What?" My shocked gaze snapped to Strauss's face.

The old man looked entirely serious. "Adam and I have talked about it. We both see a lot of potential in you. You possess the skills, knowledge, and experience necessary for the job. You're a good fit. We trust you." He lifted both shoulders. "So, tell me. If Adam offered, would you be willing to become a sentry for the Black Rock Guardians?"

"Uh…" It had never occurred to me that Adam might consider me—a former enemy, a grizzly enforcer—for a position with so much authority within the wolf pack. The rank and status would make me an insider. I'd join Adam, Zane, Remy, and the other sentries when they sat around the table in wolf headquarters and planned strategy against their enemies. I'd work with them to enhance security. The more I thought about it, the more I liked the prospect. "Hell, yeah, I'd be interested."

Strauss raised his palms, cautioning me against my excitement. "This isn't an offer. Not yet. But Adam asked me to sound you out and see if you'd entertain the possibility."

"I would," I said firmly.

"Good. Good." He gave a jaw-cracking yawn. "A couple more hours of sleep will do me good. I'm going to head to bed. Good night."

"Good night," I echoed. "And thanks for the pep talk. I appreciate it."

With a wave, he shuffled out of the dining hall. A minute later, I heard the *ding* of the elevator door opening. Deep in thought, I ate the banana then headed upstairs myself. I slipped into our dark and quiet family quarters.

Bosco nudged open the door to Hallie's bedroom and trotted over to greet me. Even the dog had handled the move well. Bosco and Loki—Marit and Adam's mutt—often played and chased each other on the rocky shores of Shooting Star Lake. Everybody in the pack stopped to pet him and say hello when he walked by.

"Good boy." After a final pat, I made my way to the bathroom for a quick shower.

Liv was a sound sleeper, so I didn't expect to find her awake when I padded across our bedroom and dropped the towel wrapped around my waist to the floor. I crawled between the sheets, careful not to jostle the mattress.

"Hey." A sleepy feminine voice told me my caution was for naught.

"Didn't mean to wake you."

"I like it when you wake me." She cuddled against my side, threw a leg over my thigh, and splayed her hand across my chest. "Any trouble during the patrol?"

"Nope. Quiet night."

I considered, then rejected, telling her about the potential job offer. She'd be thrilled and she'd want to talk about it. But right now, with her warm fingers sliding south over my abdomen, I had no interest in hijacking the woman's attention.

Don't let regret tarnish your joy.

A tall order, but I'd try.

"Good." She nuzzled my throat. "You smell nice." Her tongue darted out and she licked my collarbone. Her thumb brushed over my dick.

"You're playing with fire," I warned her.

In reply, she rolled on top of me and straddled my hips. The room was full dark, but with my bear's night vision, I saw my mate clear as day. Her hair mussed from sleep. A crease on her cheek from her pillow. Round, perfect breasts tipped with pink nipples.

"Aren't you *cocky*?" she marveled.

I arched my hips, grinning up at the woman who held my heart. "Well, yeah. Thought *cock* was the whole idea. But if you got other plans—"

She pressed her fingertips across my lips, silencing me. "How about you shut up and let me have my way with you."

I definitely liked that idea. Tucking my hands under my pillow, I gave her free rein over my body.

"I'm all yours, darlin'."

Chapter Thirty-Two

Liv

I opened the door to Grandma Freya's cabin, toed off my boots, and flipped on the overhead light, illuminating an interior that looked like something straight out of a Carl Larsson painting. Grandma had *loved* color. Whether in her small bungalow in Belle Reve or this cozy cabin on the shores of Shooting Star Lake, she splashed her favorite colors around with abandon. Sunset coral. Apple green. Cobalt blue.

My preference was for muted hues and simpler, less fussy lines, but I'd always have a soft spot for Grandma's eccentric, whimsical style.

"Whoa." Viggo lifted a brow, taking in the riot of colors and patterns.

"Grandma had a distinct sense of style, and she was a talented artist." I pointed at the painting hanging over the fireplace.

A large gray wolf stood on the lake shore, his eyes sparkling in the golden light of the setting sun. Behind him, a tall, dark-haired man lounged in the shadow of a tree, his features half obscured by the dappled light. I grew up with the painting but had never wondered about its significance. Only recently did I understand that it was a portrait of Grandma's lost love, the wolf shifter Aleksandr, in both his human and animal forms. The answer to the question of who fathered her twin sons had been here all the time, hidden in plain sight.

Viggo dropped our duffel on the floor and walked over to admire the painting.

Hallie and Bosco were at a sleepover with Emma and Tory. Owen had gone to a bowling alley in Belle Reve with Xander and Remy. Viggo and I had the night to ourselves. I'd decided it was the perfect opportunity to introduce him to Grandma's cabin and to give him a break from all the commotion in the lodge. We shared our home with a loud, gregarious pack of wolves. Viggo never complained, but sometimes I saw a look in his eye that told me he'd had enough of the hubbub.

He studied the painting then turned on his heel, his gaze sweeping over the place. "So this is the cabin that started the big dispute between the Hagen women and the Black Rock Guardians?"

"Yep, ownership of the cabin was a major source of contention between us and the pack. But it all worked out in the end."

"Fate knows what it's doing." He held out a hand and drew me to his side. "It's what brought Marit and Adam together. And Annika and Zane. And you and me."

Fate.

I couldn't deny the evidence of my own eyes, but my rational brain had a hard time accepting the notion of an otherworldly force that predetermines events.

"You *still* look skeptical." He unzipped my coat and tossed it onto the apple-green-and-white striped sofa. His strong fingers pushed my collar aside, exposing my mating bite. He traced a fingertip along the edges of the scar then lowered his head and lightly pressed his teeth over the mark. Instantly, goose bumps skittered across my arms and shoulders. My knees went weak and I clung to Viggo's waist for support. A groundswell of love surged through my veins. I shivered, feeling connected to Viggo in a way that defied sense.

"Viggo," I gasped.

His lips quirked. "Still not sure you believe in fated mates?"

I blinked, regaining my equilibrium. "If anything in the world could convince me, it's your teeth on my skin. It's practically an out of body experience."

He kissed me, his mouth staking a claim to me, body and soul.

I pulled away reluctantly. "I need to put the salad and dessert in the fridge." I nodded toward the basket of kindling and split logs sitting near the hearth. "It's chilly in here. Could you light a fire?"

He waggled his brows. "I can think of better ways to keep my woman warm."

"You've got to wine and dine me first." I laughed. "I skipped lunch so I'd have room for both a rib eye and dessert."

He swung me up into his arms and deposited me on the sofa. "If you're light-headed, you should sit and rest. I'll put the food away in the refrigerator and get the fire going."

I started to protest—to tell him I was fine and didn't need to be babied—then reconsidered. Annika and Marit had told me how much Zane and Adam enjoyed taking care of them. Shifters were hardwired to tend to their mates' needs, not just to protect them from harm, but also to make sure they were warm, comfortable, and well-fed.

I was finally getting used to Viggo lifting a bite of food to my mouth. It soothed something elemental inside him to have me eat from his hand. It felt silly at first. A grown woman was capable of feeding herself, but it made him happy, so I adapted. None of the losers I used to date were a fraction as attentive and considerate as Viggo. His attention to detail left even the nice guys in the dust.

"I'm a lucky, lucky girl," I said under my breath.

Viggo touched a match to the kindling then hopped to his feet and joined me on the sofa. Twining our fingers together, he stretched his long legs out on the coffee table.

"No, I'm the lucky one," he said quietly.

I bumped my shoulder against his. "You want to arm wrestle to decide the winner of the who's-the-luckiest contest?"

"Hmmm…" He pretended to think about it. "If you want to wrestle, I'm down with that."

The sudden mental image of a naked, oiled Viggo grappling with me—like an ancient Olympic athlete—made my thighs soften and my pussy twinge.

Viggo tilted back his head and inhaled a deep breath. His nostrils flared. "Somebody likes that idea."

It was impossible to hide desire from a shifter. But why would I want to when the inevitable outcome was so damned gratifying?

I swung my leg over his, straddling his lap. His body was massive. I had to spread my thighs wide to encompass his hips, making me very aware that beneath my black leggings, my sex was open and vulnerable. I sighed. Open and vulnerable to Viggo was a very, very good thing.

I forgot I was hungry. Grabbing the hem of his tee, I yanked it up over his head and tossed it aside.

Firelight played across the bronze skin of his broad shoulders and wide chest. His eyes glittered, the grizzly flashing in their golden depths. I hummed with pleasure as I scratched my nails through the dark hairs sprinkled across his pecs. All heat, hard-packed muscle, powerful limbs, and rugged features; he was the embodiment of masculine perfection.

And he was mine.

Viggo laid a hand on top of mine. "You need to eat."

Dear God, what an opening. I was tempted to run with his suggestion, to turn it into a lascivious retort, but his concern for my well-being was so sincere that I resisted the urge.

"Later," I said.

I was hungry all right, but for something other than food.

"You sure?"

I pressed an open-mouthed kiss above his right nipple then lifted heavy eyes to meet his. "Absolutely sure."

Not so long ago, when we were still enemies, Viggo told me how he propositioned a woman. "No games. No pussyfooting around the subject. I tell her exactly what I want to do. Ask what she wants."

I'd follow his example.

I dragged my fingers over his shaved head, smiling at the rough rasp of stubble scraping against skin. "Let me tell you what I want."

"I'm all ears." His hands slid around my hips and cupped my ass.

"I sincerely hope not." I wriggled, pressing close against the denim-covered bulge in his jeans. "I want *all* your parts."

"Smart-ass." Shaking his head reproachfully, he smiled.

I continued. "I want to get naked. Right now. Right here." I patted the sofa cushion then grabbed his beard. I pushed his head back, parted his lips, and touched the tips of his still-human canines. "I want you to bite me again, over your claiming mark. Then I want you to fuck me so hard I can't remember my name."

With every word I spoke, lust flamed hotter in his eyes. By the time I'd finished, his heated gaze scorched me. The spit in my mouth dried up, and my lungs seized.

"You up for that?" I croaked, following through on my resolution to ask him what he wanted.

Instead of answering, he jerked my shirt off over my head. His fingers found the clasp on my bra and threw the lacy confection across the room. It landed on the Little Red Riding Hood cookie jar sitting on the kitchen counter.

Remind me not to tell Annika that we festooned Grandma's cookie jar with my black lace bra.

In fact, I'd better not tell Annika or Marit that we'd gone at it on the sofa. They'd never again look at it the same way. Unless, of course, I wasn't the first of the Hagen women to desecrate the spot.

"Up," Viggo grunted, pulling my leggings and panties down over my hips. I rose up on my knees. He peeled my pants off my legs and shoved them to the floor.

"Your turn," I ordered breathlessly, pointing at his jeans. He kicked off his boots and stripped out of his pants.

I settled astride his hips once again, very aware of his thick cock pressing against my heated core. We locked eyes. I traced a fingertip over one dark eyebrow, along the bridge of his nose, and across his firm bottom lip.

"I do love your face," I said.

He snorted. "This ugly mug?"

"Ugly mug?" I repeated, scandalized. "Dude, you're gorgeous."

His brows drew together in a skeptical frown.

"Take the compliment," I ordered.

"Yes, ma'am." His hand tunneled through my hair. He tugged, tilting my head to one side, exposing my mating bite. "Did I ever tell you you're the prettiest woman I've ever seen? And the bravest? And the feistiest?"

Feistiest? Was that even a word?

Before I could decide one way or the other, Viggo distracted me. He sketched a leisurely chain of kisses from the corner of my eye to my chin. His lips descended on my mouth. He took his time, going deep. When he finally broke off the kiss, my legs were trembling. He slowly peeled back his lips and allowed me to watch his canines descend.

I jerked back, a primitive, involuntary reaction to the sight of a predator flashing his fangs. His fingers tightened in my hair, and he easily held me in place.

"I love you, but I need you to hold very still."

Before I could react to the command, he struck. Sharp teeth broke through my skin. It wasn't a mating bite—we'd already mated—so there was no need to sink his canines into bone. It was a facsimile of the claiming bite, a vivid reminder of the bond we'd created. I rode the pain, my fingernails digging into his chest.

His fangs withdrew and he licked over the spot, a healing balm that immediately diminished the hurt to a mere ache.

I levered up on my knees and kissed him, tasting my blood on his tongue.

"I love you, too," I murmured against his lips.

Strong hands seized my hips, lifted me up, and positioned my slick slit above the broad head of his cock. Bracing my weight on his chest, I slowly lowered myself onto his shaft, refusing to stop until my butt struck his thighs. I dropped my forehead against his and gulped in air. Deep. His cock was buried deep in my pussy, and it took me a moment to adjust to his size.

"You good?" he asked.

"Yes."

I lifted up onto my knees then plunged down, taking him to the hilt. I set the rhythm, riding him like an enthusiastic cowgirl. Viggo arched his hips, meeting me thrust for thrust.

After a few minutes, his strong hands grasped my biceps and lifted me off his cock. I whimpered, bereft. My deprivation didn't last for long. Viggo flipped me onto my back, propped my ankles over his shoulders, and drove his cock deep inside me.

Light and shadow flickered across his rugged features. Time lost all meaning as he rode me hard. I was so caught up in sensation that I was only vaguely aware of his cock swelling inside me, of the bulbous head locking in place. He shifted the angle of his incursion, dragging the slick shaft over my clit. One, two, three strokes and pleasure exploded from my core and rippled out through every inch of my body. Gasping, I felt Viggo shudder and spill hot cum deep inside me.

He rolled us onto the hardwood floor, landing on his back and absorbing the fall while I sprawled on top of him. He pulled out, leaving a familiar sticky coating on my upper thighs.

"What the heck was that about?" I laughed, surprised by the tumble.

He made a rueful face. "I realized Adam and Zane might not appreciate smelling grizzly cum on the couch."

I batted his chest. "The slip covers are machine washable, doofus."

"Well, *now* you tell me."

He pulled my head to his shoulder and held me against his chest while our heartbeats slowed and our breathing returned to normal. I reached for his face and rubbed my knuckles across the bristles of his beard.

"I've been thinking about something," I said.

"What's that?"

"There are several abandoned cabins on the lake shore, ones the Black Rock Guardians bought when they were trying to evict all the leaseholders."

His big hand stroked up and down my back. "What about them?"

"I know—" I hesitated searching for the right words.

His hand stilled. "You can tell me anything, darlin'."

"I know it's not easy for you to live in the lodge, surrounded by so many people. I was thinking, we could ask Adam if we can fix up one of the old cabins. We could live there with Hallie and Owen and Bosco. Have our own place close to the lodge. Give you some privacy and a break from noisy, boisterous wolves."

He sucked in a breath, and I thought he was going to go for it, leap at the suggestion. "You *are* a softy."

"Am not," I grumbled.

His shoulders shook with a chuckle. "Are too."

"So what do you think?" I asked.

"I can't tell you how much I appreciate the offer, but I'd rather stay put in the lodge. Hallie loves being right down the hall from Emma and Tory. Owen's made friends. You've got Annika and Marit nearby. Hell, even Bosco would miss the place and all the attention he gets."

"And what about you?" I asked.

He shrugged. "I get a little overstimulated sometimes, but I can go on a run or retreat to our quarters for a break. And this place—Grandma Freya's cabin—is a perfect getaway spot when I need time alone with my mate."

"You're sure?"

He kissed the top of my head. "One hundred percent. My family is safe and my life is better and happier than I ever dreamed it could be. All because of you and the Black Rock Guardians."

In the space of a few weeks, my life had turned upside down. I'd mated the man who'd kidnapped me and dragged me to the wilds of Alaska. Never in a million years would I have seen that coming.

"I'm happy," I murmured, snuggling into the heat of his chest. The fire warmed my back. I felt drowsy and content. My eyelids drifted shut and I dozed, more at peace than I'd ever been.

"After dinner, we need to talk about the future." Viggo's deep voice tore me from sleep. "Adam and Grandpa Matthew have some ideas about what I might do to help the wolf pack, and later, maybe even the grizzlies."

My eyes snapped open. Suddenly, I was wide-awake. I lifted my head and met his gaze. *What did that mean?*

"Dude, you can't leave me hanging. Tell me everything."

Epilogue

Remy

Two weeks later

I should've known better than to stay up late playing video games with Owen. Whether I got a measly three hours of sleep or a solid eight, my alarm was set to go off at an ungodly five thirty a.m.

I'd offered to help Marit, Annika, and Liv box up the pastries for Freya's Bake Shop, but after I dropped a cranberry scone, they booted me from the kitchen. They told me to come back and help load up the van after I got some caffeine in my system.

Now, with a cup of coffee in one hand, and a bear claw in the other, I stumbled half-awake out of the communal kitchen and into the dining hall. I spied our newest lieutenant sitting at a table overlooking Shooting Star Lake. He nodded at me, which I took as an invitation to join him. I dropped onto a chair opposite the big man and took a bite of my pastry.

"Nothing I like better than sinking my teeth into a bear claw." I smacked my lips.

Viggo rolled his eyes but refused to rise to the bait. "How much longer till they're ready to pack up the van?" he asked.

"Probably ten or fifteen minutes," I guessed.

Freya's Bake Shop was open for business only four days a week. Every time the Hagen women set foot in the place, they were accompanied by at least two bodyguards. Today, Viggo, Xander, and I would go with them to Belle Reve and stand watch all day.

"I heard Owen come in at two in the morning." Viggo took another sip of black coffee. "No wonder you look beat."

I lived alone. Owen and I played video games at my place so the sound wouldn't disturb the rest of his family.

"What were you doing up at two a.m.?" I asked.

He grinned and wiggled his brows.

I shuddered and waved both hands in the air. "Never mind." The absolute last thing I wanted to think about was Viggo Creed getting busy with Liv. I still had a hard time wrapping my head around the notion that the former grizzly enforcer—once our sworn enemy—was now family.

"You asked," he said blandly.

"Yeah, I did." Time to change the subject. "How are you liking the new job?"

"I like it fine," he said. "It's good to be useful, and I welcome the responsibility."

"You miss Alaska?"

He lifted a shoulder. "There are some good people in the grizzly pack, and I miss them. I miss the cheeseburgers at Howling Jack's. And I miss my old house, which your grandpa tells me was once your family's place."

"What?" I hadn't heard that.

"Yeah," he nodded. "The wolves who lived in the house left their furniture behind when they left the state. There was a wooden trunk and a pair of nightstands in my bedroom, covered with hand-carved animals and birds. The name Jacob Hunter was etched onto the trunk."

"Jacob Hunter was my great-great-grandfather. He was a furniture maker, like Zane. He died in the war. His widow and two sons fled to the lower 48 with the rest of the pack."

Viggo settled back in his chair, shaking his head. "It's weird, isn't it? To see how our lives have been enmeshed for so long."

"My family fled with nothing but the clothes on their backs," I said. "I'd like to see Jacob's handiwork."

"Someday—after I go back to challenge Medved—you'll get that chance. There's nothing I'd like better than for the Black Rock Guardians and grizzlies to end up allies."

"Amen to that," I agreed.

We clinked our coffee cups together in a toast.

Liv walked out of the kitchen and dropped down onto Viggo's lap. "All the pastries are packed up, and the boxes are ready to be carried to the van."

At the sight of Liv, his expression morphed from hardass to playful. He wrapped an arm around her waist, pulled her close, and nuzzled her nose. First Adam, then Zane, and now Viggo. The toughest shifters turned into the biggest pussycats once they found their mates.

"Did I ever tell you how much I love spending the day with you at the bakeshop?" Viggo asked.

Liv smiled fondly at her mate, her unguarded expression showing none of her customary snark. "You mean you love hauling boxes, sweeping floors, taking out the trash, and handing cookies to children?"

"As long as I'm with you, Liv Hagen Creed, I'm good."

She stretched up and kissed the tip of his nose. "I love you, too, big guy."

I groaned and simulated sticking a finger down my throat. "Dammit, woman. I was counting on you to be a snarly hellcat forever."

"Oh, she still has her snarly hellcat moments." Viggo chuckled.

"Hey!" Liv protested, swatting his chest.

Viggo lowered his chin. "Am I wrong?"

She tilted her head to one side, her eyes sparkling, and bit her lower lip.

"Well, am I?" Viggo persisted, his voice a deep rumble.

She shivered and wriggled on his lap, a movement that made him suck in a breath. His eyelids lowered to half-mast, and he tightened his grip on her waist.

"Darlin'," he breathed.

"Will you two cut it out?" I held up my bear claw. "Some of us are trying to eat."

Liv's gaze sliced my way. "Just you wait. When you find your mate, you'll turn all lovey-dovey, too."

Would it happen to me? Would I go mushy and mawkish if I mated?

Hard to imagine, but if it could happen to my grumpy brother, Zane, it could happen to anybody.

Marit stuck her head out of the kitchen and whistled to catch our attention. "Time to load the van and hit the road."

"Yes, ma'am." I hopped to my feet and jogged to the kitchen, Liv and Viggo on my heels. Viggo, Xander, and I made short work of loading the boxes of pastries into the van. I helped myself to an apple fritter for the road. The Hagen women insisted that unlimited pastries were a perk of the job.

During the summer months, the drive to Belle Reve took about an hour. In mid-December, ice and snow often slowed the commute. We gave ourselves an extra half hour and pulled into the alley next to the bakeshop right on schedule.

Summer was the busiest season in the riverside resort town, but every December tourists descended on Belle Reve for the annual Christmas Festival. All the shops downtown were decorated for the season. Cedar garland draped across each storefront, and a wreath hung on every door. White lights twinkled on the street trees. Giant outdoor ornaments dangled from the branches. Wide red ribbons wrapped around the old-fashioned white lampposts gave the appearance of peppermint sticks lining the main street.

A holiday overload, if you asked me, but most folks loved it.

We passed only a handful of cars on our way into town. Within a couple of hours, downtown would be crammed with visitors and finding a place to park a nightmare. This early in the morning, no stores or restaurants had opened for the day. The sidewalks stood empty. The parking spaces along Main Street were vacant.

All except one.

A white sedan had pulled up next to the door to Freya's Bake Shop. Condensation fogged the windows, but as we drove past I caught sight of a figure sitting behind the steering wheel, a blanket wrapped around their shoulders. I saw a flash of coppery red hair. My gaze skated to a back seat piled high with boxes.

By all appearances, the driver had slept in their car. It could be perfectly innocent—somebody passing through town who couldn't afford to rent a room, or who hadn't anticipated the holiday crush and forgot to reserve a bed. Maybe parking outside Freya's Bake Shop was nothing more than a coincidence.

Or maybe not.

My spidey senses tingled.

The coyotes and grizzlies both had an ax to grind with the Hagen women. Waiting in plain sight for the women to show up at their bakeshop? A lamebrained tactic at best. Still, I'd be a fool to reject the possibility that our enemies were up to something.

I brought the van to stop next to the bakery's back door, cut the engine, and set the brake. "I'm gonna go check out the car parked in front of the shop."

"You need help?" Viggo asked, sliding open the van's side door.

"Nah. It's probably nothing. I'll see what's up then come back and help you unload."

I jogged up the alley to Main Street and strode over to the white sedan. Through the steamed-up glass, I saw a young woman with auburn hair huddled under a blanket, sound asleep. I rapped on the driver's-side window. She jerked awake, turned her head to the window, and stared at me, unmoving.

Shit. I probably scared her.

I took a step backward and lifted my hands into the air, trying to appear harmless and friendly.

She slowly rolled the window down a few inches and called out through the opening. "Can I help you?"

I kept my distance. "Is there a reason you're parked outside Freya's Bake Shop at this time of day?"

"Do you… do you work there?" she asked.

Standing guard was work, although probably not the kind she meant. I nodded. "Yeah, I do."

She rolled the window all the way down, and I got my first good look at her. Tousled red hair fell past her shoulders. Her wide-set gray eyes were bloodshot and rimmed with dark circles, as if she hadn't slept well for days. Freckles dusted too-pale skin stretched tight over her high cheekbones. Fatigue and stress rolled off her, so thick, so pungent, I could taste it.

Instantly, my protective instincts roared to life. Beneath my skin, my wolf lurched to his feet, on high alert. I glanced around, scanning the block for any sign of danger, but spied nothing to warrant the warning bells going off in my head.

"Are you all right?" I asked.

Her forehead wrinkled, as if the question surprised her. "Yes," she said. "I'm fine." A lie, but one told with little art and no malice. "By any chance, are Annika and Marit here?"

I rocked back on my heels, surprised. "How do you know Annika and Marit?"

She hesitated, clearly reluctant to answer a stranger's question.

"Annika is… um...married to my brother, Zane." I stopped myself before I used the word mated in front of a human. "And Marit is married to my cousin, Adam."

"They're married?" An adorable dent formed between eyebrows the same bright hue as her hair. "I had no idea. The last time I saw them, they were getting ready to move to Belle Reve to open a bakery."

"You were friends in Seattle?" I guessed. My breath frosted the air, reminding me how cold it was, especially for a human who'd spent the night sleeping in a car.

"We went to pastry school together. After we graduated, I got a job at a restaurant near Pike Place Market. The restaurant recently changed hands." She swallowed. Her chin trembled. Her lips tipped up in an unconvincing smile. "I decided it was time to move on."

Another lie, or a partial truth, one that had my agitated wolf pacing back and forth beneath my skin. I balled my hands into fists, fighting the impulse to reach out to her.

C'mon, man. What are you doing? You don't even know her name.

"Annika and Marit are filling the pastry cases. Why don't you come inside, get a cup of coffee, and warm up."

She opened the car door, stepped outside, and tossed the blanket onto the front seat. She turned to face me, a slender woman, no more than five feet tall. Her rumpled appearance confirmed my suspicion that she'd slept in her car.

"With the Christmas rush, I was wondering if they might be hiring?" Hope colored her voice.

The door to Freya's Bake Shop swung open, and Annika rushed outside. Spying the red-haired woman, she shrieked and dashed forward, pulling her into a hug.

"Oh, my God, Skye. I thought that was you. What are you doing in Belle Reve?"

The Black Rock Guardians series continues in *Beneath a Shifter's Sky*.

Thank you for reading *Marked Under the Midnight Sun*. I hope you enjoyed it. If you have the time and inclination, please visit the site where you purchased it and leave a rating or brief review.

Want More Susanna Strom?

Sign up for Susanna's newsletter for book news, sales announcements, and exclusive content.

When you subscribe, you'll receive a free short story set in the World Fallen World. http://eepurl.com/h6WRRb

Join my readers group, Susanna's Stormers: http://www.facebook.com/groups/1572291033136914

Follow me on Facebook: https://www.facebook.com/susannastromauthor/

Follow me on Instagram: https://www.instagram.com/susannastrom.author/

ACKNOWLEDGMENTS

Most of the time, writing is a solitary pursuit. My cats keep me company, but I'm otherwise alone, sitting at my desk, banging out words. Or I'm pacing back and forth in my office, mumbling possible lines of dialogue or contemplating plot points. I may write alone, but an amazing team of people help me get the book ready for publication. Without their advice and support, I'd be lost.

Many thanks to my wonderful developmental editor, Christina Trevaskis, aka the Book Matchmaker. We've worked together on eight books. Every book has benefited from her advice and expertise. With endless enthusiasm, she teaches me how to craft better stories and encourages me to write fearlessly.

Raven Dark—my writing BFF—is the first person to read everything I write. Raven is my go-to person for brainstorming, advice, and the occasional pep talk.

My proofreader, Brittany Meyer-Strom, is persnickety in the best possible way. The correct use of language, grammar, and punctuation genuinely excites her. She's saved me from some truly boneheaded errors.

Lori Jackson designed the gorgeous cover for *Marked Under the Midnight Sun*. Lori is one of the best cover designers in the business and is a dream to work with.

Thanks to the very talented photographer, Golden Czermak, for providing the perfect cover image. Every time I reached out to him, Golden was friendly and helpful, a consummate professional and all-around great guy.

My friend, author Michael Aspen, is one of the wisest and most generous people I know. I come to him with the most obscure questions, and not only does he know the answer, he patiently answers all my questions. As a pilot familiar with bush planes, he was especially helpful with this book.

Additional thanks to everybody who helped me along the way: Jennifer Connor of Romance Rehab, Sharon and Harry Shook, Debbie and Mel Springer, and Becca Syme.

And finally, a big thank you to my endlessly-supportive and endlessly-loving husband, John Hoefer. I couldn't do this without you, baby.

Other Books by Susanna Strom

THE WORLD FALLEN SERIES

Pandemonium
Maelstrom
Bedlam
Cataclysm
Requiem

THE BLACK ROCK GUARDIANS SERIES

Secrets of Shooting Star Lake
Havoc Under the Hunter's Moon
Marked Under the Midnight Sun